A Pacifica Resort Novel

A Liar and a Thief

DEE ROLLINGS

A Liar and a Thief: A Pacifica Resort Novel

First paperback edition May 2023

ISBN 979-8-9861581-3-6 (Paperback)

ISBN 979-8-9861581-2-9 (eBook)

To my village.
*Thank you for your love and support. I wouldn't be who I am
without you.*

Chapter One

"Am I really letting you talk me into this?" I downshifted my thirty-year-old Miata and made a right-hand turn into the most familiar neighborhood I'd ever known.

"Look, Lina, I'm not telling you to break into the house, but if you wanted to, for hypothetical reasons, right now would be the best time." My best friend's voice echoed through the tinny aftermarket Bluetooth radio I had installed in my little blue convertible.

I pulled to a stop and killed the engine four houses down from my parents' old house. "There aren't any lights on inside." The line was silent as I listened to the quiet ticking of my engine cooling down. "I don't know, Val, maybe I should just call the real estate agent in the morning and ask him to let me inside."

"You really want to deal with him calling you honey and standing way too close to you again? That guy's gross. I'm pretty sure he touched your mom's butt."

"You weren't even there, so you couldn't possibly have seen that." I thought about the meeting with the agent this morning when my mom had signed the final paperwork.

"I looked him up online. He seemed like the type to do that." She was right. The realtor was a scumbag. The last thing I wanted was to be alone in a room with him again. Luckily, he had sold my mom's house for way over her asking price, so hiring him had been worth it.

"Focus, Valerie. What am I even doing here?"

"All you have to do is climb up the tree, wiggle through the window, get it, and climb back out. I bet you can do the whole thing in under a minute. Two at the most." She sounded encouraging, but the pit in my stomach wasn't budging.

When I'd helped my mother with the movers this morning and they'd asked if we were sure we'd collected all of our belongings, I never thought I would be sitting here, contemplating breaking back in to get my most prized possession.

Sure, I had totally forgotten I owned it until an hour ago, but that didn't make it less special.

"Are you sure you can't just meet me here and do it yourself? I would love you forever."

She ignored my plea. "I'm the only one at the store right now. If I left, I would have to close for the night, and I'm supposed to be open for three more hours."

"You own the damn place. Who is coming to buy records at nine anyway?"

"You would be surprised by how busy I get right before closing. Audio aficionados are night owls."

I turned off the Bluetooth and held my phone in my hand. Getting out of the car, I closed the door quietly and crept up the sidewalk, making sure my long braid was secured tightly behind my back. I whispered, "Okay. I'm walking up to the house now." I tugged my black beanie over my head, trying to turn as invisible as possible.

"Okay, look for Ester's window." Val's voice was barely loud enough to hear.

I crouched in the bushes. "Why are you whispering?"

She replied, louder this time, "Because you were. Do you want my help or not?"

I kept my voice as low as possible as my irritation increased. "Please, Val. You're the only person I know who has snuck into this house."

"That's not true. Your sister was the one who taught me that the easiest way to get into your house was through her window." I resisted the urge to complain that I was so sorry I wasn't nearly as cool as my older sister when we were teenagers, and instead I focused on the task at hand.

When I didn't reply, she asked, "Can you see it?"

"Yes. I'm about ten feet away from the tree." I scanned the yard but didn't see any movement. "I think I'm clear."

"Okay, good. I'll see you at home. Unless you get arrested. In that case, call me and I'll bail you out."

"Don't put that bad luck on me, Valerie."

"Break a leg. Love you." The line went dead, so I put my phone into the side pocket of my black yoga pants and estimated how tall the tree I had to climb actually was.

I took another deep, steadying breath, watching the windows for any signs of life. The entire house was dark. I peeked in the front window on my way to the base of the tree; nothing looked any different from how it had when my mom and I left this morning. The house was completely empty.

I had spent my life playing it safe. Never taking chances. Taking the easy way out.

Well, tonight was the night I grew some guts.

I patted my right pocket and felt the flashlight and the flathead screwdriver I would need to peel up the floorboard in my room. Then I went over the plan one more time.

My old room would be more difficult because the tree didn't quite reach it and I wasn't even sure if the window would open. But if Val was right and they never fixed Ester's window, it would slide up and I could slip inside without making a sound.

I never thought Ester's partying ways in high school would give me an advantage later on in life.

Okay, Lina. You can do this.

After one more deep breath, I scaled up the tree.

The window slid open silently, and I sent a quiet thank-you to the universe. I stood up and got my bearings.

Listening to the house and not hearing a peep, I found the courage to flick on my flashlight. I made it through the bathroom and into my old room.

I scanned the space with my flashlight and found it unnerving, seeing it dark and vacant. I hadn't lived here for several years, but I guess I never thought about it not being mine anymore. It was a little sad to think that I might not have a place to land if I needed one.

I shook my head. This was not the time to have an existential crisis. I stepped soundlessly to the spot where I had hidden all of my treasures throughout my childhood and crouched down. Holding the flashlight between my teeth, I felt for the floorboard that I knew would pop open. With my fingers in place, I wedged the screwdriver in and lifted the board as quietly as possible.

I thought I heard a noise down the hall, and I froze. Blood pumped through my veins like a bass drum as it rushed through my body, but after a few breathless seconds, I decided it must have come from outside.

Probably a tree branch hitting the window.

I knew the house must be empty, but I didn't want to take any chances of getting caught. My mother would die of a heart attack if I got arrested. This had to go smoothly, or I would never hear the end of it.

Once the board slipped free, I set it aside and reached in, grasping the heart-shaped locket that had set this plan in motion in the first place.

A deep relief filled me, knowing that what my dad had given me for my twelfth birthday, right before he died, was safe in my hand.

Cupping it in my palm again, I felt just like I had the first time he handed it to me. It was one of the last happy moments I could remember before our lives were changed forever.

Just as I let myself relax, I heard another creaking noise. I waited a few seconds before rolling my shoulders, listening to the silence around me. This old house was going to drive me to insanity. I needed to get out of here.

I clicked the flashlight off and slid the floorboard back

into place before clutching the necklace to my chest. I promised myself then and there that I would never make the mistake of leaving it anywhere else.

Pulling my braid out of my shirt and over my shoulder, I tried to clasp the necklace securely. My hands vibrated wildly, causing me to fail a few times and whisper a curse under my breath.

Why couldn't they make these damn clasps easy for people to put on by themselves? The thought of someone finding me in here did not help calm my shaking fingers.

I was reaching up to try one more time when I heard a deep voice behind me. "If you turn the flashlight back on, I could assist you."

I threw my arms up, flinging my treasure into the air and letting out a mix between a scream and a grunt. Cursing loudly this time, I clicked the flashlight back on and scanned the room, finding the source of my terror.

He stood in the doorway, his shoulders blocking off any light from the rest of the house. I screamed like someone about to be murdered in the first five minutes of a horror movie and flung the best weapon I had, my flashlight, at him. It hit him square in the chest but bounced right off. So much for that.

"I believe you're looking for this."

The flashlight rolled across the floor, casting a warm glow on the man standing a few feet away from me, and I cursed myself for not just jumping back into the tree when he came through the doorway. I couldn't tell if it was the shadows being cast from a strange angle or not, but his presence was immense.

His features were still mostly hidden as he stepped

forward, close enough for me to feel the heat radiating from his body.

He reached forward, my locket dangling from his fingers. "I'm assuming this is important to you, judging by how you broke into my house to retrieve it."

I stared at him, unable to speak. His dark hair had a slight wave to it. It looked wild, like he had been running his hands through it. I wanted to run *my* hands through it.

"You might as well let me put this on you so you can slip back out the window and be on your way." He was quiet. Contemplative.

I was unable to think. I released a shuddering breath with the knowledge that he probably wasn't going to call the police. My eyes scanned his face. It was too dark to make out any fine details, but what I could see was gorgeous, like a brooding Henry Golding.

He cracked a sideways smile, revealing perfectly straight teeth. "Come on, turn around. Let me help you." His voice was smooth like silk; it was intoxicating. I couldn't stop myself from following his directive. His free hand brushed my hair over my shoulder, and I let out a gasp as his skin touched mine. I'm sure I imagined it, but I felt electricity flowing from him into me. The locket felt cold and heavy against my chest as he secured it in place.

His large hands wrapped around my shoulders as he spun me back around to face him. I had to lean my head back to look into his face since he was at least a foot taller than me. His eyes were too dark for me to tell what color they were, but there was a glimmer of humor and kindness in them. My gaze roved to his hair, which was just long enough to fall over his ears. I reached forward to brush away the thick lock that rested across his forehead but stopped myself when he spoke again.

"I'm Reece. And you are . . . ?"

I stood there like a fish out of water, my mouth opening and closing involuntarily. Did I have a name? What was it? One of his thick eyebrows raised in a perfect arch, and I realized that I needed to answer him before his loyalty shifted and he decided to have me arrested.

I shook my head and squeaked out, "Lina." My voice cracked over the second syllable. Utterly embarrassed, I cleared my throat and tried again. "My name is Lina. It's spelled like Lean-a, but its pronounced Lynn-a." He didn't say anything, so I quickly added my usual giggly, "Thanks, Mom and Dad, for giving me the weirdest name." His smile grew brighter, but he continued to stand there in silence. "Listen, I can explain—"

He chuckled quietly and pushed the hair that I was becoming obsessed with off his forehead. "Lina. Hmm . . . ." He paused, and I noticed that he gained a small dimple when he smiled. "I like the way that feels on my tongue."

Any sense of reality that I'd had before fled as my body filled with heat. Did he just say what I thought he said? He leaned closer to me, his breath grazing my skin. The scent of something sweet—caramel, maybe—tickled my nose.

I should be terrified of this large man filling my personal space. But I wasn't—and that scared me.

Abruptly, I took a step backward, breaking his spell on me. "Sorry for disturbing you. I didn't see a car outside, so I assumed no one was here."

He clamped his lips together for a second before saying, "I parked in the garage."

"Oh. I didn't even think of that. When we lived here, the garage was always full of stuff." His smile stayed, but he didn't say anything else. Unable to stop myself, I said, "There weren't any lights on when I peeked through the windows. I thought it was empty." I looked toward the doorway, realizing how crazy I must sound. "I should go."

"Or you could stay?" He took a tentative step forward, erasing any space between us.

"I, um . . . I have a boyfriend." I rushed through the bathroom and practically threw myself out the window.

I scaled down the tree in record time and ran as fast as I could to my car. I was halfway there when I realized that my flashlight was still on the floor of my old bedroom.

Oh well, at least it was something totally replaceable that got left behind, not the most important piece of jewelry I had ever been given.

Once safely in my car, I pulled the screwdriver from my pocket, tossed it on the passenger seat, and buckled my seatbelt, promising myself never to do something this stupid ever again.

"Wait, wait, wait. You told him you had a boyfriend?" Val laughed. "So, you're a liar *and* you stole from him."

I rolled my eyes at her as I took another gulp from my wine glass. "I mean, I wasn't technically lying. Ezra is kind of my boyfriend, right?" I clutched the locket around my neck. "And I'm not a thief. I was just getting back what was mine."

My two favorite humans sat with me on the floor of the living room that Valerie and I shared while I filled them in on my adventure. At first, they didn't believe that I had actually followed through with the plan, but the longer I talked, the more they realized I had done something completely out of my comfort zone.

My father had always encouraged me to be brave, but after we lost him, I'd had too much on my shoulders taking care of Mom and Ester, even though I was the youngest. It was hard for me to come out of my shell and try new things.

Valerie and I had met on the first day of tenth grade when she sat next to me in Mr. Beckett's English class. My dad had been gone for a few years, so I was in the routine of my new normal. She and I instantly became best friends, despite being complete opposites in every way.

Her extroverted personality clashed with my tendency to want to stay at home all the time. She busted her butt after college to buy this house and her record store, whereas I buried myself in student loans and landed a job that didn't exactly leave a lot of padding in my bank account.

She paid the mortgage and rented the converted attic to me. I had a bedroom, a bathroom, and a tiny landing I used as a makeshift office away from work. Thankfully she wasn't hard up for cash, so what she charged me was easily a third of the going rate for renters these days. I owed her more than I would ever be able to afford, both for the material things she had helped me with and the mental things, like allowing me to discover myself after living through the worst thing that had ever happened to my family.

Blake rolled her eyes at me, snapping me back into the present moment. "Umm, did you and Ezra finally move beyond 'seeing each other' territory, or are you still just fooling around?" She was the general manager at the resort I worked for, which made her my boss, but in the three years I'd worked there, we'd become inseparable. She only lived a few miles away, but her roommates were annoying, so she spent more time at our place than at her own.

Our house was what you could call boho chic. We had blankets and rugs strewn everywhere, making it the best place to snuggle up after a long day at work. I understood why it was more of an oasis for Blake than the room she rented from the uptight couple a few blocks down.

"Well . . . no, we still haven't actually talked about anything serious." I finished my wine, hoping they would stop questioning me soon. Ezra and I had been on several dates, but we never spent much time talking. Warmth rushed through my skin when I thought about the last time I was over at his place. A plan to watch a movie turned into something much heavier only a few minutes into the film.

"Then he's not your boyfriend." Val raised her glass, almost spilling her red wine on the carpet. "Besides, I haven't even met him. What does that say about your relationship if your best friend in the universe hasn't even met the guy?"

I scowled at her. "You're just saying that because

you're the only one of us in a real relationship." Val and Joey had been together for a few years, which was longer than anything Blake or I had ever been involved in, so she considered herself an expert on the subject. "I'm sure you'll meet him when the time is right. Our schedules just haven't lined up yet." I was aware that I was making up excuses, but I was desperate to get out of the spotlight.

"Yes, but Joey and I were both aware that neither of us was monogamous until we sat down and discussed our future. You two need to have The Talk."

A shiver ran through my body. "Yuck. Even if we haven't verbalized that we are monogamous, the thought of seeing more than one guy at the same time gives me the creeps."

"I certainly doubt that Ezra feels the same way." Val's voice was clear as she finished her drink and reached for the bottle to add more wine to our glasses. I knew she was a better drinker than I was, but it always surprised me how she could keep her cool after drinking a whole bottle when just a single glass made me tipsy.

Blake held her hand up in that wobbly way that meant she was drunk enough to start giving sage advice. "Okay, but wait. Here's where I disagree." I knew I could always trust Blake to have my back. "I have met him. Hell, I take care of his payroll. And while I don't think he's actually your boyfriend per se, I believe that we should hang out with him outside of work before you make any life-altering decisions about him." Her shoulders weaved from side to side. "And I also think it's okay to only be with one guy at a time." She turned and looked me dead in the eye. "But I think you need to have the conversation soon so you know if you should cut him loose. Because he probably is seeing other girls."

So maybe she didn't *always* have my back, but her last boyfriend was an impulsive cheater, so maybe her opinion was a little biased.

Val cut in again, "Besides, you've been seeing him for what, two or three months, and he hasn't given you a . . . you know. . . ." She made the most obnoxious winky face before bouncing her eyebrows up and down dramatically.

I grabbed a pillow and threw it at her. "Oh my God, Valerie, you are about to make this conversation so uncomfortable." I lifted my full glass and chugged it until it was empty. "I don't know why I even told you about that!"

Blake put her hand on my knee, more to steady herself than to comfort me. She was not one to talk openly about bodily functions unless she was fully intoxicated. "Huh, I thought you guys had already slept together."

I shrugged. "Well, just the once. But his roommates were home, and it was so awkward." Thinking back to the sounds of guys yelling over a video game in the living room while Ezra's body thrummed above mine made me desperate to make the situation sound better, so I added, "We've done other stuff, though." I was getting more embarrassed by the second. "I just haven't been able to . . . finish."

"He doesn't know how to complete the transaction, if you catch my drift." Val held up her glass like she was giving a toast. "I say, kick him to the curb. Move on to the other fish in the sea!" She then drained her glass in one gulp.

"You would think a florist would know his way around your parts. Like exploring a Georgia O'Keeffe painting." Blake looked up with wide eyes, shocked at what she had just said out loud, but Val and I burst out laughing. This time, Blake picked up the bottle sitting between us and drained it into our glasses.

Chuckling, while also avoiding the burning in my cheeks, I added, "I don't think it's an issue of him not knowing his way around. We get along really well, and he turns me on." I shrugged, realizing I was tipsier than I thought I was. "I think my flower is defective."

Blake tilted her head to the side and blinked slowly, reassuring me that if I was hammered, at least she was, too. "Oh, Lina. Have you never been to O-Town?"

"I don't know." I hadn't planned on my sex life being the topic of conversation this evening.

Val giggled like a little kid, "O-Town? Is that what we're calling it these days?" Her eyes met mine. "You would know if you've had an orgasm before. Believe me."

I sighed. "I have . . . I mean, maybe." I tucked my free hand into my lap while the two of them stared at me like owls. "Okay, probably not."

Val leaned forward, whispering for dramatic effect, "Not even by yourself?"

"Valerie! I can't believe you asked her that!" Blake's jaw was practically on the floor.

I sheepishly answered, "I don't think so? Like I said, my body is defective."

"No, I'm not accepting that answer. I am taking you

shopping for tools. Both of you." Valerie sat there rubbing her hands together with a grin on her face.

"Can we please talk about something else?" I was grasping at straws to change the topic to anything other than my inability to orgasm. "How are the contracts going with the sale of the resort, Blake?"

The way she growled led me to believe that I struck the right chord. "It's bad. Oh, it's so bad. I'm not supposed to say anything, but this new company has a history of coming into boutique hotels like ours and laying everyone off. They're going to turn it into another boring chain and ruin all of our lives." She threw herself onto the floor.

Blake sometimes had a flair for the dramatic, but I had heard from a few other people at work that massive layoffs were on the horizon.

"Do you really think they are going to get rid of all of us? Who else will they hire?" I took another sip from my glass, trying not to take drunk Blake seriously.

"We need to prepare for the worst. These jerks are coming in here thinking that just because their company dropped a ton of money to buy The Pacifica, I'm just going to hand over my hard work. Well, they've got another thing coming."

Val frowned sympathetically. "Would the new owners really change what's obviously working? I thought the Vandenburgs were only selling because they wanted to retire and none of their kids wanted to take the property over?"

Blake shook her head. "I really don't know, but I promise I'm going to fight them with everything I've got!

The new CFO is supposed to stop by my office sometime this week to introduce himself and fill me in on the budget. I'm sure he's going to be some rich asshole who thinks he's God's gift to the universe. He probably doesn't even have a business degree." She stared at the wall with a look that could kill. "I hate him already."

Val put her hand on my knee. "You should just quit. Take this as a chance to start your own photography business."

I cringed. "I'm not close enough to my goals for that. I don't have the money in my savings or the social media followers to even think about it."

"Why are you even thinking about those ludicrous goals? Shit or get off the pot, right? Just quit your job already." Val was drunker than I originally thought. I wouldn't be surprised if I found myself holding her hair out of her face in the bathroom later.

"You know I can't do that. I have bills to pay." I thought about the color-coded chart I kept in my planner. I had about 10 percent of the savings and 1 percent of the social media following I needed to start out on my own. Until then, I belonged to the resort, regardless of the new management rolling in.

We talked about work for a little while longer, but it was all gossip and speculation. When I finished my glass and stood up, the room spun around me. I probably shouldn't have mixed dee adrenaline from breaking and entering earlier with so much alcohol.

"Well, ladies," I said, "tonight has been grand, but I have an early day tomorrow. I had two sessions today that I need to edit in the morning so I can send proofs before the guests check out." I loved being a photographer, but I wasn't sure if I was *in love* with being the only on-call photographer for Santa Barbara's fanciest beach getaway.

"Just because you're leaving the room does not mean that I'm going to forget our earlier conversation," Val said. "You better know that I'm holding you to our dirty shopping trip."

I stuck my tongue out at Val, jealous of her ability to still be cognizant after drinking so much wine and started walking toward the staircase.

"Wait, before I forget, Joey has a gig Saturday night. I know you're usually slammed this time of year, but it would be cool if you could join us. Maybe see if Ezra wants to come, too? I've got a bunch of extra tickets." Valerie's boyfriend played in an indie rock band that was right on the cusp of making it big.

"Yeah, maybe. I'll have to—"

Blake cut me off. "We know, you've got to check your planner." She grabbed a blanket and curled up on the couch, following the unspoken rule to never get behind the wheel after drinking.

"Whatever. Say what you will about my planner, but you know that both of you depend on my organizational skills to keep your lives together."

They both laughed, and I flipped them my middle finger in response, something I would not have done without the liquid courage flowing through my veins.

I climbed the stairs to my room and fell into bed. I lay there, trying to fall asleep as the room spun around me, but our conversations played over and over in my mind.

First, I worried about my job. Between my student

loans and how much it cost just to live in California, I didn't know how I could survive without this job. Would the new owners really get rid of so many of us? What about Ezra's job? If my place wasn't guaranteed, there's no way a house florist would be set in stone either.

I needed to talk to him. About work. About us. About a few things.

Maybe I did need to go with Val to see what I could do to prove that my body didn't work like theirs.

But when I thought about the possibility of mind-blowing intimacy, I couldn't help but wonder what it would have felt like if Reece had leaned down and kissed me while I stood in my old bedroom earlier this evening. I remembered the feel of his hands on my shoulders and imagined them traveling to other places as well.

 # Chapter Two

I wandered around the banquet hall, admiring the blue and purple accents on every table. One of the things I loved about shooting weddings was seeing the reception area before anyone else. There was something magical in an ornately decorated room right before the chaos began. I liked to explore while the bride and groom were getting ready since I only needed to take pictures of them putting on their final touches.

When I was in college, a friend told me that her wedding day was such a blur that she never even got to see the centerpieces in all their glory. For some reason, that story stuck with me, so I always made a point to get several shots before the reception started.

This room was my favorite reception hall at The Pacifica Resort. The natural light came in from the giant windows that overlooked the beach where we held many of our weddings. Hundred-year-old dark wood flooring and crown molding gave the room a classic feeling, and the plaster walls evoked the Spanish history of Santa

Barbara. The room was lavish and exquisite. The ten-foot crystal chandelier in the center of the room was the epitome of old California money.

Later this evening, the twinkling lights around the dance floor would transform this room. But now, in the middle of the afternoon, I had this place to myself.

I took a look around, wondering where my life would be this time next year.

Would I still be working here, or would I finally be living my dream—running my own photography studio?

Or would I be working in some strip mall taking generic family photos just to make ends meet?

Oh God, would I have to sell my camera equipment to pay the bills?

I pulled my camera close to my chest. No, I wouldn't let it get that far. I was good at what I did, and I deserved to stay. The new owners would see my work and have no choice but to keep me.

Hopefully.

I shoved my thoughts down deep and went back to work. As I snapped a few shots of the floral centerpiece on table six, I felt warm hands wrap around my waist.

"Hey, you." Ezra's voice was soft in my ear as he placed a kiss on my neck.

My skin tingled at his touch, and I wanted more. I turned around to face him, but an unfamiliar feeling rolled through me.

Uncertainty, and maybe a twinge of guilt, since he wasn't the first person who came to mind when I felt his lips on my skin. "You have really outdone yourself with these arrangements. They're beautiful."

He beamed at me, his blue eyes sparkling, and reached to adjust the flowers in the vase. My gaze caught on his sinewy biceps as I watched him rearrange the bouquet, and my mouth went a little dry. He had on a green apron over his tight white T-shirt. He didn't have a set uniform here at The Pacifica, but he always wore the same thing. I had asked him about it once when we were at his house, and he said it was just easier to wear a white shirt and jeans every day.

He plucked a browning hydrangea petal, stuffing it into his apron pocket. "This couple was pretty laid back, so they let me do whatever I wanted as long as I stuck to their color palette. I like it when they let me just do my thing." He leaned down and placed a quick peck on my lips.

I put my hands against his chest, looking around the room nervously. "Ezra. You're going to get us in trouble." As much as I wanted to be in his arms, my conversation with Blake about the resort changes had me spooked. I slipped away from him and started walking around, forcing myself to focus more on the centerpieces placed around the room rather than the freckles that were dusted across his cheeks. I began taking shots of each table. "This is some of your best work."

He tucked his hands into the straps around his apron and followed me as I worked. "I have to admit, I only came to check on the room because I know you like to come in early." He leaned over my shoulder and took a peek at the screen on the back of my camera. "I did put in a lot of work on these arrangements, but they almost look better in your shots than they do in real life. I know you said social media is too overwhelming for you, but you really should get more involved on Instagram. People need to see how good your work is."

I hated that he was right. "I have almost two hundred followers."

"And they're all people who work here or are related to you."

Social media felt too intrusive to dive into. Showing people what I ate for breakfast or pictures of cute dogs I saw on the beach was not going to get more people to book my services through the resort.

"Well, after talking to Blake last night, I think I'm going to need to start building a better professional portfolio. Maybe you could come over sometime and help me pick out good shots from the last few events we've done together?"

He gave me a kiss on the cheek, even though he knew it made me nervous. "Sure. Oh, I could put together some sample tables when this room isn't being used, and you could take shots for both of our accounts. Like a cool collab project."

I smiled up at him. "That would be really fun. Let's do it."

"Come here." He opened his arms, inviting me in.

Glancing around the room one more time to ensure we were completely alone, I took my camera off my neck and set it on the table before wrapping my arms around his waist. He enveloped me in his arms and kissed the top of my head. I felt warm and safe and imagined that we were standing together at our wedding reception.

"If the DJ was here, we could ask him to play a song for us." He grinned down at me, and I blushed, thinking about how he would look in a tux with a blue bow tie that matched his eyes. This moment was one I would always remember.

And of course, because I am the person that I am, who has to ruin every perfect moment, I blurted out, "Ezra, are you my boyfriend?"

Panic flashed in his eyes for a moment before he smiled sweetly and cupped my cheek in his hand. "Babe. Look at me." My eyes met his, which were dancing in the sunlight. "Are you enjoying the journey we're on together?"

I took a second to think before answering. He was a great guy. He had the ability to make me laugh at the drop of a hat. He never hesitated to compliment my work, and he always popped in to see me at some point during the day, even for just a quick hug. I stared at his pink bottom lip, just as his tongue darted out, licking it, like he knew I was thinking about it. He was a phenomenal kisser. Sure, there weren't exactly explosions when we did other stuff . . . but those reactions only happen in movies, right?

I smiled up at him. "I really am. Things are great."

He kissed my forehead. "Then there's your answer. Let's focus on the journey."

Before I could ask him to clarify what he meant, he pulled me against him and kissed me deeply. As his tongue danced with mine, I reached around him, feeling the muscles of his back through his shirt. He led me to the nearest table and propped me against the edge. His kisses trailed down my neck, and he reached up, unbuttoning the first two buttons of my blouse.

"Ezra, wait. I'm not sure if we should be doing this." I heard a door close down the hall. "Did you hear that?"

He ignored me and pulled the fabric of my top open, his kisses turning into gentle nibbles across my shoulder.

"We just never get any time together—we're both always here at work. I hate it. I want to have you every time I see you." His mouth took mine again, and he untucked my shirt from my skirt, sliding his hand underneath and leaving a trail of goosebumps on my skin.

Part of me worried that the DJ would walk in on us, but this was the hottest moment we'd ever had together, and I didn't want it to end. His fingertips slid under the cup of my bra just as the alarm on my phone screeched from inside my skirt.

He jumped away quickly, like my skin was on fire.

I reached into my pocket and silenced my phone, my heart pounding. "Oh my God, Ezra. We can't let that happen again." I was completely out of breath as heat pooled between my legs. "I can't lose this job." I straightened my clothes. "I need to go do some shots of the bridal party getting ready. I'm on a pretty tight schedule."

He ran his fingers through his hair and adjusted his apron. "I'm sorry I lost control. I was on my way to bring the bridal party their bouquets when I found you in here. Mind if I walk with you?"

I looked him up and down, wishing we were anywhere else in the world right now. Hell, a locked closet would suffice for what I wanted to do with him at this moment. With a shake of my head, I cleared the memory of his hand gripping my thigh. "I would like that a lot."

I stared at his lips, pink and swollen from our kisses, and reminded myself that with new management coming in, we needed to remain professional now more than ever. We had to keep our hands to ourselves, no matter how badly I wanted him to prop me against a table again.

As he grabbed his box of flowers, I slung my camera across my shoulder and pulled my planner out of my bag. I flipped open to today to double-check the room numbers of the bride and groom, but my eyes panned over to Joey's show.

Ignoring the fact that Ezra didn't actually answer my question when I asked him if we were in a serious relationship, I decided to ask him to come with me to the show.

A small voice in the back of my head screamed that I needed to ask him what he meant when he said "then there's your answer," but the last thing I wanted to do after our heated make-out session was to come off as completely neurotic. Maybe introducing him to my roommate would give me some insight into what we really meant to each other.

"Oh hey," I said, "My friend's band is playing tomorrow night. A bunch of us are going, and I have an extra ticket. Want to join?"

He smiled. "That could be cool. Text me the details, and I'll let you know."

The thought of bringing him into my small circle of friends suddenly made me nervous. Would he like them?

Would they like him? I wasn't sure which question worried me more.

I put a question mark in my planner and stuffed it back into my bag.

We walked through the hotel, not talking about anything in particular, until we stepped off the elevator on the top floor. I knocked on the door of the bridal suite, and the mother of the bride let us in. Ezra set the box of flowers on the table gingerly and said hello to everyone. The hair and makeup team was finishing with the bride, and the girls in the bridal party were rushing around, zipping each other up and giggling. I immediately started snapping candid photos of everyone.

Watching Ezra give the bouquets to the bridesmaids caused me to swoon a little. He looked like the Ken Doll I'd had when I was a little girl: tall and blond with sun-kissed bronze skin. As he smiled and handed flowers to everyone in the room, I realized that one day, sooner rather than later, I wanted to be on the other end of the camera in my own flowing white dress.

I wondered if it could be him at the end of the aisle. Maybe I was already on the road to my own happily ever after.

He finished his task and grasped my elbow gently in his hand, the motion feeling more intimate than it should have. "I'll talk to you when you get off work tonight, okay?" He leaned down and kissed me gently, and I found myself swaying toward him, despite my earlier worries.

The bridesmaids started to squeal, so I rolled my eyes at him and pushed him away playfully. He had never kissed me in front of other people before. Did this make him my official boyfriend? Ugh, I should have just asked him to tell me what he really meant.

I plastered my best work smile on my face as he left the room. I would have plenty of time to obsess over this later. "Okay, ladies, I need some time with the bride, and then I'll get some individual shots of you helping her put on her dress."

The longer I stood outside of the venue, the more I regretted coming out tonight. I checked my phone for the tenth time, staring at the last text from Ezra. I'd sent him a casual message at lunchtime reminding him of the details of tonight's show. He'd said he was hoping to meet me here but wouldn't know if he could make it until later.

I didn't want to come off as a nag, so here I stood, staring at my phone, stuck in limbo. How late was "later"? Could I text him now without coming off as needy?

I had gotten two tickets from Val just in case, but I was starting to realize I would probably only need one.

I really didn't want to go in there by myself.

My phone buzzed in my hand, and my heart raced. I looked down to see what my future would hold, only to find a text from Blake in my group chat with the girls: *I had the looooongest day ever. Arguing with new management blows. I'm totally exhausted. Gonna go home and catch some Z's. Plz tell J I'll be at the next one. Xoxo*

Before I could use it as an out and tell them I wasn't coming either, a text from Val popped up: *Girl, you gotta do what you gotta do. I'm back here doing roadie work since Dave's flaky ass didn't show up. Gonna be a long night for me. Jealous that you get to go to bed. Love ya!*

Well, this made it harder to skip out.

I put my phone in my pocket, deciding to wait five more minutes just in case Ezra showed up. If he didn't, I would be happy to pop in, say hello to the band and then go home. I could put my jammies on and finish editing yesterday's photos.

Even though I was in my midtwenties, I always got carded going into these venues, so I pulled my license out of my wallet and held it in my hand so I would be ready as soon as Ezra got here. I was already anxious and didn't want to make it worse by fumbling through my wallet.

I paced around on the sidewalk, rapping my ID against my bright yellow fingernails, trying to keep my mind off whatever was going on between Ezra and me.

Luckily, it was warm outside, so I didn't mind waiting out here, but the crowd of tourists milling up and down State Street was beginning to grow. I didn't want to wait around much longer.

I stopped, staring up at the marquee, wondering if I was being stood up. Ezra and I had been out several times, but after spending countless hours overthinking our last conversation, I wasn't even sure what I was doing with him.

"Ohhh, *Magdalina.*"

I jumped at the sound of the masculine voice in my ear just as a large hand came into my field of view, pointing at the name on my license: Magdalina Herrera.

No one on earth called me anything other than Lina,

so I turned to see who had spoken. I jumped again when I discovered I was once again face-to-face with Reece, the mysterious man who had bought my parents' house.

Without a word, he plucked my driver's license from my hand and examined it. "So this is the identity of the cat burglar who has been terrorizing my neighborhood."

I looked around him nervously, thinking that, of course, this would be the moment that Ezra would show up. But he was nowhere in sight. Apparently, I had been stood up by my maybe-boyfriend.

"I wouldn't exactly say terrorizing." I subconsciously reached up and tapped the locket around my neck. Since getting it back, I only removed it when I showered, and then I put it right back on. I didn't want to lose it again. "I only took one little thing, and it was mine to begin with, so it wasn't burglary."

The way he raised his eyebrow sent a bolt of heat through my body, and when he took my locket into his free hand, I thought I might faint right then and there. "It was a jewelry heist, and you know it."

I let out a nervous giggle—the loud kind that you end up replaying in your head when you're trying to sleep every night for the rest of your life—and looked right into his eyes. They were amber with a dark umber ring around the edges. They perfectly accentuated the warm brown color of his skin.

I could spend all night staring into his face.

He handed me my license, snapping me out of my awkward trance. "Well, Mag, shall we go in?" I thought about correcting him about my name, but in the moment, it felt more exciting having him call me Mag, like a secret nickname from a person I would never see again.

He angled his elbow out toward me, and I stood there like an idiot for a few seconds before realizing he wanted me to put my arm in his. I hesitated, but then a thought occurred to me. If Ezra didn't care enough to tell me that he wasn't coming, I shouldn't care about letting another man wrap his arm around mine, so I slipped mine into his.

As we walked together, he asked, "So, you come here often?"

A laugh escaped my lips. "Well, that was corny." He looked down at me with a crooked grin. "But no, I've never actually been inside. I've wanted to for a while now, but my job keeps me pretty busy at night."

"Ah yes, I bet it would be difficult to break into people's houses if you did it during the daytime."

"Obviously. But business is business." I shot him a conspiratorial look. We walked in the door and he pulled out his wallet. I stopped him and took the tickets out of my pocket. "I've got us covered. My tickets were free." After the bouncer took our tickets and checked our IDs, I twined my arm into Reece's again. The gesture made me feel bold, like I was playing a character instead of being myself.

Reece smiled down at me, causing my head to swim again. He really was beautiful. "Watch out, if you keep taking care of me, I might just fall in love with you."

Another nervous laugh escaped my lips. I had no idea what to say, and I worried that I was coming off as deranged, laughing at everything he said. I blurted out the first question I could think of. "So, how long have you lived in Santa Barbara?"

"I just moved here. In fact, you were the welcoming committee on my first night. It wasn't exactly how I had planned on meeting the locals, but it was a nice way to be introduced to the neighborhood." Another one of those slow smiles warmed me to my core. "What about you? Been here long?"

"Well, I was born here, so I guess you could say so. I grew up in your house. I mean, the house you live in used to be my house, which is how I knew how to get inside." I cringed before I even finished speaking. "Where are you from?"

"Most recently, Malibu, and before that San Luis Obispo, but I'm originally from Singapore."

We made our way through the entryway of the dark club, and I scanned the crowd, looking for anyone I might know. It seemed busier inside than I would have guessed from outside. I had no clue where all these people had come from. I didn't recognize anyone, but I wasn't surprised.

I looked up at Reece. "Wow, that's a big move. How old were you when you came to California?"

"We moved here when I was a toddler," Reece said, "and I've lived pretty much up and down California, so I'm really a West Coast guy at heart. My mom was born and raised in Singapore, but my dad is from the Bay Area. He moved to Singapore after college and met my mom. They started their own company and moved my sister and me here to be closer to my dad's family." He looked away from me for the first time and scanned the crowd. "Want to get a drink before finding a spot?"

"Sure." We walked over to the bar, our shoes sticking slightly to the floor, and waited for the bartender to see us. "Is your sister older or younger?"

"Older."

"So is mine!"

"Ugh. Is yours as controlling as mine?"

I nodded, and he tugged at his hair, which somehow made him look even more handsome than before.

He continued, "I've spent the last decade working for the family company, which Izzy is poised to take over soon. It's not the easiest job, and she works me like a dog, so I'm hoping the move to Santa Barbara will give me a little autonomy." He shuddered slightly before he asked, "So, what about your family?"

"It's just me and my mom here in California. My dad passed away when I was a kid and Ester, my sister, lives on the other side of the country. She works all the time, so we only see each other on major holidays." I don't know what made it so easy for me to tell him my family history, but I hoped my family rundown didn't come off as depressing as it sounded to my ears. "Actually, I just got Mom settled in her new place the day you and I met. She's in a cute little condo for people fifty-five and older."

The bartender finally made his way over to us. Reece ordered a Pepsi. I thought for a moment about ordering something strong and fruity, but I didn't want to have to leave my car here and catch a ride home with Val, so I ordered a Sprite.

Reece smiled at me. "Magdalina and Ester? Your parents must be super religious."

I grinned at him. "You know, you're the first person I've ever met who made that connection. My dad was very religious. Not, like, in a cultish way, but he sure loved Jesus. It was important to him for us to have strong, biblical names." I froze for a second, surprised that I had just shared so much with someone I had only just met. But for some reason, I knew I could trust him. "It's funny, no one really knows my full name. Just a couple of friends and, well, now you."

"So, what you're saying is that I need to discover all of your aliases before reporting your jewelry heist ring to the proper authorities?"

I smacked his shoulder lightly. "Oh my gosh, how am I going to convince you that I am not a thief?"

His eyes narrowed. "That's exactly what a thief would say." The opening band came out onstage, and the crowd cheered. Reece grabbed his soda and held his arm out to me again. "Come on, let's go find our spot."

With my drink in hand, I wrapped my arm in his, and we made our way to the ground floor.

He leaned down and spoke into my ear, sending a jolt of energy through me. "Do you mind if we stand near the back? I always feel too tall to stand in front of anyone. I don't want to spend the whole night worrying that someone is going to throw a drink at the back of my head for blocking their view."

I had noticed he was tall the first time I saw him, but now that he mentioned it, I leaned back slightly to get a good look at his height. The top of his head was well above most people in here, which could be a problem in a place like this. "The back of the room is perfect. I'm not really a fan of having a crowd shoved up against me anyway."

He leaned down and squeezed me into a sort of side hug. As soon as he let go, I wanted him to do it again. There was something enticing about having his muscular body pressed against mine.

We watched the band play—a group I had never heard of before, not that I was a connoisseur of rock bands or anything. Sure, I listened to music, but I didn't know enough about indie bands to identify them at a show. At some point, Reece and I started to bounce along to the music.

He yelled down to me, over the band, "They're really good! I've seen them a couple of times, but this is the best they've ever been."

I hollered back up, "I really like them, too! They make me want to dance!"

Without another word, he grabbed the drink from my hand and placed both of our glasses on a ledge nearby. Reaching forward, he took my hands, and we danced to the beat without any steps in mind. It was honestly the most fun I'd had in a while.

He spun me around before pulling me close to him. "I'm glad I ran into you tonight. I usually come to these things by myself. It's way more fun having someone to dance with."

I felt my face turn bright pink. "I usually have to be dragged out to this stuff kicking and screaming, but I'm glad I'm here with you, too. Do you come out to stuff like this a lot?"

"It's my favorite thing." He grinned and spun me around before pulling me tight against him again. "I would see live music every night if I could." He laughed before leaning down and nuzzling his face against my neck. "Sometimes I daydream about running away and becoming a roadie, just to have a better excuse to come to shows."

Just as I started to melt into him, he stepped back and twirled me in a circle again. I was usually a wallflower, refusing to dance in public because I'd never felt comfortable doing it, but tonight I felt like a princess at a ball. His excitement was rubbing off on me.

The band finished their last song and exited the stage, and I found myself standing quietly next to Reece. He lowered his mouth close enough to my ear for me to feel his breath. "I'm dying of thirst. Want me to get you a water or a beer or something?"

I nodded, hoping he couldn't tell how sweaty I was in the dim lighting. "A water would be great. Thanks!"

He squeezed my waist and took off toward the bar. I turned back to the stage and saw Val helping Joey and his band set up their instruments. She waved at me and then pointed in the direction that Reece had gone and gave me an overzealous thumbs up.

Cupping her hands around her mouth, she yelled out, "He's so cute!" which then caused the people around me to turn and stare.

I covered my face, wishing I could turn invisible.

When I peeked through my fingers, Val blew me a kiss and went back to work.

A few minutes later, Reece bumped his hip into mine playfully and handed me a plastic cup. "Sorry it took so long. I think there's only one bartender working tonight."

I shrugged and took a drink of water. I hadn't realized how parched I was until I gulped down half the cup. "Thank you for this." I pointed up to the stage. "I was entertained here watching them set up. The one with the curly hair is my roommate, Val, and the guy on the left is her boyfriend, Joey. I can introduce you to them sometime." I winked at him. "Maybe the band would let you play the tambourine or something for them when you decide to go on the lam."

He laughed. "The tambourine, huh? I dunno, I think my cowbell skills are probably better. I've seen them a few times, too. They might be too good for my tambourine skills."

I plucked at his shirt—a black button-up that was soft and smooth–probably the same price as a car payment. "I think you might have to trade in the Hugo Boss for an old T-shirt, though."

He looked at me in mock horror. "Oh no. There are some things I am willing to compromise on, but my clothes are not one of them. They'll have to take me as I am, Armani and all."

I looked him up and down and had to admit that his backside would not look nearly as good in a pair of jeans as it did in his slacks. They were filled out very nicely.

He nudged my shoulder. "Umm, excuse me, are you objectifying my body?"

My face immediately turned bright red, and I turned away from him because yes, yes I was. And I really only regretted getting caught.

"I wasn't complaining, you know," he whispered into my ear.

Luckily, I was saved by the band as they began playing. We continued to dance together during the entire set, and I found a new appreciation for Joey's band. They might even be my new favorite.

"Hey, hand me your phone." Reece held his hand out in front of me. I raised an eyebrow at him but unlocked it and handed it to him. He opened the camera and pressed his cheek against my temple. "Say cheese!"

He snapped a few pictures of us and tinkered around before handing the phone back to me. "I sent myself the pictures, so I have your number. And now you have mine." Before I could say anything else, he grabbed me again and swept me off my feet.

When the music had ended and people started clearing out, I awkwardly reached into my pocket for my car keys. Why the hell couldn't they make pockets in women's jeans big enough to hold all of my things?

"Can I walk you out to your car?" Reece's hand grazed my hip, and I lost my train of thought.

I smiled. I didn't remember if a boy had ever walked me out to my car before. My phone buzzed in my back pocket, so I pulled it out to check it. It was Val, reading my mind: *I would normally ask you to come hang out with us while we clean up, but it looks like you're busy. Go get some, girl! I'll see you tomorrow!*

I tucked my phone back into my pocket and wrapped

my arm in his like I had earlier. There was no way I was ready to "go get some" with a man I barely knew, but I could at least let him walk me out. "Sure, I would love that." We headed out of the venue and to the parking lot, along with the rest of the crowd. "I had a really great time tonight."

He turned his head to me and flashed that grin that made me weak in the knees. "I did, too. It was nice to have a dance partner."

"Well, I usually work weekends, and my busy season is about to start, but I'm down to join you whenever I'm free." I didn't know what compelled me to be so forward, but I liked it. Here with him, I wasn't feeling any of the usual anxiety I got with new people.

"I'm going to hold you to that." He pulled me a little tighter against him.

Now it was my turn to give him a grin. "Good. I hope so." I walked up to my car. "Well, this one's mine."

He looked over my Miata, which needed a bath but was otherwise in good condition. "Wow, you don't see a lot of these on the road anymore."

I let out a dramatic gasp. "And just what is wrong with my little roadster?"

He laughed. "I don't think anything's wrong. It's just that most Miatas have been modified to hell."

I rolled my eyes at him and backed up against the driver's door. "Oh please, I'm sure what you drive is *soooo* much better."

He chuckled. "Eh, you're probably right."

I caught myself reaching for his arm but stopped before I actually touched him. "You're so easy to talk to."

He took a step toward me; the spark between us was undeniable. His mouth was so close to mine that I could feel his breath on my skin. "I was just thinking the same thing."

For a second we stood there, staring at each other, not moving a muscle. I closed my eyes and leaned in, preparing for him to press his lips against mine.

"Ahh, shit. I'm sorry."

My eyes flew open to find him standing several feet away from me, rubbing his face. I tried to speak, but the words didn't come out.

"I'm such an asshole. The other night, you told me that you had a boyfriend and here I am not respecting your boundaries at all. I've been touching you all night like some creep. I'm so sorry."

"Well, umm, actually—" Based on Ezra's weird "journey" comment and the fact that he didn't show up tonight, let alone text me to tell me he wasn't coming, I had come to the conclusion that we weren't as serious as I'd thought we were.

Reece shook his head. "Look, Mag, it won't happen again. You're just so beautiful, but I want you to know that I respect you and I promise to behave myself better in the future."

Did he just call me beautiful? I needed to clear this up immediately, but I was at a loss for words. This good-looking man, quite possibly the most gorgeous man I'd ever seen, just said that I was beautiful. "I mean, it's complicated."

He groaned and tugged at his hair. "I'm sorry. If I

was your boyfriend, I would want to kick the crap out of any guy who touched you like I did tonight."

"It's not what you think—" My brain was refusing to communicate properly with my mouth.

Before I could explain, he said, "I promise to keep my hands to myself from now on. Friends?"

I thought about admitting that I was hoping for the opposite of what he had just said, but a trickle of self-doubt spilled in. Maybe this was his way of letting me down softly.

He put his hands up in surrender. "Well, now that I've made a complete mess of things, I should go. Maybe I'll see you later sometime."

"Yeah, okay . . . ." I turned to put the key in my door, cranking it to the side to unlock it before continuing, "But what if we—" I looked up from the keyhole to find only empty space in front of me.

Maybe I should have called out his name. I should have clarified that I was sure I did not, in fact, have a boyfriend.

If anything, after tonight, I kind of wanted Reece to be my boyfriend. Instead, I let the doubt crash against me.

Maybe I wasn't the kind of girl men wanted to date. The last one I had slept with didn't even show up tonight. My thoughts drifted to what the girls said about me in high school. According to them, I'd never find a man who could love a girl like me.

I scanned the parking lot, looking for Reece's masculine frame in the dark, but he was long gone already. I slid into the driver's seat wondering what it would have been like if I were brave. If I would have kissed him the first time I had wanted to. But that wasn't me. I'd never been the kind of girl to make the first move.

As soon as I started the engine, my phone buzzed and lit up. I felt my heart skip a beat, thinking it was Reece asking me to come over to his house or something.

I read the incoming text, which was actually from Val in the group text: *I hope you ladies are having more fun than I am right now! At this rate, I don't think I'll be home until the sun comes up.* Attached was a picture of her sitting in a pile of wires, cords, and other sound equipment.

And because I had no self-control and was borderline pathetic, I went back into my texts to see the picture that Reece had taken of us together. Right before I re-opened that text, however, I noticed that I had an unread message from Ezra from about an hour ago.

If I were being honest with myself, I'd have to admit that I would have much rather it been from Reece than Ezra, which bothered me.

His text said: *Babe, I'm so sorry for not meeting you tonight. I got hit with a bad case of food poisoning and I can't get off the floor of the bathroom. Gross, I know. I feel really bad for missing our date. I hope I'm feeling better soon so I can take you out to lunch.* His text was punctuated at the end with three kissy-face emoji.

I shot a quick reply to him: *Sorry, I just now got your text. I hope you feel better soon!*

As I put my car into reverse, feeling more confused than before—and a little guilty—I backed out of the parking space, wondering what my evening would have been like if I had never bumped into Reece.

Chapter Three

I sat in my office, catching up on edits from last week. Mondays through Wednesdays were usually pretty quiet around here, so I used them to get files compiled and sent to clients. But this Wednesday was not normal. I checked the clock for the third time in just as many minutes, trying to not worry about my imminent future. My interview with the new owners of the resort was in an hour.

I would know by the end of it if I was going to be able to pay rent next month.

Sure, if I lost my job, I could set my own hours. Never working before 11 a.m. could be a perk of being my own boss. I would have to figure out health insurance and find out how to pay into a retirement plan, but I could think about those issues later. Hopefully later than this afternoon. Like two years from now later.

I stifled a yawn with my fist. I had tossed and turned last night, sleeping in 20-minute increments, worrying about the grammar in my resume even though Val had gone over it ten times, promising it was perfect. She even made me practice answering interview questions while we ate dinner last night. I was so thankful to be roommates with a successful business owner.

Unable to focus on the bride and groom on my screen, I got up and walked to Kathy's office, which was halfway down the hall from mine.

When I had tried to check in with her earlier this morning, as I did every day, she hadn't been here, which was odd. Kathy was the real boss of the resort, even though she would never admit it. She ran my schedule and everyone else's in the activities department at The Pacifica.

Luckily, she was here now. "Hey, Kathy. Have any of my appointments changed for today or tomorrow?"

The older woman was typing quickly, the giant computer screen casting a glow across her face. She jumped in her chair and looked up, her hand clutched to her chest. "Oh my goodness, Lina. You scared me!"

She turned back to her screen, grabbed her computer mouse, and clicked around a few times before her eyes finally met mine again. "Come in. Sit down."

I sat down in the plush white chair across from her desk. "I didn't mean to scare you. What's made you so jumpy?"

Kathy gave me a shy smile. "I had my interview first thing today. I guess they wanted to get through the easy cuts early on."

"Oh please, I'm sure they picked you to go first because this place would go to shit without you. Your office is the hub of the resort."

As the special event coordinator, she did all the

wedding planning and booked all the activities. Other than my photography sessions, the resort offered surfing, paddleboarding, and bike rentals. Kathy was essentially the administrator for anything that wasn't the hotel or spa on this campus, and every single member of this staff would agree that she was the real boss around here and always had been.

"I sure hope you're right. The suits in that conference room didn't crack a smile. Blake was there with them, sticking out like a sore thumb, contrasting with their collection of funeral attire." She clicked her tongue a couple of times. "They are going to eat her alive."

I cringed, more worried for my friend than for myself. Blake had been pretty quiet about most of the details going on at work because there wasn't much she was allowed to share. I worried that she was carrying a lot of stress on her shoulders.

Kathy and I chatted for a little while before I excused myself to grab lunch from the café. I ordered a sandwich and a coffee before going back to my office where I scrolled mindlessly on my phone while scarfing down my food.

Ten minutes before my appointment, Val sent a text in our group chat: *Good luck today, ladies!*

I replied: *Kathy told me the people doing the interviews were a bunch of robots, so I'm obviously excited to dive right in. How's it going, Blake?*

Blake replied: *Terrible. I can't wait for the next three days to be over with so I can go back to my life. There are four vultures I'm trapped in this conference room with and they're out for blood. Lizette, her brother, and two other corporate snobs. The brother is*

HOT though, so at least there's one positive to being on the firing squad.

Val popped in with: *Ooh, I wanna see hottie boss! Sneak a pic!*

Then Blake replied: *Not on your life. I don't want to lose my job, too. FYI, Lina, I didn't tell them you're my best friend. You can if you want to, but if they hate me, I don't want them to cut you because of it.*

A few seconds later she sent: *Ugh, most of them are back from our break. I'll see you soon!*

I checked the clock and saw that it was time to make my way to the conference room. I replied: *I'm headed that way! Wish me luck!*

I put my phone away, balled up the empty sandwich wrapper, tossed it into the trash, and stood up, brushing the crumbs off my dress. My fingers were tingling as my anxiety reared its ugly head. This meeting had the power to change everything, and all I wanted to do was run in the opposite direction. Steeling myself, I grabbed my laptop—onto which I'd loaded with a slideshow of my best work—and headed out the door.

I walked into the boardroom and found a small group of women sitting at the table. Lizette, the new head of The Pacifica, sat at the far end. She wore what I realized was her signature look—a tailored black suit and deep red lipstick. I had seen her a few times around the resort, but she had never stopped to say hello.

Her black hair was down today, pressed straight, and

power oozed from her glowing pores. I let out a slow breath, trying to ignore how intimidating I found her.

Two women I had never seen before sat to her right, both dressed in all black as well. One had long, dark braids tied into a knot at the top of her head, and the other had platinum-blonde hair flowing just below her shoulders like a 1970s TV star.

The woman closest to Lizette had a notepad in front of her and started writing something as I approached the chair at the other end of the table, which I assumed was for me. The blonde was on her phone and didn't lay it down until I put my hand on the back of my chair.

Thankfully, Blake sat to Lizette's left and looked like a blossom on a spring morning, with her bright pink blazer and yellow polka-dot blouse. I made a mental note to make fun of her later for obviously not getting the drab attire memo.

Lizette spoke before I could say anything stupid. "Ms. Herrera, correct?"

"Yes."

I suddenly didn't know what to do. Should I sit down? Should I tell her I brought pictures on my laptop? My palm gripping my computer was sweaty, but I was grateful I couldn't flop my hands around.

Lizette pointed to the chair I stood behind. "Please, have a seat. There's no need to be nervous."

I sat down, desperately hoping my blank expression hid my fear and didn't make me look aloof. My eyes met Blake's, and she gave me a ghost of a smile. I exhaled again and reminded myself that I was prepared and had nothing to worry about.

"You already know Blake," Lizette said.

I dipped my chin at Blake, not sure if I should reveal how well I knew her yet.

Lizette gestured to the woman who was still quietly writing notes. "This is Aniyah. She's our third in command with this project." Aniyah looked up from her notepad and gave me a brief nod before she scribbled more information down. I smiled at her through gritted teeth, offended that the resort I'd built my career around was just a project to them.

Then Lizette pointed to the blonde. "This is Aimee. Her company is handling our marketing as we move forward. She is going to decide what departments will be the most lucrative and will bring in the type of customer we have in mind for the resort."

I smiled brightly at Aimee, hoping she saw it as an olive branch. "What firm are you with? My sister works for Hamilton and Rowe in Chicago. They're one of the largest marketing firms in the nation."

Before I could continue, she cut me off. "I know who they are. You wouldn't know my firm, we only cater to . . ." her pause gave her a moment to look me up and down like I was a browning banana peel, "an exclusive clientele."

So much for any peacemaking I had in mind.

The door opened behind me and Lizette stood. "You'll be joining us after all?" She sounded condescending and skeptical of whoever had just walked through the doorway.

I turned in my chair and my body temperature seemed to drop twenty degrees.

He reached out for a handshake without looking at me. "Nice to meet you, I'm—"

I took his hand in mine as his name left my lips in a whisper.

Reece.

He finally looked into my eyes and I could tell he felt the jolt of electricity flowing through our hands. Or maybe he felt the same panic I did in that moment.

"Mag." It was barely loud enough for me to hear, let alone anyone else in the room.

He rubbed the back of his neck with his free hand and I finally realized why Lizette had looked so familiar. She was his sister, the one he called Izzy.

His hand was warm in mine, a strange comfort for this intrusive situation. My first instinct was to bolt out of the room, but my bones were frozen to the seat.

Lizette's voice boomed across the room as she sat back down, snapping me out of my trance. "This is our house photographer, Lina Herrera."

Before I could correct her on the pronunciation of my name, Reece and Blake's voices echoed off the walls as they both said, "It's Lynn-a, not Lean-a."

Lizette's eyes went from Blake to Reece in a fraction of a second. "Have you two met before?"

I twisted to face her, about to explain how I knew Reece, but he spoke before I could.

"No, I haven't had the pleasure yet. It was just a lucky guess." His fingers tightened around mine. "Reece Howell. I'm the new CFO of The Pacifica Resort."

I looked back at him, catching the dimple in his smile, and my heart skipped a beat. Maybe his was also skipping because he didn't start shaking my hand for several seconds.

He finally let go of my hand, and his eyebrows scrunched together. "You have a little something . . . ." He pointed to my cheek. I rubbed at it frantically but didn't feel anything.

"Here, let me." His thumb grazed my cheek. I thought I was nervous before, but now I couldn't find enough oxygen in the room to fill my lungs.

He pulled his hand away and looked down at the pad of his thumb before glancing at me and smirking. "Mustard?"

Reece wasn't doing a stellar job of hiding the fact that we knew each other. That we had almost kissed each other. But I didn't want the look on his face to ever go away.

Heat finally traveled through my body, unfortunately out of embarrassment, and maybe something else. I should have stopped in the bathroom to check for food on my face. That's probably what Aniyah was writing when I walked in.

I remembered how to speak again as he grabbed a tissue from the box on the table and wiped off his dirty finger. "It's nice to meet you, Mr. Howell."

"Please, call me Reece."

He continued staring at me, probably reading my emotions, until Lizette finally spoke again. "Reece, please have a seat so we can get started."

His shoulders bunched when she spoke to him, like he was a child being chastised, but he tossed the dirty tissue into the trash and slipped into the chair next to Blake. We still had a couple of chairs between us, but it felt like he might as well be sitting in my lap.

Aniyah shuffled her papers and tapped them on the dark cherrywood table, straightening her stack before laying them down again.

Reece reached across the table toward her. "Can I see those for a second?" She handed them to him and he read through the first page quickly.

"So" He pointed to the bold name on the company document, "Do you go by Magdalina, or is Lina just fine?" The corners of his eyes crinkled teasingly. I already knew he wasn't going to call me either.

Aimee repeated my name, shaking her head. "I don't know why you pronounce it that way. It's kind of weird."

Reece's eyes shot to her. "The girl who spells her name with two e's at the end has no room to tell anyone that their name is weird, Aimee." He emphasized the last syllable of her name like it was sour.

Instead of giving him a retort, she just shot him a glare from her side of the table. Reece passed the papers back to Aniyah, ignoring Aimee's gaze.

"I didn't have much time to prepare for this one. I apologize." He motioned for them to begin.

Aniyah leaned forward in her chair, asking, "So, Lina, how long have you been employed at the resort?"

I slipped out the resume I had tucked into my closed laptop and slid it across the table toward her. "I've been here for almost five years."

She picked up the paper and scanned it briefly. "Do you not have any other experience as a photographer outside of this resort?"

I knew that would be one of my weaknesses, so I tried to sit up a little taller to show her I was confident. "I was hired here right after college and haven't needed to work anywhere else. I've done a few side gigs for friends or relatives, but I've never been paid for them, so I didn't feel comfortable putting them on my resume." I pointed at the document in her hand. "I did work at the camera shop while I was in school. I can give you the owner's contact information if you would like a reference."

She looked over the paper one last time before handing it over to Lizette, who looked down at it but didn't actually read it before pushing it to the center of the table.

Aniyah went on, her voice dismissive, "I don't think that will be necessary at this time."

Then Lizette jumped in with a question. "Do you have any reviews of your work from former guests at the resort?"

I smiled and opened my laptop. "Yes, actually, I do." I opened the document that I had created with copies of emails from clients.

I pushed my laptop closer to her and she scrolled a couple of times.

"These are nice, but I was wondering if you had anything more substantial. Possibly from a third-party website. Not some list of personally curated responses." She pushed my laptop back across the table toward me.

Shaking my head, I replied, "Sorry, I don't. There might be reviews on the resort's TripAdvisor or Yelp pages, but I don't have anything like that ready to show you today."

Lizette sent a sideways glance to Aniyah, who scribbled down whatever they were communicating wordlessly.

Blake finally spoke up, "Did you bring any photos to show us? A portfolio, maybe?"

Thank goodness for Blake. I opened my presentation on my laptop and showed it to the group. I was glad I had already shown her most of these pictures, so she knew which ones were my favorites. The room filled with oohs and aahs, which was surprising, considering my audience.

I even got a comforting smile from Reece. Until then, he hadn't said anything or even really looked at me. I wasn't sure if that was a good thing or not.

Aniyah put her pen down, finally interested in me, and even Aimee flashed me a smile, which just made me more proud of the work I had done over the years. Lizette's expression didn't change, but I had a feeling she always held any emotions she felt locked tightly inside.

The women took turns asking me more questions after I ran out of photos, but Reece stayed silent. I was honest with every answer, telling them I wasn't sure what kind of income I brought in for the resort, but that I had been working steadily since day one and my workload compared to the few photographers I was still in contact with from college.

Aniyah went back to writing on her notepad and Aimee even picked her phone up at one point, completely ignoring what I was saying.

As the interview was winding down, Aimee leaned forward, folding her arms on the table in front of her. "So, tell me about your social media presence."

"Well, I have a couple hundred followers, but I'm willing to work on that."

Her smile was condescending. "Could you give me your name on Insta?" I gave her my Instagram handle, which was the very creative use of my name followed by the word "photos," and she looked up my account on her phone. "There's some good stuff here, but not enough engagement. You're going to have to make a bigger commitment if you want to be more successful."

I smiled, wondering what she had against me. "I'm willing to do whatever it takes. I'm a team player."

Aimee's lip perked in a smile for the bricfest of moments, but it felt like I was looking at a shark. "You're going to have to be to stay with us. It's a lot harder than it looks, you know."

"Hard work doesn't bother me at all."

Aimee nodded, staring at her phone, clearly done with her questions.

There was a knock at the door and a woman with a clipboard and a radio headset like the one Blake always wore stepped in. She kept her eyes on the carpet like she was bracing for something painful. "Excuse me, Mr. Howell, but, umm, the senior Mr. Howell is on the phone for you."

Reece looked up at her. "Did you tell him I'm in the middle of something?"

She cringed. "I tried to, sir, but he said it was urgent."

He pulled his hair into his fists and—was that an actual growl? "Did you try to tell him I would call him back?"

She shook her head, her eyes large and traumatized.

One of the Mr. Howells in question must have caused her some undue stress recently.

Reece stood and looked at her, his eyes soft. "I'm sorry, Janine. I hate when he puts you in the middle of our arguments. I'll be right there."

She ran out the door without a second glance. He shot a pleading look to his sister, who kept her face neutral but after a few seconds quietly said, "I'll talk to him."

He answered her with a curt nod before his eyes turned to me. I couldn't quite comprehend the look he gave me, but I hoped we would have a chance to talk later. Privately.

Once the door closed behind him, Lizette tapped her perfect nails on the table. "Actually, I do have one more question."

I gave her my undivided attention.

"What is your stance on relationships in the workplace?"

I wasn't sure how to answer. Was she asking about my friendship with Blake, or was this about Ezra? Or did she pick up on whatever was clearly happening between Reece and me? "Could you elaborate?"

I glanced at Blake. The way she propped her elbows on the table told me that Lizette had clearly gone off script.

"What is your history with your coworkers? Is there anyone here at the resort that you are close with? Anyone that is closer than a friend?" Her eyebrow went up, and she looked so much like her brother that I didn't know how I'd missed it earlier.

Honesty is usually the best policy, but I didn't want to say something that might get me in trouble. I was desperate to please these people. "Well, Blake is one of my best friends, but we don't openly discuss work if that is what you're worried about."

Lizette nodded. "Yes, we are aware that the two of you are friends. But I'm trying to discover if there is anything else going on. Maybe with other employees?"

Aimee leaned forward again, flashing the biggest mean-girl, you-can't-sit-with-us smile. "Lina, are you sleeping with anyone at work?"

My jaw dropped.

Before I responded, Blake jumped up, "Okay, I think we can all agree that we are done here."

Lizette turned to Aimee. "Well, that was unprofessional and uncalled for."

I glanced sideways at Blake, who was turning red, preparing to pounce.

I turned to Aimee, angry for the way she treated me and now for what my friend was dealing with. "I don't understand what any of that has to do with my job and how well I perform here at the resort."

Out of the corner of my eye, I caught Lizette shooting daggers at Aimee. She pointed to Blake, barely looking at her. "Sit down, you're making this bigger than it is." When Blake sat back down in her chair, Lizette focused her brown eyes on mine. "It's just that we are worried that a lovers' quarrel could cause undue stress, making it difficult for you to do your job. That's all."

Blake laid her palms flat on the table. "This meeting is over. You asked all the questions we discussed previously."

Lizette turned her viper's glare on her, and for the first time, I worried for my friend's job, too. "We need to discuss company policy with Lina, and we haven't even brought up the terms of her future employment."

I finally responded, shell-shocked. "Well, I guarantee that anything I do in my personal life has not and will not affect my professional life. That is all I am willing to say at this time." This had to be about Ezra. One of them had to have seen us the other day. What a stupid mistake.

Blake cleared her throat, shuffling through a stack of papers in front of her. "According to company policy, there's a rule about not dating within the chain of command, such as an employee with their manager." She scanned the page and read a section silently, following along with her fingertip. "But there's nothing in here about staff members who are on the same employment scale."

Aimee jumped in. "Just because it's not in the company handbook doesn't mean it's not frowned upon."

Trying to remove the focus from me, I asked, "Are you going to let us have a copy of the handbook so we know what rules we're supposed to be following? I would like the opportunity to read them before being accused of breaking them."

Aniyah flipped a few pages in her notebook, writing something down. "Consider it done. I'll send it out to the whole company as soon as we adjourn."

Lizette steepled her fingers, tapping them slowly against each other. "Fine. We're almost out of time and need to move on anyway. Here's what I'm thinking. Since you don't have a strong social media following, and we don't have valid reviews from customers, we're going to keep you on as a probationary member of our staff."

Sure, they were putting a pin in my dating life, but this was even more terrifying. I thought I had interviewed well today, despite the emotional roller coaster. "I'm not sure I know what you mean. What is it to be a probationary staff member?"

Lizette looked at Aniyah to answer this one. Aniyah smiled at me, and for the first time, I felt it was genuine. "We're going to retain you as a full-time employee for the next three months. At the end of June, we'll reconvene to review your data. We'll share your reviews, your productivity, and you can share with us any strides you have made in networking and social media." She paused, tapping her pen against her notebook. "If you impress us, you'll remain an employee at The Pacifica. If not . . . ." She turned toward Lizette, who made eye contact with her but didn't complete her cliff-hanger of a sentence.

I looked to Blake, who mouthed, "I'm so sorry."

My voice was flat as I clarified, "So I have three months to prove to you that I should keep my job."

"Precisely." Lizette stood, indicating that our interview had finally come to an end. She came around the table and opened the door, ushering me out.

I thanked them all, solely from habit, and walked down the hallway. I was in a daze on my way to my office.

I had a nagging feeling that they were setting me up to fail.

I made it back to my tiny office and knew I needed to talk to Ezra before his interview later today.

I sent him a text: *911, we need to talk.*

He replied a minute later: *OMW to your office.*

I didn't think it would help either of us if we were seen together after my disaster of an interview, so I sent: *No. Meet me in the West Garden. We need privacy.*

After locking my office, I went through the maintenance entrance at the rear of the building, hoping to not be seen by anyone.

I walked into the small garden, which was surrounded by tall hedges, making it the most private spot we had access to without room keys. I paced back and forth for a couple of minutes before Ezra stepped through the arched entryway.

One of his hands landed on my hip and the other cupped my cheek. Forgetting any animosity I held for him after standing me up, I melted into his embrace.

"I'm so sorry for missing our date. I really wanted to go out with you."

I shook my head. "We can talk about that later, right now I need to tell you about my interview."

He tipped his head forward, concerned. "How did it go? Are you okay?"

I took a few steps back, nervous that there could be eyes everywhere. "Ezra, it was terrible, but you need to know that they are not happy about our relationship."

"There's nothing wrong about you and me, Lina."

"I know, but I don't think we can be affectionate at work anymore. My job is on the line here." I felt myself starting to hyperventilate. "I can't afford to get laid off."

Ezra guided me to a bench. He sat down next to me but left several inches between us. He rubbed my back slowly. "It's not that big of a deal. Your talent greatly outweighs the fact that we're seeing each other."

I looked into his crystal blue eyes. A thought occurred to me. If our relationship was solid and had been established before the takeover, there wouldn't be a problem with us seeing each other. "Maybe if we told them we were boyfriend and girlfriend, it wouldn't be an issue anymore."

He pulled his hand away from me and tucked it into his lap. "Listen, Lina. I like you a lot, but I'm just not there yet."

"Ezra, we can just tell them. It doesn't have to be true."

His lips drooped in a grimace. "I'm not comfortable doing that." He looked up at the sky. "I'm not looking to settle down yet. I'm only twenty-six."

I kicked at the cobblestone path, wondering if I was going to lose the job and the boy all in one day. "I understand. I'm just grasping for solutions."

He looked back down at me. "I'm glad you get me, babe. What we have is working. There's no need to complicate things."

I nodded, but I wasn't sure if I fully agreed with him.

He laid his hand on my leg. "I'm so happy when I'm with you, but I just have too much going on to be someone's boyfriend. It's a big commitment. Can we just keep it like it is for a while longer?"

I stood up, ready to be anywhere other than this resort. "Yeah, it's cool. I just wanted to warn you that they might bring me up at your interview."

I didn't even pay attention to what he said next, I was

too eager to get to my car so I could go home. I gave him a quick goodbye and walked back to my office.

I grabbed my purse and thought about bringing my camera bag so I could do some work from home. I decided against it, though. I wasn't up for spending the next couple of hours analyzing tiny details of happily married people.

I locked the door again and made my way to the lobby. Sending a weak wave to the concierge, I dug through my purse, looking for my keys as I shoved the giant wooden door open.

I thought about calling Reece when I got home, but I wouldn't know what to say to him.

Sorry I work here?

My life is complicated and I'm a mess, so it's best that you keep your distance?

I felt, rather than heard, someone step in front of me. Looking up from my purse, keys in my hand, I almost bumped into Aimee.

She had that mean-girl look in her eyes again. "I don't think you're going to make it one month, let alone three, so you should probably start packing your things now."

I took a step back from her. "Is there something I did to offend you?"

She put her hands on her hips, "No. I just don't think you're a good fit for the future of our resort. You should quit so we can hire your replacement already."

My eyes started welling up. No. I couldn't cry in front of this woman. This bully. I just shook my head and walked away from her, knowing if I said anything, she would bask in the knowledge that she had upset me.

I walked through the parking lot and made it to my car in record time. Once I got inside, the tears pushed their way out again, but I wiped my eyes with the back of my hand. I wanted to call Blake and tell her what Aimee had just said to me, but I knew I couldn't.

I thought about calling my mom to ask her if I could come over and curl up on her couch, but I didn't want anyone to know how humiliated I was after letting this afternoon affect me so much.

It was probably best that I didn't talk to anyone, so I put my phone on "do not disturb" so I wouldn't be tempted to use it and stuffed it into the bottom of my purse. I knew Val was working the late shift, so I drove home, ready to ignore the universe for the next several hours.

Chapter Four

As soon as I got home, I ran upstairs and changed into my favorite pajamas—an old shirt that was peppered with holes and flannel pants that were so thin you could read a newspaper through them. I threw my hair into a messy bun and plopped on the couch. I had cried the whole drive home and knew my mascara was probably dried in streaks down my cheeks. I probably looked like a member of an early 2000s emo band, but I didn't care enough to wash it off.

Knowing I would be alone in this quiet house until it was time to go to bed was a small comfort. Here, I was safe. There were no mean-spirited women or corporations that were intent on destroying my pleasant life.

In our cozy little house, I could dwell on everything that was ruining my life in peace, not giving a shit what I looked like in front of our giant TV.

I flipped through the channels, not really caring what I was going to watch, when the opening scene for the original *Jurassic Park* appeared on the screen. It had been my dad's favorite movie, so I stopped channel surfing and tossed the remote onto the coffee table.

When I made it to the part where the kids were hiding in the kitchen, a scene that had given me nightmares for weeks the first time I saw it, I realized that slouching into the couch cushions wasn't miserable enough for me, so I got up and grabbed a pint of ice cream and a spoon from the kitchen and found my way back to my nest on the couch.

It wasn't so I could avoid a movie moment that still scared the hell out of me as an adult. I was much braver than that.

As the credits rolled, I had my feet propped up on the coffee table while I continued to stuff cookie dough ice cream into my face. Of course, I was crying again. But this time it was because the T-Rex saved those people, even though it was against her nature. Was this movie really a love story from the dinosaurs to us? I felt a strong emotional connection to this strong female lead and had the urge to tell the world that she was just misunderstood.

My dad had loved how this movie ended. He said it was absolute perfection, especially since it wasn't the original plan. Aaannnd now the tears spilling from my face were from missing my dad. He would know how to handle all of my problems.

My spoon was scraping the bottom of the container for the last bite of mostly melted ice cream when I heard a knock at the door. It made me wonder which one of us ordered from Amazon, but I didn't care, so I ignored it. I would grab the package on my way up to bed later.

The knock repeated again. Dammit.

I mumbled to the person on the other side of the door from my spot on the couch, "You better not be some jerk trying to sell me something, because I don't want any."

Another knock, louder now.

Fine. I'll get up.

"Just a second!" I yelled, turning off the TV. With the curtains closed and all the lights off, the house was bathed in darkness. I stood up and spooned the last drop of ice cream into my mouth, preparing to tell them to take their solar panels or whatever else they were peddling and shove them where the sun doesn't shine before I swung the door open.

I couldn't imagine how I looked with a spoon hanging out of my mouth as I stared at Reece standing on my front step. I whispered an incoherent curse before he started laughing.

"Well, hello to you, too."

I had forgotten how smooth his voice was. And of course, he was still dressed immaculately just like I had seen him earlier, in a dark blue oxford shirt and slacks that looked like they had been handwoven by God himself.

"Are you stalking me?" I shoved the spoon into the empty container and set it on the table by the door.

He held up his hand, and a flashlight dangled by its thin braided handle from one of his fingers, the one I had left on the floor when I ran out of his house. "I was worried you would need this for your next robbery. Wouldn't want you to get lost on the way out of someone else's bedroom window."

I narrowed my eyes at him, ignoring his jab. "What

kind of person just shows up randomly at someone's house without calling first?"

His teeth flashed in a smile as he looked me up and down, "Well isn't that kind of how we met? At least I knocked on the front door."

He did have a point.

After watching his eyes scan my body, I became very aware of the way I was dressed. This was the universe telling me that we were polar opposites and I should send him on his way. I tugged at the frayed hem of my stained shirt, attempting to make myself more presentable. "I appreciate you bringing back my lost property, but why are you here? Did you look up my address in the company files or something?"

He gave me a mischievous half-smile, placing the flashlight in my hand. "I remembered it from your ID Saturday night."

My eyes practically doubled in size. "You memorized my address?"

He shrugged. "I'm freakishly good at memorizing things."

"You've got the freak part right, I guess."

He crossed his eyes, causing me to burst out laughing. "Well, Mag, are you going to invite me in?"

I smiled to myself, confirming that he had been messing with me when he asked what I wanted to be called during the interview.

I looked over my shoulder into the house, judging how messy it was before deciding whether he could come in or not. There weren't any bras hanging from the kitchen chairs, and the sink was actually empty for once, so I found myself gesturing for him to follow me inside.

"Would you like anything?" I asked. "A glass of wine or water?"

He shook his head. "No thanks, I'm perfect just like this."

We sat down next to each other on the couch, and I silently agreed, he was absolutely perfect.

"So, why are you really here, Reece?"

"Someone told me you left the resort right after your interview. I didn't think it had gone that badly. But I wanted to check on you." His voice was even deeper when he spoke quietly.

I was willing to bet a crisp hundred-dollar bill that I could guess who went running to the bosses telling on me for leaving. Would he believe my story, or would he believe his colleagues?

I shrugged. "Some stuff happened, I guess, and my schedule was clear, so I came home."

He twisted to look into my face more easily while keeping his knees a good three inches away from mine. "Well, that's a lame answer." When I still didn't speak, he went on. "There's seriously nothing you could tell me that would shock me. I've seen it all."

I drew lazy circles on my thigh with the tip of my finger to distract myself from the emotions brewing inside of me. "Well, Aimee basically accused me of sleeping with someone at work, and your sister didn't exactly stop her."

"Oh, Mag, I'm so sorry." The nickname he had given me was now the only thing I ever wanted to be called again. Before I lost all focus, he said, "I've known Aimee for years, and she's a complete asshole. I've tried having her removed from our marketing team, but unfortunately, she's really good at what she does."

When I didn't respond, he asked, "Did she accuse you of sleeping with me?"

I pinned him with an icy stare. "Why? Did you know I was going to be in that room today?"

He shook his head quickly. "No, I didn't. I swear. I'm just trying to figure out why they would accuse you of something like that. Aimee and I are not friends, by any means, and I could see her making things up to make this job even more miserable for me." His smile had disappeared. "Does your boyfriend work at the resort?"

I picked at a piece of dirt under my fingernail and said, "I lied to you."

"About what?"

There was something undeniable between us, something pulling me toward him. I knew the reason Aimee accused me, but since it wasn't going to be something that happened at work anymore, I didn't want to tell Reece about Ezra. Besides, Ezra was clear that we weren't exclusive. He wasn't my boyfriend.

I inhaled deeply and conjured up some bravery. "When I told you I had a boyfriend the night I met you, I wasn't exactly in a clear state of mind. I panicked and blurted the first thing that came out."

He turned in his seat, his knee grazing mine, and warmth pooled in my chest. "I don't want to be the other guy." The conviction in his voice was heavenly.

I tried to shrug like I hadn't spent several hours this

week obsessing over my relationship with Ezra. "You have nothing to worry about. I don't have a boyfriend."

"Okay. So, just to clear things up: You're single, and you feel this thing between us, too?"

I nodded. "Correct. On both counts." I tucked my legs under myself, adding space between us. "But, you're my boss. I literally just endured an interrogation that made it very clear that this can't happen."

When he didn't respond, I shook my head and buried my face in my hands. "I'm sorry. I think the interview hit me harder than it should have because my mom just moved to her new place, and my sister is doing so well at her firm." I don't know what compelled the words to leave my mouth, but somehow I felt safe talking to him. "All of my people are on amazing paths to happiness, and I'm just trudging along in a job that's good but isn't my life goal. And now I'm not even sure I'll have it in a few months."

I gave him another long look. He looked so welcoming, so kind. I wanted to snuggle against him and kiss him until we passed out together on the couch. Instead, I said, "And in a cruel twist of fate, we shouldn't even be sitting here together because I work for you."

He looked up at the ceiling and let out a long breath. "Not for long, though."

I cringed, "Shit. I guess Blake was right and I probably should find a new job." Needing to burn off the nervous energy jolting through me, I stood up and walked into the kitchen, pulling a glass out of the cabinet. "Are you sure you don't want anything to drink?"

"I'm fine, thank you. And I didn't mean you won't have a job soon."

I filled the glass with water and walked back toward the living room, meeting his eyes.

"I'm leaving the company. Especially after the way they treated you today."

"I can't let you do that. I won't be the reason you walk out on your family business."

"I've been planning to leave for months. I should be ready to move on by the end of summer. Plus, once you meet more of my family, you'll understand why I can't stay." I made it almost to him when I tripped, sending my glass of water spilling all over the coffee table, the couch, and of course, him.

He laughed, but the pitch of my voice rose. "I'm so sorry. I didn't even want that stupid water anyway." I ran back to the kitchen, grabbed a hand towel, and rushed back to him, attempting to soak the water up from his chest.

"Calm down, please." He continued laughing as he unbuttoned his shirt.

I tossed the towel onto the coffee table and jumped back. "You're taking your shirt off in my living room, and you want me to calm down?"

"I think I pulled it away before my undershirt got too soaked." He winked at me, and the way heat flowed through my body reminded me that we really shouldn't be alone right now. Or possibly ever. "I promise I won't undress completely."

Without asking, I took the wet shirt from his hands.

"I'm going to throw this in the dryer. You stay right there. Don't take anything else off while I'm gone."

I went to the hallway and opened up the laundry closet. I may or may not have sniffed his shirt before tossing it in the dryer and turning it on "delicate."

I came back into the living room, but this time I sat on the puffy floor pillow across from the coffee table. One less layer of clothing between us made the room feel much smaller than before. I tried to remember what we were talking about before I drenched him. "So why would you take over a new property if you were planning on leaving?

"I'm sort of obligated to stay with the company for four more months."

That was a specific number. "Is your contract almost up?"

He pursed his lips like he was debating something. "I'm assuming you won't let me answer with 'some stuff happened and I have to do some things,' huh?"

I shook my head but didn't press him. I was, however, a little concerned.

His lips pressed together in a grimace before he responded. "So, I had a pretty tight-knit group of friends growing up. We went all through school together and essentially were all brought up only to take over our family businesses with no other goals."

The idea of having a career planned before you're even grown was foreign to me. I couldn't imagine the weight on his shoulders.

He went on, "Long story short, we spent more time

partying than studying, and eventually I got myself into a bit of trouble and I had to go away for a while."

"Oh my God. You didn't kill anyone, did you?"

"No, but I did damage some property during a DUI. Thankfully it was enough of a wake-up call that I went into treatment and got help. I've been sober for a little over a year now, but I have four months left of my probation. My dad has to sign off on my paperwork showing that I'm working and I'm a productive member of society and all that. Without his signature, they'll send me to jail."

"And I offered you a glass of wine earlier. Wow, I'm such a jerk."

He chuckled. "Don't stress, I'm good being around other people when they're drinking. Just don't offer me any cocaine and we'll be fine."

I wasn't sure if he was joking or not, but I had a feeling he was being totally serious. "Well, I've never even seen cocaine other than in movies, so I think you're safe with me."

"I do feel safe with you." His voice was steady and low. We sat quietly, just staring at each other for a bit. It was as if we were in a bubble neither of us wanted to pop.

He broke the silence but spoke quietly. "Most of my friends are still living that lifestyle, so I don't have a place with them anymore."

I wanted to get up and cup his cheek in my hand, but I knew if I touched him, I wouldn't be able to stop myself from going further. "Do you miss them?"

"Not really. I only stay in contact with my best friend,

since the rest of them kind of suck anyway." He chuckled. "And besides, I have been so overwhelmed with work lately that I don't have time to miss anyone."

"What do you do for the company, exactly?"

"I'm usually the guy that comes in and fires everyone as soon as we buy a new property, leaving destruction in my wake." He must have noticed the frown on my face because he laughed a little. "Really, I'm just a puppet for whatever idea my dad has up his sleeve, and I fucking hate it.

"When the company purchased The Pacifica, they promised that I would get to run it the way I wanted to, but of course, they pulled the rug out from under me on the first day and handed it to my sister. So now I'm the CFO instead of the CEO, and I'm ready to get out."

That had to be mentally jarring, to have a plan only to have it taken away. I wouldn't have been able to hold myself together as well as he did. "What would you want to do instead?"

He thought for a minute before answering. "Honestly, I think I would love the job if they trusted my decisions. I'm hoping that buying a house will prove to them that they can trust me financially. It would be fun to run my own small collection of properties." He paused for a second, thinking. "But really, I'd like to walk away from all of it and get into the music industry. Managing a band would be cool."

He had seemed in his element at Joey's show. Thinking about him running the day-to-day life of my favorite bands brought a smile to my face.

His smile turned shy. "How about you? Is working for a resort your dream or is it holding you back?"

I laughed a little. "I enjoy it, but it's not my end game by any means. I need the money, but I don't know if it'll be sustainable for much longer."

"What don't you like about it?"

"Blake—she's one of my best friends, by the way—mentioned that the new management . . . well, you and your sister, I guess, aren't interested in our boutique-style services, so all of the people like me are most likely going to get laid off. So, the things I don't like don't really matter, do they?"

He sounded concerned. "I really need to talk to Izzy about this."

I crossed my arms across my chest absentmindedly. "Would it even help? They are giving me a three-month deadline to bring in more clients and prove my worth, but maybe I don't want that. Maybe I want my own thing." If I were closer to my goals, it wouldn't be an issue. Right now, however, I knew it would be an uphill battle to start my own business.

"Have you thought about opening up your own studio?"

I felt like he had read my mind. "I have a five-year plan. Which is actually a four-year plan because I'm already a year into it. If I can save up two years' worth of rent and have enough of a social media presence to bring in a steady clientele I'll be able to start my own company."

"You know you can get started without all that, right?"

It was my turn to laugh. "My friends are constantly saying the same thing to me." I shrugged. "I just want to make sure I have somewhere to land if I fall. I'm not exactly a risk-taker. I know it sounds like I'm lacking ambition, but not having to handle scheduling and paperwork and only being responsible for my own creativity has been a huge perk with this job. I would hate to lose that."

I kept my deeper reasons to myself. When my dad died, a lot of responsibility had fallen into my lap. I had to step up and keep my mom organized those first few years, or we would have lost everything. I didn't want to worry like that ever again.

"I bet we could find you something like that somewhere else." He tilted his head back and forth a few times, deep in thought. I tried not to think about his use of the word we and what it could mean in the future. "I can find out if there's an opening for a photographer at one of our other properties."

I giggled nervously. "Slow down there, cowboy. I'm a big fan of baby steps."

"Okay, fine, I'll let you take your baby steps. But when you're ready to run, I'd like to help you."

I smiled up at him. He seemed genuine, like he really wanted to help me and he actually cared about the resort. But I also had just met him and needed to get a better feel for him first.

The dryer buzzed, letting us know that his shirt was dry. When I stood up, he got to his feet, too, and stood directly in front of me. "I know we don't know each other very well yet, but I promise to support you however I can.

Want me to call Izzy and tell her to go fuck herself? Or I can help you launch your own business. Whatever you need, I'll do it."

I blinked back the tears forming in my eyes. Why was I so emotional over his offer? "Thank you. I'll think about it." I let out a deep breath. "I think it's a mixture of how rude they were in the interview and my mother's move. Like all the emotions of being a loser in high school are bubbling up to the surface."

Reece's thumb rubbed back and forth across my cheek, and I might have noticed a flash of anger in his eyes. "I cannot believe what Aimee said. They had no right to ask you personal questions."

I stepped away from him before I did something I would regret and walked to the laundry to pull his shirt out. "It doesn't matter. It's not the first time I've dealt with mean girls."

I hadn't realized how late it had gotten until I heard the jingling of keys unlocking the front door. "Holy crap, my roommate! Put this on." I tossed Reece his shirt in a panic.

He slid it over his arms and started buttoning it. I spotted the glass I had dropped laying under the coffee table and crouched down to reach for it.

Valerie opened the door and flicked on the light in the entryway. Not expecting to see a man standing there, dressing himself, she screamed at the top of her lungs. "I have pepper spray! You better watch out!"

"Wait!" I called out from the ground, having retrieved the glass. On my way up, I slammed the back of my head into the coffee table. "Fuck."

"Oh, you're home." She then looked Reece up and down, noticing that we were both a little disheveled, before repeating in a different tone, "*Ohhhhh*, you're home." She tossed her keys, attached to a still-full pepper spray keychain, onto the table next to my empty ice cream container and flashed us a knowing smile.

I rubbed the back of my head where a knot was already growing. Before I could speak, she held out her hand to greet him. "Hi, I'm Valerie. You must be Lina's boyfriend Ezra. I've heard so much about you. It's so nice to finally meet you!"

This was going to be one of those moments that I would replay in my mind at three in the morning on restless nights forever. I could see it now . . . the memory would come to me, forcing me to break out into a cold sweat, and I would fight the urge to throw up all over myself.

Reece reached forward and shook her hand, but he faced me. "No, I'm definitely not her *boyfriend* Ezra. But I would love to hear more about him when you have the time." The smile on his face had to be the one he kept plastered on when he met with a client he hated at work. On the outside, he was dazzlingly beautiful, but I knew I had some explaining to do.

I turned an equally fake smile on my roommate and spoke through gritted teeth. "Hi Valerie, this is Reece. I met him the other night at my mom's house. And I was just walking him out."

"Wait. The house guy? The one you robbed?" She popped her hip out in her cute socialite way and smiled even brighter at him. "Nice to meet you, Reece."

I cleared my throat. "Wanna give us a minute?"

She jumped at that. "Yeah, sorry. I'll see you tomorrow." She shot Reece a little wave before scurrying off to her room. "Have a good night!"

I waited until Val had closed the door to her bedroom. "Okay, I know how this must sound, but he is not my boyfriend."

Reece tucked his hands into his pockets and stared down at the ground. "But there is another guy that your roommate knows all about?"

"I wouldn't say she knows all about him. Otherwise, she wouldn't have thought you were him, right?" I walked to the front door, pulling it open. He joined me outside, and I closed the door behind us, hoping Val wouldn't be able to hear our conversation.

He paused, pursing his lips.

I put my hands on my hips. "Just say what you're thinking."

"Are you sleeping with him?"

My bottom jaw just about hit the floor. "That's none of your business, you big oaf!"

He took a deep breath and released it in a grumble. "I don't even know why I asked that, it was not a fair question." He rubbed at his face and cursed, chastising himself.

I raised my eyebrow. "You don't see me disagreeing."

He reached forward, taking my hands off my hips and holding them in his own. "Mag, I'm kind of a mess, but I promise if you give me a chance, I can make it up to you. I've made so many mistakes in the past, but this thing between us feels important."

"I can't give you any chances. It won't work."

He squeezed my hands. "Why not?"

"Really? Reece, you sign my paychecks." I pulled my hands out of his and gestured to the entryway of the house. "Which I need so I can continue paying rent and buying food."

"Okay, so we'll be friends. Friends who spend a bunch of time together. The moment my probation is over, I'll walk in there and tell them I quit. Problem solved."

"That's insane, and you know it. We only just met."

He stretched his fingers and closed them tightly a few times. "I can't see you every day at the resort and not spend time with you. It'll be miserable."

I stepped back, leaning against the door. "Look at us. We're completely different. We'll date for a month and realize we're not compatible."

He reached forward, brushing a loose strand of hair over my ear. "I bet if you spent more time with me, you would see just how much we have in common. Please. Just friends."

His puppy-dog eyes were crushing their way through any resolve I had left. "Fine, but we have to keep our feelings in check. I need this job, and I don't want it being swayed one way or another because I want to sleep with management."

He grinned and leaned in, his lips almost brushing mine. "So you do want to sleep with me?"

I rolled my eyes and pushed him away from me lightly. "Eventually, I guess." I looked down at his feet and ran my eyes up his body. "Could you blame me?"

He gave me a smile that told me he knew just what I

was talking when I looked at him that way. "We won't hang out at work. It will be like you don't even know me there."

"It will be our secret. We could even pretend that we hate each other," I said, wondering what that could look like.

He ran his hand down my arm, taking hold of my wrist. "I don't know if I could go that far, but we'll just have to avoid each other when people are around." Without warning he stepped close to me again. The tickle of his breath ran across my lips, and I had to lick them to stop myself from pressing them to his. I wondered if he used sandalwood aftershave or if he naturally smelled warm and earthy.

"I'm going to have so much fun proving to you that I'm a better man than . . . what's his name—Erick?" he mumbled.

It took me a few seconds to remember who he was talking about. "Oh, Ezra." Then it hit me—work was about to get so awkward. "You probably met him today, actually. His interview was after mine." Heat rose in my throat. The thought of the two of them together was mortifying.

"Wow. Mag's a player. Okay." He bit his bottom lip lightly. "I was summoned by the devil to our corporate offices during your interview, so I didn't have the pleasure of meeting your other guy."

I was a little relieved, but still embarrassed. "Can we please talk about something else? Anything else? What kind of sports do you like?"

His fingertips grazed my neck, ignoring my question.

"I don't want to talk about sports right now." His eyes closed as he leaned forward, his nose touching mine. My heart raced as those strong fingers dug into my hair, pulling me closer to him.

His eyes shifted to a spot over my shoulder when we heard a knock on the door, Val's voice loudly following it. "Umm, guys, I forgot my wallet in my car and need to go get it. Can you let me out?"

Reece stepped back, and I planted my feet firmly on the ground.

"I should go," he said. "Can I call you tomorrow, after work? As a friend?"

I smiled, my lips tingling from the kiss he had almost given me. "Sounds good to me."

He licked his lips and gave me another mischievous wink before turning and making his way down the walkway.

"Okay, it's safe to come out now," I called out to Val, and she opened the door behind me.

Reece turned and waved. "Goodnight, Valerie! It was nice to finally meet you, too!" He smiled at me before making his way down the sidewalk.

"Well, here I was thinking I totally screwed things up for you two," Val said. "I had to come up with some stupid excuse to come check on you to make sure you weren't out here arguing."

"No, I think he's a good one." I grinned into the dark street before turning around. "Please don't tell Blake he was here. I'm not sure how to tell her about him yet."

She began to sing "Secret Lovers."

I held up my hand, stopping her. "He is my boss,

which would make that wholly inappropriate. We are going to be friends. That's it."

She giggled. "That sounds like a terrible idea. I love it."

I rolled my eyes at her and walked inside. "Goodnight, Val."

I laid down in my bed, full from the leftovers I found in the fridge after Val went back into her room. I had tried to watch TV after Reece left, but I couldn't focus.

Just as his name traveled through my brain, my phone lit up on the nightstand, illuminating my dark bedroom.

I grabbed it, swiping at the screen to answer. "Hello?"

"Hey Mag, what are you up to?"

I paused, curious. "I thought you said you were going to call me tomorrow?"

I heard him rustling around in the background. "Friends can call each other whenever they want, you know."

I barked out a laugh. "What friends in our generation call each other, anyway?"

I heard a smile in his voice. "Oh, okay, I'll let you go then. Talk to you tomorrow."

"Wait, no. Don't hang up. We can talk. Since we're already on the line and all."

He released a huff, like he was lying down. "I missed you."

I pulled my phone away briefly, looking at the time. "You were here like an hour ago."

"So first I can't call my friends, and now I can't miss my friends." His voice was light, and it was impossible not to crack a smile at his words.

"No, you can." I paused for a moment, glad that he called. "I missed you too."

"Tell me, what would you have been up to tonight if today had been a good day?"

"You mean I'm not supposed to come home and cry into a bucket of ice cream every day?"

He laughed, and it felt like he was lying right next to me. I rolled onto my side, closing my eyes, pretending he was in bed with me. "I don't know, I probably would have gotten some takeout and watched a movie. Maybe gone to dinner with Val or Blake. I don't really go out much." I ran my hands across the sheets like I was reaching out toward him. "How about you? What would you have done if you hadn't felt compelled to show up on my doorstep earlier?"

I swear I heard him stretching, and my mental image of him went straight for the gutter. Being only friends with him was already proving to be difficult. "There was a band playing tonight that I was hoping to see, but I ended up getting slammed with paperwork, so in reality, I was just going to sit at the kitchen counter looking over spreadsheets for hours on end."

"So is that what a CFO does? Crunches numbers all day long? I wanted to ask you earlier, but I didn't want to make it weird."

His laugh was quiet and breathy. "Basically. I oversee the finances of the property, see what investments are working, and plan for the future."

"So what do you like about it?"

He paused, and with the sound of his deep exhale I could imagine him being close enough to touch. "I love solving puzzles and finding solutions to important problems. I love manipulating numbers to see what works and what doesn't. It's kind of like a game."

"So he's cute and nerdy."

There was genuine delight in his voice. "You think I'm cute."

"Shut up," I laughed, "that wasn't my point."

"So yeah, I enjoy being a bean-counter. I just want to do it elsewhere, away from corporate life."

I shifted in my bed as a yawn pushed its way out of me.

"I'm sorry. I'm keeping you up. I should let you go." He didn't sound like he wanted to, though.

"No." I protested, "Tell me about the band you wanted to see tonight."

I imagined him sitting up excitedly, his voice suddenly energetic. "They're a folk hip-hop-rock band."

"A what?"

His laugh was infectious, "I can't describe them in any way that does them justice. Hold on." I heard him moving around before a song played through the phone. I lay there, listening, amazed that a banjo hip-hop percussion could sound so good together.

The song ended and he simply asked, "Right?"

His happiness had spread to me through the phone. "Next time they come to town, let me know. I want to go with you."

The line was quiet, but I could feel his presence. "I'd

like that, Mag." Then he asked, "What kind of music are you into?"

I told him about my fondness for emo and pop punk, but I admitted that I also liked singers like Taylor Swift and Ed Sheeran. He replied by listing several bands I had never heard of but that he thought I would like. He played a few snippets of songs, and I even recognized a few.

After a while, his yawns made me yawn, and we couldn't keep them from happening like falling dominoes.

His voice was deep and relaxed as he said, "I had a really good time tonight."

I smiled. "Me too. Talk to you tomorrow, friend?"

"Yeah, I'd like that. Friend."

Chapter Five

6:30 a.m. was early. It wasn't the earliest I'd ever trudged across the front lawn of the resort with my camera equipment hanging over my shoulder, but it was still too early. It had been a week since my interview, and I was determined to prove my worth. So here I was, sucking it up before the sun had risen above the horizon.

I stared out at the ocean, thinking that I wouldn't feel so tired if I had slept until my alarm clock went off at 5:30. I'd slept like a rock last night, which made up for my last several sleepless nights, until about 3 a.m., when I woke up after a particularly explicit dream regarding a certain dark-haired man. The image of me running my fingers across his cheek while I looked deeply into his brown eyes was going to live rent-free inside my head forever. Our nightly phone calls were probably not such a great idea if they were going to trigger any more dreams like this.

If only I didn't have so much debt.

If only I didn't have to pay rent.

Maybe then my heart could be happy.

I rubbed my hands up and down my arms, which were freezing under my sweater. I didn't want the clients I was about to meet to find me shivering when it was fifty degrees outside. They were from New York, and our lowest temperatures in early April were their highest.

I found them standing under the streetlight near the pier. At least I assumed it was them since they were the only ones dressed in formal attire this early in the morning. Everyone else on the sidewalk had on activewear and headphones and was either jogging or riding a bike.

I reached my hand out. "Hi, I'm Lina. It's nice to meet you."

They introduced themselves as Patrick and Brita. They had come to Santa Barbara to celebrate their engagement and wanted to have photos from their romantic getaway.

Either Brita was a pro with hair and makeup, or she had hired someone to get up even earlier than I did to style her. Her braids were twisted into an elaborate waterfall down her back, and her eyes were dusted in gold.

I took them down below the pier, just as the sun sent its first rays across the sky. Perfect timing.

The shots I got were dark and romantic, perfect for her emerald green dress and his charcoal suit.

We walked down the beach as the light got brighter, and I felt a little jealous of the way he looked at her like she was the only other person in the world.

As I did with all my clients, I asked them about

themselves to ease any of their anxiety and to get some sweet candid moments. Patrick told the story of how he proposed in the middle of Central Park and how it took him weeks to plan. Brita told me how she knew it had been coming for a while because she accidentally found the ring box when she was putting away his laundry one day, but she swore she hadn't opened it. She'd wanted to be surprised.

The two of them were beautiful and seemed happy together. Just as we finished and were walking back toward the hotel, I asked, "I'm starting to branch off from mostly shooting weddings and was wondering if I could use some of these images to promote my work on my social media."

Brita squealed. "Oh, I would love that. What's your Insta? I'll follow you, and then you can tag us." She turned to Patrick. "My followers are going to love getting a sneak peek of this!"

I blushed and told her the name of my account. "I don't have a lot of followers right now, but I'm working on it."

She giggled a little. "Well, I will do my best to help you out." Her knowing smile told me that I was going to find out more about her than I ever could have during this hour-long session. A little spark of pride flickered in my chest.

I dropped Brita and Patrick off in the lobby, promising to post some pictures soon, and took a second to admire the flowers. Ezra had knocked these out of the park. The bouquets on the table and the concierge desk looked better than some of his best wedding centerpieces

—the pink and blue flowers perfectly complemented the light green color of the walls.

I kept my eyes open for Blake. I hadn't seen her in person since my interview. I knew she was slammed with meetings all week, and I'd planned on ignoring that entire area of the resort anyway. I knew I couldn't keep a secret from her, but I didn't know how to tell her about Reece yet.

I also didn't know how my body would react to seeing Reece at the office, and I desperately needed to keep things G-rated around here.

It would be best for all of us if I stuck to my wing of the property and didn't venture anywhere else. As I walked to my office, I noticed more flowers than usual on display. Ezra must be more worried than he had let on.

I stopped walking and looked at myself in one of the mirrors hanging on the wall. Did I really go from thinking about one guy to another in the space of a second?

I was starting to break free of the ridiculous rules that I had set for myself, and I kind of liked it.

I grabbed a cup of coffee from the café since it was on the way. The last thing I needed was to pass out on my desk and have Lizette or Aimee find me. With my caffeine boost, I settled in my comfy office chair to edit the pictures from this morning's shoot.

While the images took their sweet time uploading onto the computer, I pulled my phone out from deep inside my camera bag and opened up Instagram. The notifications said I had two new followers, Patrick Morgan and Brita Jackson.

I clicked on her profile first to follow her back, and my

heart skipped a beat. She had over a million followers! After I clicked to follow her, I went to his profile and followed him. He had about half of her following, which was still more than I could ever dream of.

I laid my phone on my desk and focused on the edits. These were some of the most amazing photos I had ever taken. The two of them knew how to pose perfectly, and the lighting was exquisite, which meant I didn't have to modify my shots very much.

Half an hour later, I picked five pictures I thought stood out more than the rest. My favorite one showed Brita in Patrick's arms as he spun her in the air, the tail of her dress and little bits of sand floating behind her. The love in their eyes was matched only by the spontaneous joy they had felt when I asked them to do something so silly.

I emailed them full-resolution files of the best ones and then grabbed my phone and uploaded them to Instagram.

It took me a few minutes to write a caption, but I finally settled on a simple, "Thank you for coming to The Pacifica for your engagement photos. You looked amazing!" and I tagged Brita and Patrick before hitting "share."

My body felt like it was carbonated as nervous energy flowed through me. A lot of people were going to see my work, for better or worse. But I was proud of my shots from this morning and knew my clients would be, too.

Since I had nothing else to lose at this point, I spent the next hour going through my old files, compiling a Google Drive containing my favorite photos from the past few years. I wanted to have enough material to post something every day in hopes of growing my following.

It occurred to me that I should think about copyright and who actually owned the images, but I stopped myself before I got too far down that rabbit hole. Until I was officially laid off, I was still promoting the resort, which was what they wanted.

I hit a groove, and before I knew it, I had finished creating a rather impressive calendar for my social media posts and I had caught up on all the edits from my photo shoots from last week. I even went through the last two years' worth of wedding photos and made a drive for Ezra, showcasing his floral arrangements, and sent it to him.

I finally had a plan to show those bitches that I was worth holding on to. I was going to spend the next three months working harder than ever before, so they would either see that I was their most prized employee, or they would at least have trouble letting me go.

I popped into Kathy's office once I had checked off the last box on my to-do list. "Any changes to my schedule today?"

Kathy greeted me without looking away from her screen. "I just got off the phone with someone who said they saw your pictures online and want to book you. If this keeps up, I think you're going to be pretty busy."

I plopped down into the chair across from her and played with the leather tassel at the end of the zipper on my bag. "What do you mean? I'm always busy."

She laughed out loud. "Get your planner out, girl."

I opened my bag, pulled out my planner, and laid it

on the table. She turned back to her screen and clicked a few more times. "Whoever you had a session with this morning was a very special person. I've already gotten a couple of emails asking for information about our photographer. Did you know your client was famous?"

I frowned a little, unsure of what Kathy was talking about. "She had a lot of followers online, but she seemed like a normal person."

I sent a quick text to the girls' group chat: *Either of you know of Brita Jackson? She came in for a session this morning.*

Then I pulled up my earlier post to see if anyone had commented, maybe leaving a clue about who Brita was. Instead, I saw that I had a bunch of notifications and a ton of new followers.

I clicked a notification from Brita's account, which went to her post of my pictures. The caption read: *My girl Lina did a fabulous job making Patrick and I look like royalty this morning! Check her out if you're ever in Santa Barbara!*

"Oh my gosh, Kathy." I glanced up from my phone. "I have a thousand new followers and seven direct messages."

She clapped her hands. "See? Just from one of her posts. That girl's got to be important."

I checked the first couple of messages. "Holy shit. These people are asking to book me. What should I do?"

"Give them the resort number and my extension, and I'll take care of the rest."

I felt absolutely giddy. "I can't believe they all liked my work."

She focused on her screen and clicked her mouse a few times. "One of the emails I just got is asking if someone could book your services if they weren't staying on site. I don't think I've ever been asked that before."

"Are we even allowed to do that?" I asked.

She shrugged and shot me a sly smile. "Do either of us care anymore?"

This was all too much to process. I took a screenshot of Brita's post and sent it to the girls in our group text: *I think I might be on the verge of becoming internet famous. Viral? Is that still a thing? This was my client—check out how many followers she has!*

Val sent a text back within a minute: *Lina!!! Of course we know Brita Jackson! Her dad is a music producer. She's a hella famous influencer.*

Blake jumped in: *I thought I saw her checking in yesterday, but her name wasn't in the computer system. She must have used a fake name. How fancy! Remember us little people when you're taking pictures for Vogue or Rolling Stone!*

I looked up at Kathy. "According to Val and Blake, she's an influencer. This is going to be good for all of us."

She moved away from her screen to look at me. "Speaking of Blake, she told me that you left a Lina-shaped hole in the wall when you ran out of here the other day. Everything okay between you two?"

I cringed. "Things between Blake and me are fine. The rest of corporate, I'm not so sure." I didn't trust myself to not spill the beans about Reece, so I asked, "What about you? Do you want to stay or go?"

She thought for a few seconds. "I'm not sure. Maybe I'll find something better to do than the same job I've had for twenty years." She paused, thinking about something before clapping her hands together. "Anyway, write these appointments down. I haven't had a chance to add them to your digital calendar yet, and I know how you get."

She rattled off several bookings, and I scribbled the information down in my planner. She was right about being busy. I was booked pretty solidly for the next two weeks. "Holy crap, Kathy. When am I going to find the time to edit and send pictures out?"

She tapped a quick, repeating pattern on her desk with her short fingernails. "Hmm, I didn't think about that. I think I can move a few of the afternoon ones around, but many of them were adamant about wanting to get in ASAP."

I packed my planner back into my bag and stood up, already thinking about the next few evenings in my head. "No, let's just leave it like it is. I can make it work for a little bit. But going forward, can you make sure I have at least an hour or two in my office each day?"

She nodded. "Sure thing, Lina." Then she propped her fists on her desk and leaned into them. "Whatever happens will be really good for you. You're so much better than this place."

I fought a blush rising in my cheeks and said goodbye to her as I made my way to my office. Things were going to be busy but that was good. I would be able to show the new regime that I was worth keeping.

I had just barely sat down at my desk when my office phone started ringing. "This is Lina, how may I help you?"

"Hey babe, what's going on?" I know it was stupid to think that it could have been Reece on the other line, but somehow I felt deflated.

"Oh, hey Ezra. Just about to do some editing. What's up?" I should have been excited to hear from him. Just over a week ago, I was planning imaginary nuptials with him.

"Look, I feel like I haven't been able to apologize properly for missing our date the other night, and I'm sorry I've only sent a few texts since then. That food poisoning kicked my ass, and then the interviews were crazy. Now I'm slammed keeping up with the new guidelines for fresh arrangements in every room. It's been a lot."

"You know, I've been meaning to talk to you about our date. I totally would have come and taken care of you instead of going to the show. All you had to do was ask." A little voice in the back of my head wondered how hard it would have been for him to just shoot me a text when he started feeling unwell, but I'd been telling myself to ignore it since that night. Maybe I shouldn't have even brought it up just now.

He cleared his throat before speaking again, "No, it was bad. I wouldn't have wanted you to see me like that. I think I lost, like, five pounds."

The anger I had felt about him standing me up had mostly dissipated by now, especially when I thought about him being so sick. Even though he did leave me hanging, feeling like a loser.

"Now that I feel like myself again," he said, "I really want to see you. You busy today?"

I opened my planner, which was never far from my reach, and checked my schedule. "I've got a shoot at two, but other than that I'm free." In fact, today was the only day this week that didn't have me booked until the sun went down.

"Awesome. Want to have lunch at the pizzeria on Milpas? If we go now, we'll be back in plenty of time for your appointment."

I chose to put the night of the show behind us and agreed to go. I double-checked that my work was saved on my computer and shut it down before wondering if my simple sundress and jean jacket were fancy enough for a lunch date. But we were only going for pizza.

I walked to the lobby and found Ezra's familiar face among the crowd of guests checking in. When those blue eyes met mine, my heart did a little flip. Sure, he had been kind of distant lately, but we did have a good connection. We had a history, and I genuinely liked him.

I smiled at him. "Hi, stranger."

He leaned in, about to kiss my cheek, but stopped himself. "I know I said it before, but I'm sorry again about last week." He motioned for the door, guiding us across the lobby. "I should have called as soon as I started feeling off, but I kept hoping that I would feel better and could catch up with you. I regret not talking to you about this sooner."

I followed him, wondering who might see us leaving together. "It's okay, you didn't miss much." A twinge of guilt ran through me. He'd actually missed a lot, and I wasn't sure how I felt about it.

He opened the door, and walked me to his car, his hand grazing my lower back as we made it to the parking lot.

I thought about stepping away from his hand, but

then I remembered I wasn't doing anything wrong. Ezra was not my boss. Company policy couldn't keep us apart. We could show affection if we wanted to.

When we got to the restaurant, he held the door for me and even pulled my chair out at our table after we ordered our slices at the counter. The little mom-and-pop shop felt so fancy all of a sudden.

"How have you been? Other than the food poisoning, I mean?" I asked.

He flashed me a smile. "Good. I've been busy at the resort, which is a blessing and a curse. I've got some friends coming to town soon, too, and I'm really looking forward to seeing them."

"I'm sure that will be fun." I leaned forward, not sure if what I wanted to ask was crossing a line. "Umm, how did your interview go?"

He tapped a beat against the table with his hands. "Really great, actually. They told me they like the work I do and even brought up hiring an assistant for me. It's so weird that yours went so poorly."

What the hell? They were nice to him?

I stared at a scratch on the edge of the table for a few seconds before picking at it with my thumb. "I think I'm going to look for something else. I don't know if the resort is the right fit for me anymore."

"And that's not going to mess with your crazy vision board?"

I laughed. "It's not a vision board, it's just a plan. And it works for me."

He reached across the table and tapped my locket. "I

meant to tell you this was really pretty when I saw you wearing it the other day. Is it new?"

My hand grabbed the locket instinctively. "No, I've had it for years. I just discovered it again when my mom moved into her new place, though." I opened it up and showed him the pictures that were glued to the inside. "My dad got it for me when I was a kid."

"Is that you and him?"

Instead of thinking about my dad when I held it in my hand, I remembered Reece clasping it around my neck.

For the first time during our conversation, I hesitated. I imagined a little Val sitting on one shoulder, telling me that there was no reason to explain that I was seeing another man, but on the other shoulder, there was a smaller and super judgmental version of me, whispering that I needed to come clean about my "friendship" with Reece.

"Yeah." I glanced down at the two tiny pictures of me and my dad, trying to think of him and not our boss as I clasped it shut again. "You would have liked him. Our house was covered in houseplants when he was alive. There wasn't a flat surface that didn't have some sort of vine or fern on it." It had been a while since I thought about my dad without a pinch of grief in my chest. It was nice to talk about him like this, remembering happy things.

"That's really cool. I'm sure we would have had a lot to talk about." His lip curled into a smile. "So, where should I take you to make up for missing our date?"

I found myself smiling back at him. "I dunno, we could go see a movie or something."

"Did you end up going to see that band the other night? I heard from a friend that the show was really awesome."

And there they were again, the little shoulder-assistants all up in my head. One side was telling me to blurt out that I had a great time with someone else, and if Ezra wanted me for himself, he needed to up his game. The other side was telling me to keep my head down and forget about that other guy entirely.

Why was I so nervous?

Just as I started to speak, the waitress saved me with our food. I thanked her and nodded at Ezra. "I did. It was nice."

I hoped my answer didn't make him think I was up to something. Because I wasn't. According to Val, it was totally normal for a girl to see more than one person at a time. Even if one of those people was totally off-limits.

He smiled and bit into his pizza. We ate quietly for a few minutes before he shot me a wicked grin. "So my roommate is going to be out of the house on Saturday, and I was thinking that you could come over and spend the night. We could finally pick up where we left off last week. No distractions stopping us this time." He reached up and ran his hand down my arm, making my skin feel hot. The invisible little Lina on my shoulder whispered that this is what I should be doing. Going out with a guy that doesn't have so many strings, so many red flags, road blocks stopping us from being together.

My thoughts drifted to the conversation I'd had with

the girls the night I rescued my necklace from Reece's house. As much as I tried to keep what happened in the bedroom to myself, those girls were always able to pull information out of me, much to my chagrin.

Sure, Ezra had never taken me to "O-Town" as they called it, and the other two guys I had slept with had been just as young and inexperienced as me.

The one time Ezra and I had sex, his roommates killed the mood as soon as the condom was unwrapped by being way too loud on the other side of the thin walls. We had tried to fool around a couple of times at my place, but Val was home every time, and I couldn't concentrate. Maybe we just needed more time for the real magic to happen.

I started to say yes to his invitation, but I remembered my schedule and groaned. "As enticing as that sounds, the wedding we have booked that night is going to knock me on my ass."

"Come by after the event? You could sleep over and we could stay in bed all day Sunday." His smile was salacious, and I really wanted to take him up on his offer. Before I answered him, he leaned across the table and said, "You know, I've always thought that pizza and sex are pretty similar."

I raised my eyebrow at him. "Oh really?"

"Yeah, even bad pizza is still delicious."

We laughed, which released my worries. We finished our food, and the conversation made its way back to work. Ezra told me that he'd already started looking into who he could hire as his assistant.

I made a mental note to add "Look for backup jobs"

to my planner when I got back to the resort as I stood up and piled my dirty napkins onto my paper plate. Ezra stood and took the trash from my hands, adding it to his stack, and walked over to toss it in the can.

I felt my phone vibrate in my pocket and pulled it out to check. It was a text from Reece: *I hope this isn't weird, but I miss you like crazy. Your friendship, I mean. Can we hang out tonight?*

Ezra came up behind me, startling me, and I jammed the phone back into my pocket without replying. He put his hand on my elbow and kissed me on the cheek. "Ready to go?"

I squeaked out, "Yup. Sure," hoping that he hadn't seen my screen over my shoulder. Thankfully he didn't say anything about the text burning a hole in my pocket, but I couldn't stop thinking about it the whole way back to work.

Chapter Six

I rushed out to my car, calculating how much time I had to get home, shower, and dress for whatever this was with Reece. It wasn't a date, really. A hangout, I guess?

This had been the busiest Tuesday I had ever had at The Pacifica, hopefully a sign of my future success with the resort, so I hadn't had time to focus on the semantics.

I had a little over an hour before Reece said he would pick me up and not a clue about where he was taking me. I tossed my bag into the passenger seat and started the engine, wondering what I should wear tonight. Just as I pulled out of the parking lot, my phone rang.

"Please don't be calling to cancel on me," I murmured to myself as I hit the answer button. "Hi," I called out to whoever was on the other line.

"Thank goodness you answered." I was relieved to hear my mother's voice, even though she sounded panicked. "My garbage disposal is stuck, and I need you to come over and fix it."

"Mom, you literally chose that condo because it has

an on-call handyman. You don't need me to fix little things anymore."

"I did call him, and he said he can't get here until Friday. Can you believe it? All that money I paid for this place and they can't even fix a garbage disposal."

I stopped her before she could continue her rant. "I can be there in ten minutes, but I can't stay. Do you have the tool bag I used to keep under the sink?"

"Yes, it's right here in front of me. I opened it up and had no idea what you used to use to unstick the old one. Please hurry."

I told her I loved her and hung up the phone. When I got there, she opened the door without me needing to knock, which meant she had probably been staring out the window my whole drive over.

Walking through the small living room to the kitchen, I felt like I was having a dream about being home instead of actually being there. The furniture was the same, but the layout was all wrong. It was a comfortable place, the blue walls and dark green carpet perfectly matching Mom's snuggly brown couch, but it was surreal knowing this was her home now.

I ran through a few troubleshooting tests before determining that I needed to get the blade spinning from the bottom. I climbed into the cabinet and used an Allen wrench to twist the blade from underneath. "Okay, try it now," I called out to her.

She flipped the switch and the little motor whirred to life. "Hooray! Lina, you're amazing."

I stood up, wiping my hands on my skirt, and handed

her the wrench. "Next time it sticks and the handyman can't come, use this."

She grabbed me in a bear hug, her floral perfume making the dreamlike feeling of home even more prominent. "What would I do without my baby?"

I peeled her off me and checked the clock. "Oh shoot, I need to head out."

She flipped her hair over her shoulder. It was longer than mine and gray at the roots. I had always been told that I looked just like her growing up, but I hadn't started to believe it until recently. "Why, got a hot date?"

My arms broke out in goosebumps, as they always did when she read my mind. She knew instantly that I had plans with a boy tonight.

Before I could answer, she propped her hip against the counter. "Ooh, tell me all about him."

I chewed on my cheek for a second. "I can't really. It's nothing serious, anyway."

"Are you still seeing the florist from work?"

I shifted my weight from one leg to the other. "I am, but he's not who I'm going out with tonight." My mom was a total prude, so I waited for her to tell me I was making a poor decision.

Instead, she shocked me when she said, "Good for you!"

My phone started ringing in my bag, which was lying on the kitchen counter, but I ignored it. Then it rang again, and my mom pointed to it. "Someone is trying awfully hard to get ahold of you. You should answer it."

I grumbled, not wanting to have an awkward

conversation in front of her, but she was right. I pulled my phone out and answered it.

The voice on the other end was sweet when she asked, "Hi there, is this Lina Herrera?"

"What is this regarding?" The last thing I wanted was to end up on some telemarketing list because I'd answered this call.

"Please hold for Ms. Cohen." The line cut to classical music, which seemed sketchy as hell, so I hung up and set it back on the counter.

"Who was that?"

I pointed to the phone. "I have no idea. They called me and put me on hold."

Then the phone rang again, the same number as before. "I'm just going to let it go to voice mail."

But it rang again. And again, so I answered it. The voice from before spoke again, "Sorry Ms. Herrera. I must have pushed the wrong button when transferring you. Ms. Cohen doesn't have another opening today in her schedule and would very much like to speak with you. Please hold and I'll connect you to her line."

My mom mouthed, "Who is it?"

I put my free hand up in question and whispered, "I have no idea."

Ms. Cohen's voice came through my phone. She sounded older, like she had been chain-smoking cigarettes since before The Beatles broke up. "Yes, hello, is this Lina?"

"Um, yes. And this is?"

"Darling, this is Sylvia of Cohen International. I have a

great opportunity for you and our full-service agency." She laughed, and it sounded a bit like rocks spinning in a tumbler. "We don't usually have openings available this time of year, but I wanted to extend an invitation to you personally."

What the hell is a full-service agency?

I had never heard of Cohen International and had no idea what this woman was going on about. "I'm sorry, but who are you?"

Another laugh came out, like what I'd said was the funniest thing she had heard all day. "We can take care of all of your business needs. I would like to meet with you to discuss your future."

Yup, sounds like a scam.

"No thank you, I'm not interested. Have a great day." I hung up on her before she could say anything else. These telemarketers were getting crazier every day.

I stuffed my phone back into my purse, which I hung on my shoulder.

"Sorry about that, Mom. What were we talking about?"

"Your special someone." She gave me a cute little wink.

Mom was always willing to listen, but we never really got too deep when it came to my dating life. "Two someones, actually, even though I shouldn't even be seeing one of them."

"Ooh, I'm dying to hear some drama. Fill me in."

I sighed. "I'll tell you, but you have to promise not to tell anyone."

She motioned around the room with her hands.

"Who am I going to tell? Barb in 3B who bores me to death with pictures of her grandchildren?"

I laughed a little. "Okay, so I'm still dating Ezra, the florist, but tonight I'm seeing someone new."

She let out a little whoop. "That's my girl!"

I was so confused. "Aren't you supposed to tell me everything I'm doing is going to ruin my chance at happiness or whatever?"

"You're an adult, and I feel like I can be honest with you. You should take your time, see which one you really want. Maybe even pick up a third. Or dump both of them if you want to."

"Where is this coming from?" She was usually the kind of mom who told us boys were gross and kissing got you pregnant.

She looked off into the distance, and I knew she was thinking about Dad. "Did I ever tell you the story of when I met your dad?"

I smiled. "Only a thousand times. He accidentally ran his cart into yours at the grocery store."

She grinned, looking into space for a few more moments before her eyes met mine again. "Yes, but did I tell you that I was there because I was buying groceries for me and my boyfriend?"

I stood up a little straighter. "What?" My whole life, she had never mentioned dating anyone other than our father. I knew she hadn't been a nun before they married, but I didn't know about this guy.

"I thought Sebastian was the love of my life. Until your dad came around the corner of the canned food aisle and slammed right into me in search for some cream of mushroom soup. He had been singing and dancing, planning a dinner for his friends, and hadn't even noticed my cart until he collided with me."

My stomach sank. "Are you telling me that you cheated on your boyfriend with Dad?"

She shook her head. "No. Sebastian and I had been together for a few years and things were . . . comfortable, I guess. Boring. When your dad literally came crashing into my life, he looked into my basket and asked me what I was making. I was honest and told him that I didn't know how to make anything, really."

She picked up a kitchen towel and wrung it between her hands. "Your dad told me he had some great recipes that would go with what was in my cart. I was so naive that I didn't realize he was flirting with me when he wrote his number on the back of a crumpled receipt from his pocket." She laughed, and I saw that faraway look in her eyes again. "It took me a couple of weeks to call him. Long story short, I met up with him at his apartment for a cooking lesson." She stopped and touched my hand, "He was the perfect gentleman, didn't even try to kiss me. But when I walked out the door that night, it hit me that I wanted more out of my life than being comfortable."

"Why didn't you ever tell me this version of the story? I didn't even know you had a long-term boyfriend before Dad."

"I don't know. You were so young when he died. I didn't want to say anything that might muddle what I had left of him. Like if I thought about anyone else, I might lose my memories of him. But now that I've finally gotten

the courage to move on, I know that's not the case at all."
She pointed to her chest. "He's still in here."

She rubbed the counter with the towel, even though it
was spotless and dry. "I just wish I would have discovered
this years ago. I feel so free."

I smiled and realized for the first time that my mom
had transitioned from parent to friend, and I was happy
for the change. I wanted to ask her more about moving
on, but I had a question that burned deeper.

"How did you know it was Dad and not Sebastian?"

She contemplated for a second before answering. "I
don't know. I didn't really think about your dad that way
until I figured out that it wasn't working with Sebastian.
Your dad was just a friend of mine that turned into
something else slowly over time."

She looked up at the clock on the microwave. "Do
you have enough time to tell me about your boys?"

This was uncharted territory with her, but I figured
she was the only person who could give me an unbiased
opinion.

I only had a few minutes, but I figured Reece would
be fine waiting downstairs for me if I was a little late.
"Well, first there's Ezra. He's so pretty. Like, Men's
Fitness-cover-model pretty. We spend a lot of time
together at work, but not a lot of time alone, if you know
what I mean."

"What's your favorite thing about him?"

I had to think for a few moments about that. "Well,
he's relaxed and doesn't take anything seriously. He's fun
to hang out with, and he makes me laugh."

"And the other one?"

I glanced down at the counter, not sure what to share and what to keep to myself. "The other one is more . . . complicated."

She looked more excited than concerned, "What kind of complicated? Married, kids, old?"

"No, none of those. At least I don't think so." I realized I would have to tell her everything eventually. "He, umm, bought your house."

She laughed a little. "So he's rich?" When I gave her a shocked look, she shrugged and responded, "He paid way more than my asking price. Which was already California-ridiculous."

"And he's my boss."

Her forehead scrunched up. "I thought Blake was your boss."

"Well, he's more like Blake's boss, I guess. His family bought the resort."

"Wow, that is complicated. How did you start seeing him?"

I hesitated for a second, not wanting to admit to breaking into his house, so I bent the truth a little. "I met him when I was out one night before I knew he was the new CFO at the resort. We were both surprised when we saw each other at the office."

"So which one do you like better?"

"I'm not sure. I keep going back and forth, like my favorite one is whichever one I spent time with last." It felt like a bit of a lie when it left my lips. I think I knew which one I liked better, but I didn't want to give myself false hope that I could have him.

"Have you made your pro-con list yet?"

I looked up at her, surprised. "What do you mean by that?"

She giggled. "Lina, you are my logical baby. You've never made a decision without analyzing it to death. Maybe you should make a list of their best qualities to help you decide." She paused before whispering conspiratorially, "Or just keep dating them both forever. That could be fun, too."

I smiled with her and then followed her eyes back to the clock. "Oh gosh, I've been here longer than I thought I would be." I gave her a kiss on the cheek. "I have to get going, but I'll let you know how it all pans out."

The doorbell rang, and I jumped way too high for someone who was trying to keep it casual. I hadn't had enough time to wash my hair, so I just brushed it and braided it again. At least I didn't look like I had spent my day outside and then wedged myself under a kitchen sink.

The only hint Reece would give me about tonight was that it was well out of town and I should dress comfortably, so I threw on jeans and a nice blouse.

I stopped myself from rushing to the door and inhaled deeply. I was nearly out of breath from rushing to get ready, but I wanted to seem cool and collected like Reece always was.

I usually wasn't the type to get excited about a date, but having that conversation with my mom about her dating life had thrown me for a loop. I wanted to see where this was going, but I also didn't want to seem like my thoughts were somewhere else.

I was really doing this—I was seeing two guys at the same time. I had a feeling that this was going to blow up in my face.

I wiped my hands on my pants and walked to the front door. A breath left me as I pulled the door open and laid eyes on him. He had a little freckle above his upper lip that I wanted to kiss. How had I never noticed it until now?

God, he really was beautiful.

"I could say the same about you." He leaned in and gave me a hug.

"Did I say that out loud?" I giggled, trying to hide my awkwardness.

He nodded, nuzzling his nose against my temple. "Your hair smells amazing tonight."

"Thanks. Um, I didn't have time to wash it." *Really, Lina?*

He gave me his brightest smile. "You're wild." My checks heated up as his eyes scanned over me. He stepped back and asked, "Ready to go?"

"Yep. What's the plan?"

He took my hand and pulled me through the doorway. "I thought we'd go bowling."

"I haven't been bowling since I was a little girl. I have to warn you, I'm not very good at it."

"Well, I haven't been since I was about ten years old, and I was terrible."

I laughed at his admission. "So you want to go do something you're bad at?"

"What could be more fun than being awful at something together?" He had a good point.

I locked the door behind me and jingled my keys. "Your car or mine?"

"You drive. I want to go for a spin in your little roadster."

I laughed at him. "Where's your car? Maybe I want to ride in it instead?" He led me down the steep driveway and pointed to the most obnoxiously bright car I had ever seen.

"That thing practically glows in the dark!"

He threw his head back in a laugh. "That's not usually the first thing I hear when someone sees my car."

"I had my nails painted green like this once for an 80s party, and you could see them a mile away under the black light."

"We'll have to find a light big enough to see if it does, too, won't we?"

I walked down the sidewalk to stand next to his car. Hanging out with my dad when I was younger taught me enough about cars to recognize a Porsche when I saw one.

I looked at him in disbelief. "This is what you drive? Like every day?"

He shrugged. "I liked the color."

"I feel like I learn so much about you every time we hang out." I wandered around the car, spying the black GT3 RS badge on the back. "Aren't these, like, as expensive as a house?"

He tilted his head back and forth like he was

calculating. "Maybe not the housing market in Santa Barbara, but I'm sure there are cities out there where that would be comparable."

I shook my head at him, bewildered. "And you're not afraid of driving it? What if someone hits you? Or slams a shopping cart against it?"

He tucked his hands into those dark slacks that made my heart race. "It's just a car. It's got insurance."

I looked at my car parked down the street and then back at his. "Let's take yours. We can drive mine next time."

"I had a feeling you would say that when you saw her. Your eyes lit up like it was Christmas." He opened the passenger door and helped me get in.

There was a canister strapped to the bottom of my seat. "Is this a fire extinguisher? Maybe we should take my car."

"Don't worry, they all come with those. She's never lit on fire before; we'll be fine." He closed my door. I was practically vibrating with excitement.

As he got in and buckled up, I had to ask, "Why are cars always girls?" I ran my finger down the center console. "This one seems pretty masculine to me."

"I don't know." He turned, facing me. "I just loved her the moment I laid eyes on her and knew she had to be mine." He turned the engine on, and it rumbled through me. He chuckled. "In total honesty, she's a company car, so not technically mine."

"Ooh, you mean your parents bought it for you?"

"Ouch. Not like that. There are just certain . . . perks

that come with what I do. This car happens to be one of them."

"So when you quit your job, you'll have to give her back?"

He put his finger up to his lips. "Shhh, I haven't had a chance to have that conversation with her yet."

I shifted in my seat a little. "So the company is cutting jobs to save money, but the suits get to drive cars like this. Seems a little unfair."

He cringed but nodded. "You know what, you're absolutely right. But I'm working on it. I think the company can do better for its people."

"I'm sorry. I didn't mean to get all judgmental. We haven't even left my house yet."

"No, Mag, I always want you to tell me what you're thinking." His eyebrows popped up in excitement. "But you've got to see what she can do. I think you'll understand why I love her so much."

He put the car in gear and launched us down the road. It accelerated at least a hundred times faster than my little car.

"I could get used to a perk like this," I said, my stomach flipping.

He shot me a smirk that sent warmth into my core. "She's really amazing, huh?"

"I think she and I could become very good friends."

We made our way to the highway, and he reached over, taking my hand in his.

"Tell me more about work. Are things really as bad as Blake thinks they are?" I asked.

He let out a low grumble. "'Bad' is an understatement. It's fucking miserable right now."

"How so?" I didn't think I could give him any advice, but I got the impression that he didn't have anyone to talk to about this stuff.

"I can't really get into it, but there are some choices being made that are out of my control, and I'm doing everything I can to convince my father that his decisions hurt real people."

"I get it. I feel like I go into work every day just waiting for the other shoe to drop."

"Have you put any more thought into going into business for yourself? I could help you set up an LLC or find someone to build you a website."

"I don't know what I want to do. I think I'm just going to cruise along the next couple of months and see where life takes me."

"No offense, but that doesn't really sound like you."

I smiled, finding it sweet that he already knew certain things about me. "Really, the thought makes me feel reckless, like I'm jumping out of a plane without a parachute. But I need to try something different." Both with work and with my dating life, I guess.

We made it to the bowling alley, which was forty-five minutes from my house, in record time thanks to his peppy Porsche. Tuesday night was apparently Cosmic Bowling, so our clothes lit up under the black light. 80s music blasted from the overhead speakers, which matched the decor of the place. Luckily, the bright-colored vinyl seating was clean, even though the smell of popcorn and fried food wafted through the air. I plucked at his glowing button-down. "If we could just figure out how to get your car in here, we could end the will-it-glow debate."

He looked around the alley, a grin on his face. "Too bad there isn't a door wide enough to pull her through, or I would test your theory."

We stopped by the bar and ordered greasy chicken fingers and french fries before getting situated in our own lane. He only teased me a little about the differences in our shoe sizes. It looked like my rental pair could fit inside his.

He sat down on the stool and put our names into the computer. I popped a fry in my mouth and looked over his shoulder. He had typed in "Maggie" for me, so I reached over and typed his name as "Reecie." When I finished, he pulled me down into his lap, making it very clear that he didn't think we were pretending to be two friends just casually hanging out anymore.

I looked around the alley, scanning the faces around us. "Calm down, Mag. No one is here but us. We're totally incognito."

I pulled away from him and stood up. "We should probably try to play this game we both suck at."

He pulled me back down into his lap and pressed his forehead into my temple. "Or we could just sit here until our time is up."

I leaned into his embrace, wondering what it would be like to actually be with him. It was a dream that couldn't come true—not just yet. I extracted myself from him and picked up my bowling ball.

"We have to play at least one game, okay?"

It didn't take us very long to learn that both of us had been right—we were bad at this game. The bar food we had been snacking on between turns was more impressive than our talent.

"With scores like this, we might as well be playing golf." I leaned down to roll my ball down the lane.

"I really don't care about points with views like this."

I laughed and turned to face him, ignoring my ball that had just landed in the gutter. "Smooth, Reece. I bet you say that to all the girls."

"Nope, just you." He put his hands on my hips and pulled me close. Being touched by him made me feel free—less restrained by everyday life.

I rolled my eyes and patted his cheek. "I find that very hard to believe from a face like this."

He stuck out his tongue. "Oh, you mean this face?" I leaned forward and tried to bite his tongue, and he laughed. "I mean it, though. I know a lot of people like to play the field. I'm just not one of them."

I had a hard time believing him. He was way too good-looking and smooth to not have women throwing themselves at him wherever he went. I started to tell him just that, but he went on. "I'm not saying that there's anything wrong with it. I don't want to pressure you in either direction."

"You're rambling." I pointed up at the screen above us. "And it's your turn."

He stepped back and took his ball from the return. "Look, I'm no angel. I've had plenty of . . . adventures. But after my life flipped upside down last year, I learned that nothing I was doing was working, so I'm being mindful about who gets my time and attention."

He stepped away to take his turn, which gave me a chance to contemplate what he had just said without him staring at me.

His words felt heavy. Like choosing him would lead to something that might be more serious than I was ready for.

He hit a strike and cheered like he'd won the Superbowl, bringing me back into the present moment. I cheered and whistled as he jumped up and down and then ran to me, sweeping me up in the air.

Suddenly, his lips met mine, and I felt a shockwave of heat travel through my skin.

I pulled back an inch. "Reece. Did you just . . . ?"

He set me back on my feet and stepped away before covering his face with his hand and turning to face the opposite direction. "Oh God, Mag. I am so sorry. I didn't mean that."

I slumped into one of the hard plastic chairs bolted to the ground, ignoring the fact that the planet's tilt had shifted a degree or two. "It's fine."

He kissed me, but he didn't mean it?

Reece sat in the chair across from me, propping his hands on his knees. "I lost control for a second. It won't happen again."

I flashed him a fake smile. "Like I said, it's totally fine. We don't want things to get out of hand, anyway. We can forget it even happened." I stood up and grabbed my ball. "It's my turn. I bet I can beat your score."

The rest of the evening was awkward. We finished

our game—I beat him by eight points—and then we played another, but we didn't get back to the flirty camaraderie that we'd had before.

Maybe things would never be the same as they were before he kissed me.

We pulled up to my house two hours later, and the words finally spilled out of me. "When you said it won't happen again, was it because it was bad and you didn't want to again . . . or because of the work thing?"

His eyebrows bunched together. "What are you . . . are you talking about when I kissed you?"

I picked at an invisible piece of lint on my jeans. "Maybe."

He twisted in his seat, facing me. "Mag, I only said that because I thought it was what you wanted. I could kiss you a thousand more times and never get sick of it."

I looked into his eyes, which were shadowed in the darkness. "Prove it."

He leaned forward enough that his breath tangled with mine. For a split second, I thought he would pull back. Then he whispered, "Once we do this, I don't think I'll ever be the same."

I nodded slightly, inviting him in.

His hand slid up the nape of my neck, my breath pooling at the back of my throat.

Headlights from a car parking behind us lit up the inside of his car, scaring the hell out of me. I jumped out of his embrace and heard the "Bwoop Bwoop" of Blake's car alarm being set.

I watched her cross our lawn and walk up to my front

door. "Shit. What if she saw us?" I saw Val's outline as she opened the door, letting Blake in.

He pressed his hands into his lap, going cold once again. "You should go in, so they don't get suspicious."

I put my hand over his. "I had a great time tonight."

He tried to smile, but it didn't reach his eyes. "Me too, Mag."

Chapter Seven

I stomped in the door, kicking off my sneakers.

"Where are you coming in from?" Val asked from the kitchen. Popcorn popped in the microwave behind her.

I glanced at Blake, sitting on the couch, and decided to tell a half-truth. "I was out. With a cute boy."

Blake spun around and looked at me. "How's Ezra doing, anyway?"

"It wasn't with Ezra." As soon as I said it, I regretted it. But I knew she was going to find out soon, especially if we continued to go out in such a unique car.

Val shook the popcorn into a bowl. "Was it with the guy you met at the show the other night?"

I knew she knew who Reece was, so I was relieved that she was helping me with my fib.

"That's the one." I stretched my arms over my head, feeling my back pop a few times. "I'm going to run upstairs and put on some pajamas."

Hopefully if I spent a few minutes upstairs, that would

take them off the topic of me long enough for them to forget any pressing questions they had.

I made it up the stairs and into my room, but the second I was alone, my fingers met my lips, trying to remember how Reece's lips felt against them.

Val called from the bottom of the stairs. "Hurry up, Lina. We want to start watching something trashy."

I plopped down on the couch next to Blake a few minutes later, wondering if she was going to ask me about the bright green car she had undoubtedly seen me in when she pulled up.

Val put the bowl of popcorn on the coffee table in front of us before squeezing in on the couch. "Have we ever gone this many days without seeing each other? Are they scheduling you for a billion shifts on purpose?"

I sighed. "Ever since my interview, I haven't had a spare moment. I'm happy that I'm bringing in so many people to the resort, but if it goes on like this much longer, I might lose my mind."

Blake grabbed a blanket and snuggled into the corner of the couch as she turned on the TV. "No more work talk. What should we watch tonight?"

I answered, "Nothing about brides or engagements or family reunions. All I do is hyperfocus on the composition of the camera angles."

Val chimed in, "I thought we were going to watch that new reality show—the one where people get married without ever seeing each other?"

I covered my face with my hand. "That literally checks off all the boxes on my list of avoidances."

Blake agreed with her. "Yeah, but it's a disaster, and I feel like we all need to see people who are more miserable than we are right now."

I nudged her with my elbow. "You make a good point."

After three episodes of the train wreck, we had collapsed into a fit of mindless giggles. "Okay, you were totally right. These people are insane," I admitted.

Val had a mischievous look in her eye as she took a sip from her bubbly seltzer drink. "I dunno, Lina. Have you told Blake the details of juggling two guys right now?"

"Yeah, how long has this been going on? I'm so out of the loop." Blake moved the empty bowl of popcorn off her lap onto the coffee table and gave me her full attention.

I sat up from my makeshift nest of pillows and looked up at Blake. "Don't get too excited. It's not going to last."

Blake looked sideways at Val, who blurted out, "She's dating the dude who bought her mom's house!"

"The one she told she had a boyfriend before fleeing the scene? How did that even happen?"

Then Val said, "Oh my gosh, Blake, they were in here hanging out the other night, and I thought he was Ezra!" Blake looked down at the couch and cringed playfully. "So how do you go from breaking in to making out?"

I tossed a pillow at her. "First, I wasn't making out with him at all. And second, it's not going to work out, so there's no point in getting excited."

Guilt burned through my stomach like sulfuric acid. I was not the kind of friend who kept secrets, and I didn't want to be anymore. "Blake, the next part gets really complicated, and you need to promise not to tell a single soul before I tell you the rest."

I looked at Val, who clapped like a little kid. "Come on, Lina. She needs to know."

I rubbed my forehead, worried that I was about to make a terrible decision. "I need to know I can trust you both to keep it to yourselves. The fewer people who know my secret, the better chance I have at keeping it."

Valerie sat straight up, looking at Blake. "It's not as scary as she's making it sound."

Blake looked at me with an eyebrow raised before giving me a skeptical "Okay."

I pursed my lips for a few seconds and closed my eyes. "He's our new boss. Reece."

I opened my eyes a moment later, catching Blake's frown. "The asshole from the interviews? The guy who's been stomping around making all the financial decisions that make my life so much harder?"

"He's not an asshole. He's actually really sweet."

"Why didn't you say anything when I texted you that he was hot?"

"I didn't know he was our boss yet. I only found out in the interview."

Val didn't say anything, but I noticed her huge brown eyes bouncing from Blake to me and back again.

"Like as he walked in the door?" Blake asked. I nodded, and she said, "Damn, I thought about asking him out until they started bitching about relationships at work. And then they were all assholes to you, so I decided he wouldn't be worth my time." She jumped up in her seat, tucking her legs under her. "Wait, is this why that bitch asked you if you were sleeping with anyone?"

Val held up her hands. "Wait, what the hell? Someone asked you that at work?"

I turned to Val. "So it's kind of a long story, but the girl from marketing, Aimee, brought up intra-office relationships at the end of my interview."

Val asked, "Do you think she knew about you and Reece?"

I shook my head. "No, Reece and I had only hung out at Joey's show, and he told them we didn't even know each other. I think she was just trying to stir up drama."

Blake leaned forward. "I don't know about this. You could get really hurt. Or fired."

I rubbed my forehead with my hand again. "I'm not sure what I'm doing, but I promised myself that I wouldn't get too invested. There are a few different outcomes to this mess, and none of them end well." My stomach felt weighted down, like it was full of rocks. Flying by the seat of my pants was disorienting, and I wasn't sure that I liked it.

Val wiggled her fingers at me playfully. "That's not what it looked like when he had you shoved against the front door the other night." She must have seen the color rising in my cheeks because she shrugged and said, "I looked through the window first. Had to make sure you weren't out there killing each other."

"Nothing happened."

"But something almost happened."

"Look, you guys. This is super secret. You can't tell anyone." I looked at Val. "I don't want you to make a big deal out of it like you always do." She promised, and I continued, "We agreed to keep it quiet until he . . . ." I paused. He hadn't told anyone he was going to quit yet, and it wasn't my story to tell. "Until we know more about the future of my position."

Blake leaned forward, her eyebrows knitting together. "What about Ezra?"

I laced my fingers through my hair. "I don't know! Sometimes he seems really into me, but then I go days without hearing from him. He's a whole bag of mixed signals."

Blake took a drink from her seltzer can and asked, "Would you keep seeing Reece if Ezra said he was ready for commitment?"

I stared up at the ceiling, thinking. "Maybe? I mean, up until a week ago, that's all I wanted. But now I'm not sure about anything."

Val pointed to the TV, which had gone to sleep. "You really are like one of the girls from that show."

I lay back down on my pile of blankets. "I want to just skip forward to the reunion episode of Lina's Dating Adventure. Why isn't there a producer off camera telling me what choice I need to make?"

Blake folded her arms. "Well, I know which team I am. Maybe I'll make shirts. 'Team Ezra' would look great in gold glitter on a black background."

I groaned. "No teams, please."

Valerie asked, "Is there one that you think you like more than the other?"

"I think it's too early to tell." I left out Reece's kiss since I wasn't even sure if it should happen again. Blake already seemed like she was uncomfortable with whatever was happening between Reece and me, and I didn't want to make it worse. "I had lunch with Ezra today, too, and things seemed good between us."

Blake asked me several more questions, but there wasn't much information I could give her. She finally agreed not to tell a single soul, but she also made me promise to not bring Reece around her too much so she didn't accidentally slip anything out at work. Her job wasn't on the cutting block now, but that didn't mean her future with the company was guaranteed.

I agreed but knew it would add one more obstacle to this already difficult situation. Was this a sign that we were doomed before we began?

Valerie picked up the remote. "Let's do some research then, shall we?"

Two more episodes of the ridiculous dating show had finished before I realized I was the only member of the group who was still awake. I made sure the girls were covered with blankets before I dragged myself up the stairs to bed.

Maybe I was the kind of girl who could juggle two guys at one time. Or maybe I wasn't.

Would I be the girl who ran out of the room crying when things went south, or would I get to have a happy ending?

Like clockwork, my phone rang a few minutes after I snuggled under my comforter.

I answered with a quiet, "I wasn't sure you were going to call since it's so late."

"I figured you were hanging out with the girls, so I didn't want to bug you. But I couldn't fall asleep, so I thought I'd see if you were still up." He sounded tired, which made it easier to imagine him here with me like I always did.

"You have good timing. I just crawled into bed."

"How are you feeling?" At first, I didn't know what he meant, but then I realized he was thinking about our kiss, and our almost-kiss, too.

"I'm okay." There was no conviction in my voice.

"Are you having second thoughts?"

I rolled onto my stomach, burying my face into my pillow. Avoiding his question, I said, "Blake knows about us."

His voice was steady as he said, "Good."

My mind raced at his response. The more people that knew about us, the harder it would be to keep it between us. "Why is it good?"

"She's the level-headed one. Val's great, but I get the feeling she'd encourage you to fly a little too close to the sun if you wanted to. Which isn't always a good thing."

I pulled the blankets over my head, trying to disappear. "I'm just wary. I don't want either of us to get in trouble. Maybe we should take a step back and actually try to be just friends for a little while."

His breathing changed, like he was moving around. I knew from our earlier calls that he always got into bed before dialing my number. The thought that we should probably cut out this bedtime routine made my heart heavy.

"You know I'm willing to do whatever you want, but I need you to know that this is more than just some crush for me, and it would be hard for me to step back."

After a few seconds, I replied, "We just have to be careful, okay?"

I wasn't willing to give him up just yet either.

I lay in my bed the next morning, thinking about the kiss that shouldn't have happened.

Reece and I had so much fun together, and I was definitely developing deep feelings for him. Being with him was easy, but would constantly looking over our shoulders be worth it a month from now? What was going to happen when his sister found out about us? Or his father?

Would sneaking around eventually stress us out to the point of breaking up? How soon would it go on before we started resenting each other?

It felt like I was holding my breath underwater. The pressure in my chest was too much, and I'd have to come to the surface soon. If we continued, one of us would get fired over this, and I just knew it was going to be me.

My alarm blared from my nightstand for the third time. Knowing I couldn't snooze again since it was now past ten, I shut it off and got dressed.

I walked into the kitchen just as Val was coming out

of her bedroom, fidgeting with an earring. Her phone rang on the counter. "Hey, can you answer that for me? This stupid earring is stuck in my hair again."

I picked up her phone, looking at the screen. "No worries, it says telemarketer." Clicking the button on the side, I silenced the call.

"Why do they only call when I'm right in the middle of something?" She untangled the earring finally and let out a "woot."

"I got the weirdest one yesterday when I was at my mom's house. Some bullshit about being a full-service agency wanting to help me grow my business. The lady sounded older than dirt."

She reached into the cabinet for a bowl. "I haven't gotten one of those yet. Was it, like, one of those timeshare places?"

I propped my elbows on the counter, watching her pour her cereal. "I'm not sure. She said her name was Cohen something, and that she had a great opportunity for me. What a weirdo."

Val sat her spoon on the counter. "Lina, do you mean Sylvia Cohen?"

I snapped my fingers. "Yeah, that was her name."

"Shut the fuck up." She sounded angry. Bewildered, maybe?

I was confused. "Why, is she, like, a well-known scammer?"

"Sylvia Cohen called you, personally? Are you fucking kidding me?"

"No. I told her I wasn't interested and hung up on her."

She pushed her bowl away from her. Twenty seconds ticked by before she spoke again. When she did, her voice was deep and quiet. "Don't panic. We can fix this. We will figure something out."

"Well, I wasn't panicked, but now I am. Who the hell is Sylvia Cohen?"

"Lina, she only runs the most sought-out talent and marketing agency in the entire country. Ignoring her is like ignoring God. I can't believe this is happening."

I pushed away from the counter, pacing the floor. "I should probably call her back then, huh?"

"Yes. Right now. Go upstairs and call her back."

I looked up at the clock on the microwave. "I need to get to the office. I can call her from there."

"Dammit, Lina." She was practically shrieking at this point. "If Sylvia Cohen even knew the name of my record store, I would die. Any business she touches turns to gold." She leaned forward, letting me know she was serious. "Every moment you let pass without calling her back is literally putting nails in your professional coffin. Run your ass upstairs, call Sylvia back, and tell her you are deeply sorry. Maybe tell her you had a medical emergency, like a stroke or something, anything. You don't want to miss the opportunity to work with her."

I rushed upstairs, sat down at my desk, and scrolled through my recent calls, finding the number for Sylvia and tapping it in. It rang a few times before the receptionist answered. "Cohen International. Anita speaking. How can I connect your call?"

"Hi, this is Lina Herrera. Sylvia called me yesterday, and I would like to talk to her if she has a moment."

She let out a breathy laugh. "I wondered how long it would take you to call back. What made you change your mind?"

"I didn't actually know who Sylvia was until my friend told me. So here I am, begging for her forgiveness and hoping she'll take my call."

She let out another laugh, louder this time, and I heard her typing on a computer in the background. "I think we are going to get along very well, Ms. Herrera." She paused, and I heard the tempo of her keyboard clicking go up. "Okay, I can get you in with her next week. Which works best for you, Tuesday at 11 a.m. or next Thursday at 4 p.m.?"

Luckily, my calendar was open on the desk, so I flipped to next week. "Tuesday looks best for me."

"Perfect. I'll send you the address."

"Umm, I have a weird question."

She continued typing in the background, like a multitasking goddess. "Hit me with it."

"Do you know how Sylvia heard about me?"

"It says in my notes that you were referred to us by a social media follower. I don't have any other information though."

"Thank you for telling me. I guess I'll see you Tuesday."

"Have a great day." She hung up, and I stared at my phone, wondering what I had gotten myself into. A notification popped up on my screen from an unknown number with the office's address.

I wrote the address down in my planner, grabbed

everything I would need for work today, and ran down the stairs.

"Well, what did they say?" Val was standing at the bottom of the stairs, and I had a feeling she had been there listening the whole time.

"I have an appointment next Tuesday."

"Like, with Sylvia or with one of her associates?"

"I'm assuming Sylvia, but I didn't ask. Should I call back?"

"No, that would be worse. Okay, here's what you're going to do . . . ." She started rambling about what I needed to wear, what I should say, and what I needed to bring along with me. I followed her back into the kitchen and opened my planner. I scrawled down everything she said, hoping I didn't mess this up.

I grabbed a granola bar from the pantry, and she sat back down with her cereal. "So, how do you think she heard about you?"

"She said she was referred to me by someone who follows me on social media."

"Hold on, let me pull up your Instagram." She unlocked her phone and scrolled through her apps. "Holy shit, Lina. How do you have 6,000 followers already? It took me like two years to get that many for the store."

I opened the granola bar and took a bite. "I dunno. I just post pictures and tag people."

She continued to ignore her breakfast, looking through my followers. "This list is impressive; I recognize a bunch of them. Have you been booking a lot of people?"

I started to feel a little uncomfortable. I wasn't doing

anything different from usual. "I have no idea. Kathy does all the bookings. I had one famous client, and I guess she told her friends?"

She set her phone down and smiled at me. "I'm proud of you."

At least one aspect of my life was going in the right direction.

Chapter Eight

Today I only had one gig, but it was a wedding, which meant every moment from two o'clock to around nine belonged to the client. I had always loved shooting weddings, but with all the opportunities I'd had lately to take pictures for random occasions, all I could focus on was the monotony of the day.

Every wedding was basically the same, just changing the bride and groom. Luckily, this couple had requested to do their formal shots before the ceremony, which I always recommended because it meant I wouldn't be here until midnight.

I got to my office and checked my planner so I could put all the day's festivities into my phone, setting alarms to make sure I wouldn't be late for anything.

My mind drifted to my upcoming appointment with Sylvia, and I began to panic. What if word got out that I was meeting with her, and they decided to fire me over it? I also didn't want to get my hopes up. The way Val talked about this lady made it sound like I couldn't possibly afford her.

I needed to keep this meeting to myself. Sure, Val knew, but I wanted to wait until it had already happened before telling anyone else.

My mind snapped back to the task at hand. I loaded up my camera bag, making sure I had the charged batteries and lenses I needed for the whole day.

I checked the clock. About two hours before showtime. The granola bar I had eaten earlier had just reminded me how hungry I was, so I went to the café to get an early lunch.

I sat at my usual table near the back of the restaurant, eating my meal and checking in on social media. Kathy had mentioned something about making Instagram Reels and TikTok videos when I checked in with her today, but the task felt daunting as hell. I felt very old for a normal twenty-six-year-old; I was sure most of my contemporaries were already pros at this.

I told myself I was doing research as I sat with an earbud in my ear and scrolled through a ton of videos that had been made by photographers all over the world. Some of these seemed simple enough that I could tackle them, but others looked like they used an entire production team to create.

My attention turned to the man taking a seat across from me at the table. Reece looked immaculate as always in his deep navy suit. "What's going on today, Mag?"

I removed my earbud and set my phone down. Leaning in, I whispered, "Should you be sitting here with me right now?"

He laughed like we had been friends forever. "What's wrong with an executive sitting down and checking in with an employee? That's not against company policy, right?"

I looked over his shoulder at the empty room. "What if someone sees you talking to me? There could be rumors started over this."

"Well, when you whisper and look around like you're doing a drug deal, of course you're going to draw attention to us." He put his hand on mine briefly, and I missed the contact as soon as it was gone. "If we just talk as colleagues, no one will even notice us back here."

"Okay, fine." I used the napkin in my lap to wipe my face before laying it across my now-empty plate. I attempted to remember how normal people sat in chairs when they weren't breaking company policy by seeing their boss in secret. Was I supposed to sit up straight or lean back casually like I didn't care? I had no idea.

He shifted in his seat and cringed, so I asked, "Are you alright there?"

His hand went to his cheek. "I think I have a wisdom tooth coming in. It hurts like hell."

"Aren't you a little old for that? I had mine out when I was sixteen."

He rolled his eyes at me playfully. "It's totally normal for wisdom teeth to come in when you're thirty, thank you very much." He shrugged. "I didn't even think I was going to get them, to be honest. My sister got hers removed when she was in high school, so my parents have always joked that Izzy's the wiser one of the two of us. Just another snide comment to resent them over."

"Oh, they can't be that bad. I'm sure their intentions were good."

He shook his head. "Don't get me wrong, I love them. I just wouldn't be surprised if I walked in on them dismembering each other with their bare hands over my grandmother's antique furniture."

I shuddered dramatically. "Remind me to invite you to our house for Thanksgiving this year."

"Mag, did you just make major plans with me more than six months in advance?"

The moment felt special, like we weren't at the café I had lunch at nearly every day. To break the tension, I asked, "What are you up to today?"

He checked his watch. Judging by the logo on its face, it probably cost more than all of my camera equipment combined. Maybe all of my worldly possessions. "I have a meeting with my sister and her team in about twenty minutes, and then I'm stuck in meetings at the corporate office for the rest of the day. We have three other properties we ruthlessly took over recently, and I have to make sure they're being properly managed." He flashed me a smile. "You know, all the boring stuff."

"That doesn't sound boring to me, it sounds overwhelming. I don't know why I didn't think that there would be other properties going through what we were at the same time."

"Usually, we have three or four in a rotation at any time. We wait until the one we've had the longest is thriving on its own before acquiring a new property."

"And if it doesn't thrive?"

"Then we sell it. It doesn't happen very often, though,

since we have a pretty foolproof routine for taking over a company." He paused, looking at an invisible speck on the table between us for a moment. "The project that I was leading when I had my . . . issue . . . failed financially. At least according to my father. So that's one of the reasons I've been battling with them to let me have control over this property."

"But you're leaving, so it shouldn't be an issue, right?"

He chewed his bottom lip. "I want to, but I'm starting to think they're not going to let it be easy for me."

He must have seen the worried look on my face because he reached over and put his hand on mine, this time keeping it there. "That doesn't mean I'm not working out how we can be together. I've got a plan." He looked directly into my eyes and held my gaze for a moment. "Do you trust me?"

Without hesitation, I nodded. "Yes. Yes, I do."

He pulled his hand away and smiled. "Good." He leaned back in his chair, relaxing a little. "So, what do you have going on today?"

I told him about the wedding and all the activities it entailed. "Luckily I get to slip out about an hour into the reception. Once they cut the cake, I get my last shots and pack up for the night. Then I can stop by my office, back up my files, and head home."

"I didn't realize how much went into wedding photography. What time do you think you'll finish up?"

"It's all based on when the sun sets, really. This time of year, the sunset is fairly early, so I'm typically wrapping things up around nine. But when we get deeper into summer, sometimes I don't finish up in my office until after midnight."

"And you really enjoy it?"

I did hesitate with this question. "You know, if you would have asked me a few weeks ago, I would have said it's my passion. But I dunno, lately I've felt a little . . . burned-out."

The corner of his lip went up in a sweet little smile. "I won't say I'm glad that we have that feeling in common, but it's nice to have someone to commiserate with."

I reached up and touched my locket. This little thing had put me on a collision course with this man, and I was grateful for it.

But was he in my life for a reason, a season, or for life?

"So, do you have any plans for after the wedding tonight?" His mischievous smile told me exactly what he was thinking.

I tried to let him down gently. "Actually, Blake is coming over tonight to watch a movie, and I'm hoping to make it home early enough to at least catch the second half."

"You can always stop by my house after instead. I won't start the movie until you get there."

I wanted to say yes. I wanted to jump up and scream yes. But I'd promised myself to take this thing slowly, and he had already taken me out last night. With his news that he might not be leaving the company, I needed some time to think.

"Sorry, Reecie, I'm probably going to be tired and grouchy. I'm not ready for you to see me like that yet."

"It was worth a shot." The way he smiled made me

want to give in and run off to his house right then and there.

At that moment, I saw Ezra enter the restaurant, making his way straight toward me. He had his usual box of bouquets tucked under one arm. I sat up in my chair and tinkered with the spoon sitting in front of me. Having the ability to disappear would be pretty cool right about now.

"Hey, babe. I checked your office and you weren't there, and I knew this was the only other place you like to hide out. You about ready to head to the reception hall?"

I didn't think he had even noticed Reece sitting across from me yet, which was odd since his broad shoulders made him stand out in any crowd, let alone in an empty corner of a restaurant.

As soon as I finished my last thought, Ezra turned to Reece, as if finally seeing him sitting there. "Oh, hi there." He held his hand out. "I'm Ezra, and you are?"

Reece gave me a shit-eating grin before looking back to Ezra and shaking his hand. "Oh, so you're the boyfriend I've heard so much about."

"He's not my boyfriend." My tone was a little snappier than I'd planned, but I was not prepared for a possible pissing contest right here in the café.

Ezra's eyebrows bunched together as he looked at me.

Reece jumped in. "I'm Mr. Howell. My sister and I are in charge of the transition at the resort." He looked down at his insanely expensive watch again. "If you'll excuse me, I have a meeting to get to."

Reece stood and smiled at me. His voice dropped an octave when he tilted his chin and said, "Ms. Herrera."

His eyes stayed linked to mine and my bottom lip slipped between my teeth on instinct. The look he shot me was full of dark promise, and I wanted to follow him to his office. Now would be a great time to knock everything off his desk.

After a few beats of my rapidly pounding heart, he turned and walked out of the restaurant.

Ezra slipped into the vacated seat across from me. "That guy gives me serious creep vibes. What was he talking to you about?"

My eyes stayed trained on Reece's backside until it was out of sight. I looked at Ezra. "I'm sorry, what were you saying?"

"That management douche seems slimy. I don't like the way he was over here talking to you."

I snapped back to reality, feeling the need to defend Reece. "No way. He's . . . ." My eyes slid back to the empty doorway.

Before I could finish my thought, Ezra asked, "Wait, is there something going on between you two?"

I looked back at him, hoping my face was conveying the shock that I was trying to fake instead of the guilt that I was feeling. "No. I mean, eww, right?"

Why was I born without the ability to lie without sounding deranged?

He didn't look convinced, but he leaned forward excitedly. "I'm glad I found you here. There's a movie festival coming to town in a couple weeks. Want to come with me?"

He knew I was a sucker for movies, and I genuinely wanted to spend more time with him. "Yeah, let's do it."

"Cool, I'll get tickets for the two of us." He stood and reached out for my hand. "Come on, let's go get this wedding over with."

I assumed we would split ways at the stairwell, but Ezra made the trek with me to our largest banquet hall.

Leading the way into the room, I set my bag on the empty DJ stand so I could pull out my camera and choose the best lens for the natural light bathing the room. The large picture windows in the wall facing the ocean had gauzy curtains that I went around closing, cutting down on the glare from the glassy centerpieces. The less I had to edit later, the better.

I slipped right into my usual routine, snapping pictures of the unique decorations at every table.

While the decor was beautiful—the perfect backdrop for the happiest day of the bride and groom's lives—it felt flat. The dopamine my brain usually released while I did this job was nowhere to be found.

"Let's go out tonight after you're done. My roommates won't be home."

I had almost forgotten Ezra was in here, preening his floral creations on each table. "I have plans with Val and Blake tonight."

He came up and placed his hand on my hip. I couldn't deny the desire that coursed through me when we touched. I hadn't seen him much lately, but when we were together, he was irresistible. "I'm sure they wouldn't mind if you came out with me for one drink." He gave me a pouty face that made me melt a little.

I knew I had literally just told someone else that I had plans, but I felt like I hadn't been putting any energy into my relationship with Ezra lately. I didn't want to let him go yet, and, if I thought back to Val's words, I shouldn't have to.

"If I get out of here a little early, we can hang for like half an hour."

"Great. I'll text you around 8:30 to see where you are."

"Sure. Let's go somewhere close, though. I don't want to meet up with the girls too late." Just as he started offering ideas, my phone rang. Letting my camera hang around my neck, I pulled it out of my pocket and answered it.

The man's voice on the other line was unfamiliar. "Hi, I'm trying to get in touch with Lina Herrera. This is Casey from the *SB Weekly*."

"The magazine? How can I help you?" My heart rushed at the idea that maybe they were looking to hire a photographer.

"We had a sudden opening for our local artist spotlight, and we're wondering if you want to be highlighted in our next issue?"

"Oh wow, thanks so much, that would be really cool. What do you need from me?"

"We just need a good time and place to send a journalist to meet up with you. They'll conduct a short interview, talk about what it's like to be an artist in Santa Barbara, and get some action shots of you working."

I reached into my bag and pulled out my planner. We found a day that worked for both of us, and he told me the reporter would meet me in the lobby.

I hung up the phone and found Ezra moving around some flowers in an arrangement about twenty feet away. "So that was weird but pretty cool."

"Who was it?" He looked genuinely interested.

"It was the *SB Weekly*. They want to do an artist spotlight on me."

He grinned, showing off his dazzling white teeth. "Wow, that's huge. Congrats."

"Thanks. I feel kind of special. Is that nuts?"

"No, not at all." He wrapped his arm around my shoulder. "You are special." He looked around the room for a moment before looking down at me. "Ooh, maybe if your interview goes well, they might want to do one on me, too."

I said, "Sure," just as my alarm blared in my hand. Time for the next item on my event checklist.

Chapter Nine

Ten bridesmaids are at least six too many. Who even knows ten people that they care enough about to organize matching dresses?

This bride was one of the sweetest I'd ever met, but trying to get formal shots of twenty bridesmaids and groomsmen was a task in itself.

I had them lined up on a grassy spot right outside of the resort, and even using my wide-angle lens, I could barely fit them all in the frame. I'd made panoramas before by splicing pictures together, but it took hours, and I really wanted to avoid it.

I stepped back a few feet, and my shoe slipped over a rock on the pathway. I didn't notice anything was wrong until the entire group in front of me gasped in unison. Half a second later my butt landed in the middle of a rhododendron bush.

As the groom ran forward to fish me out, I scrolled back through my images and giggled at the candid picture. Every member of the bridal party was in the frame, and they were all panicked for my wellbeing.

The groom, James, crouched down and pulled me out. A branch had snagged on the neckline of my dress, and I yanked it free, trying to not further embarrass myself in front of these clients.

"Okay everyone, for my next trick, let's have the groomsmen stand behind the bridesmaids." They followed my directions, only after making sure that I was really, truly unharmed.

I got some beautiful shots of them, and I used most of the resort as their backgrounds. An hour later, my alarm rang again, indicating that it was time for the group to head to the I-do's.

I moved around nimbly once we made it to the beach, getting shots of the guests waiting for the ceremony to begin, which was a feat in itself with a group this large. There had to have been at least three hundred people sitting in the fold-up chairs here in the sand.

I made it to my favorite spot to shoot from just as the first set of bridal party couples started down the aisle.

Getting shots of the father walking the bride down the aisle was always the hardest part for me, but I managed to do it without choking up. I'd done hundreds of weddings, and it still hurt that my dad wouldn't be at my own. I turned the camera back on the happy couple, pushing my feelings away like I always did.

The next half hour was a complete blur, but the way the bride and groom stared into each other's eyes as they spoke their vows made me yearn for something similar in my life.

The rest of the evening passed quickly, and before I knew it, the newly married couple was feeding each other cake. Luckily, they were doing it without shoving the confections into each other's faces. The couples who attacked each other always made me wonder how long they would stay married.

I'd seen too many wedding cake disasters to not be a little wary at this part of every wedding. From tables toppling over and frosting destroying the dress to unattended children climbing onto the cake and smashing it with their fingers, there were just too many things that could go wrong near the end of the party.

I was glad this one had gone off without a single sugary mishap.

I pulled my phone out and sent a text to Ezra: *Just about to finish up here. Want to meet downstairs at the bar? I don't think my feet can handle any more steps.*

He texted me back less than a minute later: *Sure, I'm actually still on property. I'll meet you there in twenty minutes?*

I replied that I would see him soon and walked to my office so I could back up my files and lock up my equipment. I stopped in the bathroom to touch up my makeup, applying a darker shade of lipstick than I usually wore, because it was the only one I had in my purse. I got my hands wet and ran them over my hair a few times, trying to get the flyaways to resemble something other than the untamed mess they were.

I made it to the bar and found him sitting on a bar stool. He was hunched over a half-empty drink, looking adorable as he laughed at something the bartender had said. His apron was nowhere to be found, and I took a second to appreciate how his arms looked in his tight white shirt.

I propped myself up next to him and ordered a soda, right before he put his hand on my cheek and kissed me gently. I had to admit, it was refreshing to kiss him in public, not having to hide our affection.

"Hey babe, how was the wedding?"

I told him all about the session, and he laughed with me when I told him about falling in the bush earlier. My phone vibrated in my pocket, and I pulled it out, holding the screen slightly away from Ezra just in case it was Reece.

It was Val in our group text with Blake: *You headed home? We're about to start the movie. It's one of your favorites!*

I replied: *Just finishing up at the resort. I'll be there in like 30 minutes. 45 tops.*

Blake: *Try to make it quick. We have a surprise for you!*

Me: *I hope it's ice cream since I ate the last of it the other night.*

Val: *It's better than ice cream, I promise!*

Ezra nudged my shoulder with his own. "What's going on with the girls?" I noticed his eyes were trained on my texts, so I locked the screen and put my phone back in my pocket.

"Oh, nothing. We've got plans to watch a movie tonight, and they're excited. I'm sure it's some Zac Efron movie we've all seen a hundred times."

He put his hand on my upper thigh, the warmth radiating up my leg. "Well, now I feel bad about keeping you from them."

I smiled as I took a sip of my soda from the skinny

black straw. "They'll be fine without me for a while." My eyes scanned his lips, and I remembered the time he propped me against the table in the banquet hall. Remembered his hands and lips all over me. My breath hitched just thinking about it.

I pushed down my arousal as we caught up on small talk. We discussed work a little, keeping the topic light. He told me a little more about the movie festival he was taking me to. I didn't recognize the names of any of the directors, but I knew it would be fun no matter what.

Then he told me how his roommates were bugging him, and he was hoping that if things kept going well he would get a raise in a few months and finally afford a place on his own. I was a little jealous that his position was so safe that he was thinking about being paid more. Yet here I was, waiting for my pink slip. He was really good at what he did, so I tried to be happy for him.

He leaned closer, brushing his lips against my ear, making me forget about the little green monster growing inside me. "Since I only have about fifteen minutes left with you, how about we head to our cars?"

My skin tingled as his teeth grazed my earlobe. I knew what he wanted, and I was eager to get out of the bar, away from work—away from prying eyes. I pushed my empty glass forward on the bar and moved to stand up. He placed a ten-dollar bill on the counter and grabbed my hand in his.

He practically dragged me out to the parking lot, his hands wrapping around my waist as he propped me on the trunk of his car, which was conveniently parked next to mine.

His lips met the sensitive skin on my neck as he murmured, "I've been dying to get my hands on you for days. It's been too long."

His lips met mine, and his tongue pressed against my mouth, asking for an invitation. I let him in, running my hands around the back of his neck.

We kissed like we were starved for each other, and his hands found themselves in my hair, loosening the ponytail I had at the nape of my neck. One of my hands trailed down to his back pocket as I wrapped my legs around his hips. Ezra and I had made out a handful of times, but this was the best it had ever been. It felt like he was going to devour me right here on top of his car.

As he nibbled down my neck, my phone vibrated in my pocket. He mumbled, "You should probably check that." He stepped back a few inches as I dragged my phone out.

Blake: *Helllloooooo Lina, it's been 45 minutes. Zac Efron will be an old man by the time you make it home, which will break my heart.*

Ezra spoke before I could. "I'm sorry, I kept you too long. Can we finish this soon?"

I nodded, and he leaned in to kiss me again. His hands gripped my hips, and I didn't want him to stop. I knew I had to get home soon, but this was too good to give up.

After a few minutes, he broke away from me, breathing heavily. "Sorry. Again." He shot me a shy smile, and I melted for probably the tenth time in the last half hour. "I just have a hard time not touching you when you're right in front of me." He picked me up, taking me off of his car.

I reached into my purse, fumbling for my keys. "I'm off tomorrow. Call me?"

He grinned and gave me a quick peck. "Yeah, I'll try."

It took all of my willpower to get into the car and drive away from the gorgeous man still standing in the parking lot, watching me go.

I pulled up to the house and found a lime green Porsche parked out front. *Shit.* This must have been the surprise the girls were talking about.

I put my key in the front door and had to slam my hip into it to get it to open. The stupid thing always got stuck when it was humid outside, and this time it just multiplied how nervous I felt about Reece being inside my house.

I found the three of them—Blake, Val, and Reece— standing around the kitchen island. Val yelled out as I dropped my keys on the table at the door. "Lina! You finally made it!"

I replied with a slight wobble to my voice, "Sorry. Something . . . came up."

Reece let out a loud laugh. "I'm sure it did!" He took a few steps, making up the distance between us, and tucked a stray hair behind my ear. "Your sex hair is impressive."

I felt my skin turning red, the embarrassment shooting through me. "We didn't have sex."

Reece rubbed his thumb across my bottom lip. "The lipstick all over your mouth says otherwise."

I let out an audible gasp and took a step away from him. He chuckled and said, "Mag, it's okay. You just look really cute, is all." He tilted his head, raising an eyebrow, this time speaking quieter than before. "It's fine if you did, you know. I'm not threatened by your boyfriend."

Blake and Val shot inquisitive looks at each other, but I ignored them. "For the last time, he's not my boyfriend." His eyes trailed to my lips again, the evidence of my recent activities painted across them.

I put my hands on my hips. "Why are you even here?"

He held his fist up and opened it. My locket dangled from his fingers, reminding me of the last time he was here, bringing me my flashlight. "I found this on the ground at the resort earlier."

My hand met my neck, which was bare, and I felt terrible that I hadn't noticed it was gone. "Oh wow, thank you." I was a bit of an ass for being short with him just now.

He smiled and motioned for me to turn around. "The clasp was broken, and I knew you had to be worried sick about it. I took it to my jeweler and had them fix it." He put it around my neck and clasped it, just like he had the night we first met.

I spun around, holding the precious treasure in my hand. "I fell into a bush earlier. I thought it was my dress that had gotten snagged, but it must have been this. Thank you, again."

He leaned in like he was going to kiss me but stopped an inch before making contact. I felt his breath on my lips as he said, "Anytime, Mag." His eyes dipped down to my lips for the briefest of moments before he spun around, addressing my friends. "Well, ladies, thank you for the ice cream. I'll see you both soon, I'm sure." Val gave him a little wave as he turned to Blake. "And Blake. I'm sorry things are crappy right now. I'm busting my ass to make work better for you. If you can hold on for just a little while longer, I promise it will be worth it."

After she thanked him and said goodnight, he faced me again. He winked. "Goodnight, Mag. I'll see you at the office soon."

He let himself out, closing the front door behind him, and I sat down on the living room floor, crossing my legs under me. "Well, that was awkward as hell."

Val burst into a fit of giggles she had clearly been holding in. "Okay, but you have to see what you look like right now." She motioned to her own face for emphasis. "You've got this whole clown-lipstick thing going on. Did Ezra attempt to eat your face?"

I took my phone out and opened the front camera, taking a look at myself. "Holy shit! Why didn't he say something when he helped me get into my car?" I swiped at my lips with my thumb, but the damage was already done. "Oh God, I'm the worst human."

Blake took a few steps closer to me. "I thought you and Reece were keeping things quiet?"

I shrugged. "We're friends. And he was returning lost property. What's the big deal?"

She shook her head. "That was not an interaction between friends, and you know it. You have way more to lose than he does if you get caught together." Her eyes trailed to the front door and she glared, like she was giving Reece a dirty look. "I guess he has no problem breaking rules, though, huh?"

Before I could defend him, Valerie held up the DVD of *Charlie St. Cloud.* "I think it's about time to get this movie started. What do you think, girls?"

Halfway through the movie, I shifted on the couch, looking at them. "You guys, I don't feel good about this."

Val pointed to the screen. "Is it because we've watched this at least five times in the last year?"

I tugged at the collar of my shirt, feeling constricted. "No, dating two guys at the same time. It's weird."

Blake shrugged. "I don't see what's so bad about Ezra. Tell Boss Boy you can't do it, and maybe your life will go back to normal."

I clutched the locket in my hand; the thought of hurting Reece made me nauseous. Luckily, Val said, "I don't know if Ezra is the best idea, either."

Blake answered her. "She's completely obsessed over her five-year plan, Val. Reece throws a giant wrench into that. It's a bad idea all around."

Valerie scoffed. "Ezra doesn't fit in the plan either, Blake. No man does. But that's beside the point. We both think Lina's plan is ridiculous anyway."

"Stop. Both of you." I held my hands up. "I don't need this commentary right now."

Val gave me a sweet frown. "I'm sorry, Lina. We just want what's best for you." She smiled. "Give them a week or two. What if you go on one more date with each of them and then decide who you want to go further with?"

I mulled it over in my head. "You know, that might be

the best piece of advice I've been given in a long time." A couple of dates to decide was manageable.

Chapter Ten

I entered through the glass doors of the office and immediately noticed the giant black Cohen International sign hanging on the crisp white wall on the opposite side of the room. My heels clicked across the marble floor as I walked up to the chic glass receptionist desk. My palms were sweaty, and I worried that I would drop the iPad I had borrowed from Valerie. I tightened my grip, glad that I had updated my digital portfolio, including a lot of my recent work.

I was glad I had only told Val about this meeting. Everyone else was too involved in my current job or might sway me in one direction or another. Being here felt too permanent. Final.

The receptionist looked up from her computer screen and gave me a bright smile. "Welcome to the agency, Lina. I'm Anita. Please have a seat. Ms. Cohen will be out shortly."

I thanked her and listened to the click-clack of my shoes bouncing off the walls as I made my way to the low leather chairs in the waiting area. I sat down and resisted the urge to swipe through the pictures I had meticulously chosen.

The room was silent other than the occasional typing noises from Anita. The walls were bare, and there was no smooth jazz or lo-fi music playing quietly from any hidden speakers.

My only companion was my own heavy, erratic breathing. I inhaled deeply through my nose, trying to calm down, but when I heard the sound of stilettos tapping on the floor, I knew that wasn't going to happen.

She came through a doorway that led to a white bank of offices and met me with a handshake and a smile. "Lovely to meet you, Lina. I'm Sylvia."

I stood to shake her hand, and even though I was several inches taller than her, the power that emanated from her filled the room. Her gray hair was a jaw-length bob, and her skin was absolute perfection. She could be ten or thirty years older than me; it was impossible to tell.

I tried not to stumble on my reply. "It's very nice to meet you, too. Thank you for inviting me."

She pushed her round, red glasses up her nose in a motion that looked more like habit than necessity. "The pleasure is mine." She motioned to the hallway she had just come from. "Shall we?"

I followed her past several offices before coming to a door at the end of the corridor. She opened it and led me inside. The office was a stark contrast from the reception area. Plush chairs framed a deep mahogany desk. The patterned wallpaper reminded me more of a Scottish pub than a cold, calculating marketing firm.

"Well, Magdalina Herrera, I should let you know that our team has done quite a bit of research on you before calling this meeting. We wanted to make sure you would be a good fit for our agency. I will say, I was told that Mr. Howell had nothing but great things to say about you yesterday." Instead of sitting at the desk, she sat in one of the chairs and patted the one next to her.

I sat and put my hands on my lap. "I'm sorry if I'm a bit nervous. Um, you spoke to Mr. Howell? I was under the impression that someone else recommended me for your services?"

"Anita called him to verify your employment and to get a recommendation, that's all. So, what do you say, should we discuss a business relationship?" I was a little confused that he hadn't brought that up when we were on the phone last night. Sure, I didn't bring up the meeting, but I would have expected him to mention it.

I wiggled my fingers, trying to burn off nervous energy. "To be completely honest, I wasn't really thinking about going into business for myself until a couple weeks ago. I always thought I would one day, but it's all happening so quickly, and I'm still not sure if it's part of my current plan."

"These things usually do happen in the blink of an eye. That's where my firm comes in. We offer many services and can cater to whatever your needs may be."

"That's the thing. I don't even know what I need."

"Let's start with your portfolio. Mr. Howell said you have quite the eye." It made sense that they'd reached out to my current employer, but I wondered what other information he had shared with them.

I unlocked the iPad screen and handed the device to her. "This is a collection of my best work. I put a little bit of everything I do in there."

She scrolled through the images, spending quite a bit of time on each one. A smile warmed her eyes, and a couple of times I saw her perfectly shaped eyebrows lift.

I had chosen mostly wedding photos, but I had a few pieces from my last few sessions and some of Val and Blake that I had taken at the botanical garden recently.

Anita popped in, asked if we wanted any tea or coffee, and brought us our drinks in the time Sylvia spent scrutinizing my life's work. "These show a great range of talent. I think we can do a lot for you."

I thanked her as she slid the iPad back to me.

"We'll start by setting up an LLC. You just have to tell me the name you want for your business, and we'll go from there. How are you doing on social media?"

"My Instagram has several thousand followers, but I don't have much else going on."

"Well, once we get your LLC registered, I'll connect you with a social media manager. I also have a specialist in my office who can send you everything you need for your initial marketing campaign. We can manage your accounting to whatever degree you need us to. You have the choice for us to be as involved or hands-off as you want."

"Wow, this is a little overwhelming." My head was spinning, but I felt like I was in good hands with her. But was I ready? "Do you have a price list for your services? I'm on a tight budget, but I have some savings I can use until I figure out what I really need."

She reached forward and patted my hand. "Oh, Lina. Mr. Howell has already offered to pay for the first six months of our services. All you have to do is tell me what you want, and it's taken care of."

My pulse started racing. "I'm sorry, I might be a little confused. Reece . . . Mr. Howell, I mean, is paying you to start and manage a company for me?"

"Yes. His family's company is one of our oldest clients, and his parents are some of my closest friends. In fact, I've known Reece since he was a little boy. When Anita spoke to him, he said that you were thinking of leaving the resort and insisted we provide anything you would need to get started on your own."

This gave me more questions than answers. He *insisted* they help me? My future really was in jeopardy.

"I'm sorry, but I'm going to have to turn the offer down. I'm not even sure that I want to start my own business, and I don't want to start anything in debt to someone else." I tried to give her a polite smile, but the angry tears welling in my eyes made it difficult. "Thank you so much for your time, but I don't think I'm interested right now."

I was not a charity case.

Sylvia lifted her coffee to her lips and took a long sip before setting it down. Her red lips left a stain on the rim. "How do I put this nicely? The price of my time from this meeting alone is probably already above your budget. Many of my clients are working with price points in the millions. Mr. Howell is extremely fond of you," she pointed to my portfolio, "and I can see why. Please let him do this for you."

I blinked back my tears, willing my face to look as neutral as possible. There must be a way I could do this on my own. Millions of people quit their jobs to start small businesses every year. I really didn't need too much.

But, she said that Reece wanted to do this for me, and Val would kill me if I left a bad impression at this firm.

Did I even want to leave the resort? Was this Reece confirming that I was going to be laid off?

"Can I have a few days to think about it?"

She smiled. "He said you would say that." She stood up and patted my shoulder. "It was nice meeting you, Ms. Herrera."

I stood, ready to follow her out the door. "Thank you so much for meeting with me. I really appreciate your time."

She nodded. "I can see what he sees in you. I think I'm going to be fond of you as well."

I rushed into my office after my meeting with Sylvia, coffee in hand. Kicking off my shoes, I was finally relieved from the insanity that was wearing stilettos for more than a couple of hours.

Originally, my entire afternoon had been clear, but Kathy had sent me a text while I met with Sylvia that a client had booked me for a family session at sunset. With the prospect of having to start my career over from scratch, I couldn't turn it down.

As I plopped my purse on the floor at my feet, my cell phone rang. I reached to turn on my computer at the same time as I picked up my phone and answered with a "Yeah?"

"Hey, it's me. Um, I need a favor." Reece sounded nervous on the other end of the line.

"Sorry, my car is not big enough to move a body. Unless you have a chainsaw I can use to help you chop it up first."

He chuckled, and I took a sip of my coffee. "Dammit, moving a body is just what I needed you to do."

I logged on to my computer and pulled up my emails. "So what's really up?"

"I need a ride home."

"Did something happen? Are you alright?" A million worries pulled me away from my work, erasing how irritated I was with him about the whole Sylvia situation.

"Remember my tooth problem?" I nodded and then realized that he couldn't see me. But he went on anyway. "Well, it's impacted, and they need to pull it. But in order for my dentist to do that, he has to knock me out, and I'm not allowed to drive after."

"When do I need to be there?"

"They said it would be a couple hours before I could go home, so sometime around three, I guess. Think you could be my knight in shining armor? Knightess? Is there a female version of knight?"

I laughed at the image of me riding into the parking lot and scooping him up on my noble steed. "Dame, maybe? But I would still rather be a knight" I set my cup on my desk, leaned down to my purse, and pulled out my planner. "Let me see if I can reschedule my appointment."

Based on Kathy's earlier messages, I knew the family that had booked me today was pretty insistent on their appointment, but I could try to move them. I flipped through the pages, finding what I had written earlier. The family had a few more days left of their visit, and the worst they could do was cancel.

See? It paid to be overly organized.

"Hang on a sec while I call this client. Don't hang up," I said.

I lay my phone on the desk and clicked the mute button. Grabbing my office phone, I typed the client's number in.

"Hello, am I speaking with Bernice?" I asked once my call was answered.

"I sure am, how can I help you?"

"Hi there, this is Lina at the Santa Barbara Resort. I have you booked this afternoon for some family photos. I know we just confirmed your appointment, but I had an emergency come up and I was wondering if we could possibly move your appointment to another time during your visit?"

"My word, I hope everything is okay!" Her southern accent was thick and comforting, even through her worry.

I smiled. "Oh, it's nothing like that. My . . . ." I hesitated. Oh, what the hell. "My boyfriend is having dental surgery and needs a ride home. Nothing serious, I assure you, but I would rather reschedule just to be safe."

She didn't reply, but I heard children running around in the background. The got quiet pretty quickly, and I had the mental image of her giving them death stares. I tried to lessen the blow by adding, "I also have a 20 percent off coupon for the restaurant at the resort to compensate you for your time."

"Oh good." She let out a huff. "Actually, that works better for us anyway, the boys have been a complete handful today, and I was dreading getting them ready for pictures. What evening works best for you?"

"How about Friday? An hour before sunset?"

"That sounds perfect. I hope everything goes well with your boyfriend."

It felt weird telling a little white lie about Reece and me, but it was easier than saying "my boss, who I desperately want to make out with, needs me."

"Perfect. I will leave the coupon with the concierge so you can pick it up at your earliest convenience."

I hung up the office phone and realized that I had left a bit of a trail telling Bernice about my made-up boyfriend before sending her to the front desk for a coupon. Silently chastising myself for the slipup, I unmuted my cell. "I have successfully cleared my schedule for you. Text me the address, and I'll pick you up when you're done."

"You're amazing."

"This doesn't mean you're off the hook, Reece."

I could hear the smile in his voice, despite the pain he was in. "I have no idea what you're talking about."

"You know damn well that I met with Sylvia Cohen today, and she told me a few things I should be angry with you about."

"Before you try to argue about the money, just think of me as a silent investor."

"First of all, I was under the impression that I had a

job and didn't need an investor." The shock I had felt with Sylvia was boiling into anger under my skin.

"I promise that I will tell you everything later, but they are calling me up to the desk. Do you trust me?"

This was the second time he had asked me if I trusted him, and I knew I still did. No matter how crazy he made me. "Yes. I do."

He must have moved his phone away for a moment because I heard the muffled sound of him talking to the receptionist. Then his voice came in clearly again. "But you're right about your car. There is no way I'm going to be able to sit in the passenger seat comfortably. I'll leave my keys with the nurse so you can drive us home in it instead."

"You think I'll be able to handle that thing?" My palms began to sweat. "I could see if Blake will let me borrow her SUV?"

"Eh, it's just a car." I knew he didn't mean that, but then he added, "but I trust you, too."

I walked into the dentist's office, which was fancier than any doctor's office I had ever been in. There was an actual chandelier hanging from the ceiling in the lobby. I wondered what kind of health insurance Reece had to be able to go to a place like this for an emergency.

I walked up to the front counter. "Hi, I'm Lina Herrera. I'm here to pick up Reece Howell."

She flipped through the paperwork on her desk. "It says here that Mr. Howell had someone named Maggie coming to pick him up. Has there been a change of plans?"

I dug through my purse, pulled out my driver's license, and handed it to her. "Sorry, he's the only person on earth who calls me that."

She scanned my license into her computer and handed it back to me. "I need you to sign some release forms, and then I will have the nurse bring him around the east side of the building."

I signed the forms, but I lost all confidence in myself when she handed me his car keys. I reassured myself that this would be no different from driving my little Miata.

A nurse came up to the counter and handed me a stack of paperwork and a couple of ice packs. She gave me the rundown on how to take care of Reece for the next few hours: when to take the gauze out, how to pop the ice packs to make them cold, and how often to administer pain medication. I tried to follow along, but it was a lot. "Is all of this in these papers? I don't want to forget anything."

"Yes, you'll find all of this in there. Dr. De Luca sent an antibiotic to Mr. Howell's pharmacy, but he won't need to start it until tomorrow morning." She tapped her finger on the stack in my hands. "The doctor has also given him a paper copy of a prescription for a stronger pain medication that can be filled as needed."

"Why a paper copy?" I knew the answer as soon as the words left my lips, but it was too late to take them back.

She smiled knowingly. "Mr. Howell asked us not to

send any opiates to the pharmacy. He said that the prescription would be safer in your hands than his."

I thanked her for all of her help and tucked the papers under my arm.

I was just picking him up from the dentist, so why did it feel like I was crossing a precipice?

After making sure I had everything I needed in my purse, I went outside and found his car backed into a parking spot, the lime green color making it impossible to miss.

When I climbed inside, it took me a little while to get the seat situated and the mirrors all lined up, but I felt more comfortable than I'd thought I would. I turned it on, and the engine purred to life.

I couldn't deny that it sounded like a dream.

Shifting the car into first gear, I rolled forward about three feet before the engine stalled.

Maybe it isn't just like driving my car.

It only took one more try to keep the car running long enough to get around the building. The nurse from the lobby rolled Reece out from a side door in a wheelchair, and I hopped out and pulled open the passenger door.

"Maggie!!" With all the gauze stuffed into his chipmunk cheek, it sounded more like "Mallie." He threw his arms up excitedly and tried to launch himself out of the wheelchair, but the nurse placed a firm hand on his shoulder, planting him back in his seat.

"Hey Reecie, let's get you in the car." Judging by the glazed look in his eyes, I knew we couldn't talk about my career anytime soon, so I would just have to focus on getting him home.

The nurse helped me guide him into his car and buckle him up. I thanked her, and she wished me luck with a laugh.

I ran around to the other side of the car and got in, whispering a prayer that I wouldn't stall the car again with him in it.

I got lucky, and we made our way toward his house. A few miles into the drive, he put his hand on my leg and looked at me with big puppy-dog eyes. Because I didn't need him distracting me while driving a car that cost the same as an Ivy League education, I glanced over at him from the corner of my eye, grabbed his hand, and placed it back in his own lap.

"Thank you for taking care of me, Maggie." His words were muffled and slurred, which seemed to irritate him, but I found it hopelessly adorable, like some teenager on America's Funniest Home Videos.

He grimaced and opened his mouth wide, trying to remove the gauze with his tongue. I patted his leg. "No, babe, you need to leave those there until we get you home."

His head lolled over to the side, and he giggled. Actually giggled. "Did you just call me babe?"

I nodded, my eyes glued to the road, terrified of driving this ridiculous vehicle. "Yup."

"You're the best, babe. You're so helpful. And pretty." He turned to face me fully. "Like so pretty, I can't even stand it sometimes."

I gave him a quick smile and looked back through the windshield. "Just lie back and relax, okay?"

He followed my direction and lay his head against the

headrest. "The first time I saw you, I knew you were it for me."

At least that's what I thought he was saying, his M's and W's weren't very clear.

I didn't know how to respond, so I didn't say anything.

A few miles later, he jumped forward, looking scared. He wiggled his body to one side and pulled his phone out of his pocket. "Are we lost? I didn't give you directions to my house!"

I laughed. "Put that away, I know how to get you home better than you do."

"Oh, that's right, you broke into my house." He wasn't wrong, but it was funny hearing it out loud.

I continued to drive, using back roads to avoid traffic.

"You are such a life saver." His voice was sweet, dreamlike.

"I wouldn't call driving you home from the dentist saving your life. Especially after everything you've done for me."

He turned to face me. "No, you saved my life. I was going to do something bad. Something really bad. But you stopped me."

I couldn't help but laugh at how cute he was being. "Okay, Reece." I placed my hand on his thigh and left it there. "The anesthesia has done a number on you today, hasn't it?"

"I tried to tell the doctor, just pull the damn thing out, I don't need any drugs. But nooo, it was impacted, so they had to cut it out. Stupid tooth." He scooped up the paperwork that was hanging out of my purse at his feet. "And then they tried to give me painkillers."

He took the paper on the top of the pile and tore it in half.

I yelped, "Whoa, I need those!" In a panic, I reached over and yanked what was left out of his hands as he swatted at me. I stuffed the papers between my seat and the door, stopping any further damage. "I haven't had a chance to look through them yet."

"You don't need to. I don't want them." He reached across me and snatched the only paper he could get, tearing it up until his lap was littered with scraps. He pointed to himself. "Hello, drug addict here. Who gives drugs to a drug addict?"

We pulled up at a stop sign right down the street from his house, so I put the car in neutral and turned to face him. "Reece. I am extremely proud of the choices you are making right now. You are sticking to your convictions, which is great. But the papers the nurse gave me are the aftercare instructions. Can you please stop ripping them up?"

"Oh, that stuff's easy. You just take this out—"

Knowing what he was about to do, I reached up and covered his mouth, stopping his fingers from reaching in and scooping out the bloody cotton. It reminded me of when I'd had to practically wrestle with Ester to stop her from pulling her gauze out on the drive home when she had her wisdom teeth removed, too. Why did anesthesia make people so crazy?

"We're almost home. Just close your eyes and relax. Please."

He followed my directions, slumping back in the seat, and I continued on through the intersection. He mumbled, eyes still closed, "You're driving too slow."

"I am driving at a safe speed for having a passenger who could throw up at any minute."

"No, I mean you should get on the highway and let this girl stretch her legs. You would love how quick she is. She makes my body tingle." He wiggled his chest in an exaggerated shiver.

"I think that adventure will have to wait." The last thing I needed was to do something stupid to his car when he most likely wouldn't remember giving me permission to do so.

I pulled into the driveway and tried to stuff down the grief of it not being my parents' place anymore. I tucked his papers back in my purse and came around to the passenger side, helping Reece get out.

He wrapped his arm around my shoulder and put enough weight on me that it was difficult to maneuver both of us up the walkway. I guess this man really did trust me completely.

Just as we came up to the front step, the next-door neighbor waved from his front yard. "Little Lina, is that you?"

Reece called out belligerently, "Excuse me, her name is Magdalina."

I rolled my eyes at him, thanking my lucky stars that his speech was too slurred to understand. "Hi, Dennis. I'm just helping my new friend get into the house."

"I thought your mom sold this place? Did she decide to rent it out instead?"

He was a great neighbor but had always been nosy as hell. "No, it's a long story. I've got to get him inside, though. I'll see you later!"

"Is everything okay? Do you need some help?"

What I wanted to say was "Everything would be fine if you would shut the hell up and leave me alone."

But what I really said was "I've got it under control. He's just recovering from some dental surgery, but I'll put your number on the fridge when I leave in case he needs anything."

Without thinking, I pulled out my house keys and went to unlock the door before remembering that they weren't going to work. Reece put his lips against my ear and spoke quietly as if he were telling me a secret.

"I haven't had them changed." Then he threw his head back and laughed like it was the funniest joke in the whole world. I grabbed him, balancing him before he added, "You know what? You could have come in the front door that night instead of climbing that tree!"

The door unlocked with my key, just as he had predicted. I had thought about removing it from my keychain a hundred times since my mom put the house on the market, but I just couldn't bring myself to take it off. Now I was glad I hadn't. "Okay, big guy, let's get you inside," I said.

I put my bag and his car keys on the kitchen island and cracked an ice pack, shaking it to make it cold. "Here, hold this against the side of your face. They said it will help with the swelling."

He shook it around, squeezing it like a toy before finally pressing it to his cheek. He cringed at the cold temperature, and I wondered if I could find a hand towel to wrap around it.

"You should probably get your locks changed," I said. "Who knows who could get in here and steal your stuff." I scanned the first floor of the house, which was surprisingly empty. My throat constricted slightly. The place where so many of my happy memories happened was barren. In the living room, there was a couch, a painting of lavender fields in front of a barn on the wall, and a TV on a hutch. Nothing else. "Unless someone already did?"

"No, Mag, this is all I've got. I want you to come in whenever you want. My house is your house. You should live here, too."

Ignoring him, I read the first paper from the stack to make sure I was doing everything correctly.

It said we should remove the gauze when we got home, so I guided him to the bathroom under the stairs. I got the gauze out of his mouth, just as he started trying to bite my fingers when I reached in to help him.

He kissed my neck clumsily, and I took a step away from him. "We need to get you upstairs."

"I thought you'd never ask." He gave me an awkward wink before kicking off his shoes. He tucked the ice pack under his arm and started to unbutton his shirt.

I put my hand on his chest, trying to stop him. "We are going to be keeping clothes on this evening."

"I don't sleep like that." He turned away and stumbled up the stairs, tossing his shirt behind him as he went. He got to the top floor and dropped his pants as he continued to the master bedroom. He sat down on the edge of the bed and took his socks off, a feat that took twice as long as it would have under normal circumstances. "Come snuggle with me." He tossed the ice pack on the nightstand and reached his arms out, pulling me against him.

I put my hands on his shoulders, steadying myself. "I will snuggle with you under one condition."

His smile lit up the whole room. "Anything. I will do anything. I want you to snuggle with me forever."

I laughed and pinched the fabric on his undershirt. "The rest of our clothes stay on. Got it?"

He nodded enthusiastically. I kicked my shoes off and climbed into the bed with him. I laid on my side facing him, smiling at his swollen grin, absentmindedly running my hands up and down the smooth bedding. "These sheets are divine."

"Egyptian cotton. It's my favorite." His hand drifted to the side of my face. "But it's nothing compared to your hair." His hand moved down my shoulder. "Or your skin."

He leaned in to kiss me, but I blocked him with my hand. "No more kissing today, okay?"

"Anything you say, Mag. You're the boss."

Unable to resist, I reached up and ran my fingers through his hair, pushing it back behind his ear. His waves were more fitting for a surfboard than the boardroom.

He grabbed my hip and squeezed, pulling me tightly against him. I knew in an instant what was on his mind. His voice was deep and sultry. Any trace of the anesthesia seemed to disappear as he said, "But I'm your boss, huh?"

I pulled away from him. "I should have been more clear. No kissing or . . . other things tonight."

He rolled his eyes and flopped onto his back. "I'm not trying to have sex with you." He looked at me sideways and grinned. "Well, not right at this minute." He puckered his lips before speaking again. "Would you still love me if I wasn't your boss anymore?"

With that, I sat straight up. "Slow your roll. I've only said the L word to people who are related to me, and I'm not about to start throwing it around now." My nerves were spiraling out of control.

It was a few moments before I could look at him again, but when I did, his eyes were closed and he had the sweetest, most content smile on his face. He whispered, "Whatever makes you happy, babe."

I lay back down next to him, hoping he would never remember this conversation. "Let's try to get some sleep, okay?"

He spooned himself against me. "Yes, boss lady."

His arms wrapped around me and he held me tight. It might have been the sheets, or the cushy mattress, or . . . okay, most likely his body tucked against mine, but I fell asleep and had the best nap I'd ever had.

The room was dark when I woke up disoriented and hungry as hell. Stupidly, I had been so busy doing edits at the office earlier that I had skipped lunch. I slipped out of Reece's arms, looking around for a clock, but there was nothing in this pitch-black room.

"No, don't leave." His voice sounded clearer than before, so I hoped he was back to his right state of mind. He reached for me, pulling me into a tight embrace.

"Go back to sleep, I'll be back in a little while."

His whisper grazed my ear. "Right here is the only place you need to be."

"I'll be back in a little bit." He grumbled, so I whispered, "I have to pee."

"Fine. But don't go home yet?" It was more of a question than a statement, so I kissed his cheek and promised I wouldn't.

He squeezed me once again before letting me go, and I immediately missed his warmth.

I really did have to go after that last hug, and on instinct, I blindly found my way down the hall, through my room, and into my old bathroom. It was a little weird being here, knowing it wasn't my mom's house anymore. The unease became stronger after I saw the empty bedroom and the bathroom that only had a bag of toilet paper on the counter.

There were no signs of the many sleepovers with Val that had happened here—calling boys late at night and hanging up on them before they could ask who was calling. Lying on the edge of the bed when Ester climbed in through her window well after midnight, telling us all about the cool parties she got invited to. Even the rug that I spilled red fingernail polish all over when Val told me about her first kiss was long gone.

I shook the memories from my mind and finished up, rinsing my hands and wiping them on the pencil skirt I was still wearing. As I made it to the top of the stairs, I stumbled over Reece's pants.

I scooped them up, crept back to his room, and laid them across the footboard of his bed. Of course, because of my luck, his phone slipped out of his pocket and clattered on the hardwood floor.

I reached down to pick it up, and finally caught a glimpse of the time, shocked that it was already after nine. My stomach growled, reminding me that the task at hand was to find food.

Still looking at his phone, I noticed that he had two missed calls and multiple texts from someone named FC. I wasn't one to snoop, but I secretly wished he didn't have text previews locked so I could see why this person needed to contact him so badly.

I took the phone to his nightstand and plugged it in. The only other furniture in the room was the bed and a lone dresser against the wall. I wouldn't know that he lived here if it wasn't for the record player in a corner surrounded by a pile of albums on the floor.

When I finally got down to the kitchen, I rummaged through the bare cabinets, finding a mug—the only cup in the whole place—and a bottle of over-the-counter pain reliever. The fridge had several Styrofoam containers of various leftovers, but that was it. How did this man live here?

Knowing he was probably hungry, too, I dug my phone out from my purse and opened the app I had used hundreds of times to order from my favorite take-out place in this neighborhood. I wasn't sure what he would like, so I picked three different kinds of soup. That way he would have some for later. I got myself a burger and a large soda, since I wasn't sure how much longer I would be playing nursemaid tonight.

I sat on the couch in the mostly empty living room and answered my missed texts from Val, Blake, and my mom while I waited for our late dinner to be delivered.

Val, the beautiful human that she was, offered to use the spare key I kept in the kitchen junk drawer and her amazing boyfriend to pick my car up from the dentist's parking lot and take it home so it wasn't trapped alone in a parking lot all night. I told her I owed her big-time, but she said she just really liked having the opportunity to drive my car.

Twenty minutes later, there was a knock on the door, and I had food in my hands. I set the bags on the island and filled Reece's mug with water. Stacking the first container of soup from the bag, a plastic spoon, a bottle of acetaminophen, and his mug in my arms, I carefully made my way up to his room, holding the lip of the mug under my chin. Luckily, everything fit on his nightstand when I made it there.

Sitting on the edge of his bed, I patted his legs, and he moved to sit up slowly.

"If you could have any soup in the whole world right now, what kind would you want?"

He answered groggily, "Chicken noodle."

"Perfect." I handed him the plastic container and the spoon. I had chosen wisely. It was my favorite soup, too. "I asked them to make it with more broth than chicken or noodles since I figured it would be tastier than a protein shake or Jell-O." Once he was settled with his meal, I added, "When you're done with this, take some medicine for your pain." I opened the bottle and shook out just what he would need, laying them next to the mug. "I'll put the rest of the food I ordered for you in the fridge for later."

He took the soup container and stared at me with wonder. "No one has ever brought me soup before."

I highly doubted that, knowing that he came from such a privileged upbringing.

"It's nothing." My phone buzzed in the tight little pocket of my skirt I had jammed it into earlier. I hoped, it was Val letting me know that my car was home safe.

Out of instinct, I ran my hand along his cheek. "Eat up so you can feel better and get some more rest. I'll check on you in a little bit." I stood up and kissed the top of his head before heading downstairs to my burger and fries.

I finished my meal and had read through all the paperwork by the time I heard quiet footsteps behind me.

Reece's hands gripped my shoulders and rubbed them slowly, which felt divine. His voice was back to its normal timbre as he said, "Should we stay up and talk, or do you want to come back up to bed?"

I wiped my face with a napkin and faced him. "I think we should go to bed. We'll have plenty of time to talk later."

Chapter Eleven

I woke up slowly, like the warm cloud I had been wrapped in all night that was dissipating around me. As I made it back to planet Earth, I remembered I was not in my own bed and at some point had changed into a shirt three sizes too large.

I started to slip out from under Reece's arm, but it tightened around me. "Five more minutes," he mumbled in my ear.

"I have to go to the bathroom," I whispered back to him.

"Fine, but come back soon, please." His voice was low and gravelly. I knew if I looked at him, I would want to slip back under the sheets and run my hands across his chest, so I tiptoed to his bathroom in the dark.

I took care of my needs and thankfully found a bottle of mouthwash on the counter. After taking a swig and rinsing it out, I padded over to the bed.

Reece was sitting up, rubbing his face gently, so I asked, "How are you feeling?"

He put his hands down and looked over at me. "I'm a little sorer than I thought I would be, but otherwise I feel great."

The color was back in his skin and the light was back in his eyes, but I still asked, "How did you sleep?"

He grinned and reached for me, pulling me back into the bed. "I had the best night of sleep in forever."

We snuggled for a few minutes before his alarm clock started beeping. He reached over and turned it off before slipping out of our cocoon of smooth sheets.

He leaned down and brushed a piece of hair out of my face. "Sorry it's so early. I need to go work out for a little bit before my first meeting. What time do you have to be at the office?"

"Should you be working out? The paperwork said you can't lift anything heavy for three to five days."

Reece started to say something but stopped. He thought for a second and then answered, "Working out every day has been the biggest help through my recovery." He looked down at the bed, pulling a wayward string from the comforter. "Honestly, I hate almost every minute of it, but it's a routine that gets me out of my head enough to keep going. If I take a day off, I don't know how long it would take me to get back to it."

"I think your vulnerability is the sexiest part of you." I stood up and wrapped my arms around him.

I realized then that I didn't want to wait until one of us left the resort to see where things could go between us. I wanted to start dating him now. We had already developed a strong emotional connection—hell, I was his emergency contact. I knew in my heart that I was ready to take it further. We could figure out a way to do this under the radar at work. I opened my mouth to tell him exactly that, but his phone rang on the nightstand.

He picked it up and let out a groan. "Sorry, I have to take this."

He pushed the button to answer the call. "Izzy, this better be an emergency." I could hear her yelling on the other side. "Tell him someone else will have to do it." He mouthed "sorry" to me before replying to whatever she had yelled in response.

"I literally had dental surgery less than twelve hours ago. I told him I wouldn't be available until this afternoon." He trudged into the closet shaking his head.

He came back out a second later with a suit in one hand and hung it on a hook on the back of the door. "No, I am not using again. I just don't think that I need to rush in to meet with them. I told you I had the situation under control . . . ."

Wanting to give him some privacy, I went down to the kitchen, looking for my own phone. I found it sitting facedown on the island, and when I unlocked the screen, I found twenty-seven unread texts and 20 percent battery left.

The first was from Kathy, telling me that she had a last-minute client asking to book for nine this morning and to let her know ASAP If I could be there.

An entire conversation between Val and Blake played out in front of me. They had been predicting what I was doing while I wasn't texting them back. Some ideas were gruesome, but some were outright smutty.

My phone buzzed in my hand. Val had asked: *Okay*

Lina, all joking aside, it's time to send positive signs of life or we start looking for you!

I held up my phone and snapped a picture of myself standing in Reece's kitchen. Then I typed in the caption: *I'm alive and life is great. Hope you're both having a beautiful morning, too.*

I received a reply from Val almost immediately: *Is that his T-shirt you're wearing??* Followed by a string of eggplant emoji. I laughed out loud. Reece came into the room, fully dressed and ready for the day.

He asked, "What are you up to over there?"

"Oh, I'm just letting Val and Blake know that I didn't get kidnapped last night." Just then, the floodgates opened and I received a bombardment of GIFs from both of them, ranging from excited women screaming to graphic scenes that were definitely not safe for work.

So I wrote the only thing I could think of to get them to stop: *Nothing happened last night, we didn't even kiss. I promise to tell you the moment anything magical happens, though. Love you guys!*

"I'm sorry about that call. I have to run in to the office. You can stay if you want, or I can take you to your car?"

"Val and Joey picked up my car last night, but I would love a ride home. Kathy just asked me if I could come in early for a session, anyway."

I started for the stairs. "I'm just going to get dressed real quick, and I'll be back."

His hand brushed my elbow as I walked past. "Thank you. For taking care of me. You didn't have to do that, and I'm so thankful that you did."

I smiled at him. "No problem." I continued up the stairs, texting Kathy that I would be there soon.

We got into his car a few minutes later. I apologized for not moving his seat back when I parked in the driveway last night but couldn't stop laughing as he tried to play it cool all stuffed in there like a sardine.

He drove us toward my house, which was only a few blocks away. I inhaled deeply before saying, "So there are a couple things I think we need to talk about. Do you think we could get together later?"

He glanced at me before making a turn. "Oh, God. Is this about something I said after you picked me up? I was worried I would do something embarrassing."

There was no way I was ever going to repeat the words he said last night. "Nope. You were just a little loopy."

He glanced sideways at me. "Are you sure? I vaguely remember having a conversation with the next-door neighbor."

"Oh, Dennis was just making sure I got you in okay. He's the neighborhood busybody, but he's not obnoxious or anything."

"Well, I hope I kept my thoughts to myself and was the perfect gentleman."

"You totally were." I pointed to the scraps of paper at my feet. "I mean, other than tearing up your release forms."

"I feel like there's a whole lot you're not telling me."

I twisted in my seat so I could see him better. "You know all the important stuff, at least." The early morning sunlight came through the windshield, making his skin glow. There wasn't a single imperfection on his face, even with his swollen cheek. I wanted him, maybe more than I wanted to keep my job. And based on Reece's slurred confessions last night, I knew that he wanted me, too.

No, that wasn't totally true. I still couldn't lose my job, but I couldn't help but wonder if I could have both. Reece and The Pacifica. It wasn't part of my plan, but maybe the girls were right. Maybe there were a few flaws in my plan.

We could be careful for a few months—only going places far away from prying eyes. This could work.

Ezra's face flashed in my mind. I didn't want to stop seeing him, either. There was a spark between us I needed to keep exploring. I felt a little bad for spending more time with Reece than with him lately.

The longer I looked at Reece, the more I realized that I could totally be the kind of girl that dates two guys at the same time.

Neither guy I was involved with cared that I was seeing other people, so why should I?

I could ride this wave until the end of summer, and then when I knew what my future looked like, I could decide which boy was best suited for me.

This could totally work.

There were exactly three stoplights between Reece's house and mine. In all the time that I've lived with Val, I'd never once made all three of them on green.

But of course, because I was about to tell this beautiful man that I wanted something a little more serious, every light on the drive was green.

"Are you going to tell me what you want to talk about

later, or should I start guessing?" His voice wavered a little.

I hadn't realized that I had left him hanging when I zoned out, thinking about us. I didn't want to talk about the LLC stuff knowing that he had to rush off to the office. "Just work stuff. It can wait." *Oh, and that I want to kiss your face off. . . .*

He pulled up to my house, and all I could think about was the last time we were here. When I almost did get to kiss him. I wanted to close my eyes and lean forward, but his damn phone rang again. He pressed the button, answering it, and his sister's voice filled the tiny space.

"Reece Lingyun Howell, where the hell are you?"

"I'll be there in ten, Izzy."

She exhaled angrily. "I don't have ten minutes. These investors want to see your numbers now." She screeched the last word into her phone.

I unbuckled and opened the passenger door, but he reached over and put his hand on my leg, stopping me from slipping out.

"Just offer them coffee and show them pictures of your dog. It never fails."

I slipped out from under his hand and stepped out of his car. He leaned across, reaching for me. "No, wait," he said quietly.

I whispered, "You have to go. I'll see you later."

Lizette's voice exploded. "Are you with a girl right now? Are you in bed with her?" She let out a frustrated grunt. "Did you even have surgery or is that another one of your lies? Oh my God, this is a disaster."

He pinched the bridge of his nose and I waved at

him. I heard him say, "I don't even know what you're talking about, Iz. I'm in the car driving to The Pacifica right now," right before I closed the door.

He rolled the window down and muted his phone. "I'll find you later, okay. We still need to talk."

I reached into my purse to get my house keys, but I found the other ice pack the nurse had given me. "Wait, I almost forgot this. You just have to crack it in half and it'll get cold." I passed it to him through the window. "You're probably going to need it today."

The look on his face was appreciative, but a little sad. "Thank you. For everything." His sister continued to lecture him in the background, unaware of our conversation.

I pointed down the street. "You better go before she comes looking for you and kills both of us."

He stared for a few more seconds, and I had a feeling he was thinking about our almost-kiss. I knew I was.

"I swear I'll figure out something soon, Mag. It won't be like this forever."

"Goodbye, Reece." My voice wobbled as I waved again, and he took off down the road.

Sure, I trusted him, but we were in an impossible situation. Both of us had a lot to lose, and I worried we were letting our hearts do the thinking instead of our brains.

I sat down at my desk after my insane last-minute session. The woman was in her early twenties and was one of the most demanding clients I'd ever had. She had an opinion about every pose and every location I set up for her.

I'd fantasized about telling her to kick rocks and walking away from her the whole last half hour of our appointment, but the last thing I needed was a bad review right now, especially from someone who droned on and on about how famous their dad was.

I unpacked my camera bag and started uploading pictures. I opened my planner, put a checkmark next to the session that had just ended, and scanned the page to see what was up next today. While planning what I would need for this afternoon, I heard a knock at the door. "Come on in."

Reece opened the door, stepped in, and closed it behind him. He looked through my tiny window and then pulled down my little cloth curtain before turning around and leaning his back against the door.

"What are you doing in here? Did anyone see you?" I tried to keep my tone down, but my voice gave away the panic I felt.

"I didn't see anyone in the hallway when I ducked in. I think we're clear."

I stood up, attempting to peek out the window, but he wrapped his hands around my waist and pulled me toward my desk. He propped himself on the edge and tucked me between his thighs. My heart rate practically doubled in speed. "Reece, you can't be in here."

There was no real fight in my words. I didn't want anyone to find us in here together, but I really wanted to be with him in this moment.

He nuzzled his face into my neck, and I melted

toward him, all of my walls crumbling down. His voice rumbled through me. "I have been waiting for you to be alone all morning, and I was afraid that this would be my only chance."

I pulled away from him and locked the door without saying a word.

He gave me a devious smile and tugged me close. "I came in here to just talk, but now that we're alone, I don't think I can resist you."

"I can't resist you anymore, either."

His lips joined mine in a frenzy, causing a soft moan to escape me. He crushed me against his chest, digging his fingers into my hair, and I ran my hands up the corded muscles of his back.

His touch left a tingle down to the base of my spine, and all I wanted was him. This was better than anything I had ever imagined. Better than any kiss I had ever had—probably better than any I would ever have again.

"Oh God, Maggie. I can't stop thinking about you." He released my lips, kissing down my neck. I slid my fingers into his hair, and he slipped the strap of my dress off my shoulder, leaving kisses in its wake.

I was ready to let him take me right there on my desk but knew we couldn't go any further. "Reece, you have to stop. You have stitches in your mouth. You're going to hurt yourself."

"I don't care," he mumbled against my skin as he lightly bit just above my collarbone.

My skin tingled with the promise of what would come next, but my better judgment stepped in. I put my hands on his shoulders and pushed him away.

"Reece. Look at me."

He stopped, listening to my demand, but the heat of his eyes made my stomach flip.

My office phone rang, but he picked it up and slammed it right down again. "No more phones. I can't take another interruption."

I stepped away from him and ran my fingers through my hair. "That could have been important. You're going to get us caught."

"Nothing is more important than what is happening between us right now." His stare was molten, singing my skin.

I pulled the strap of my dress back up my shoulder as the phone rang again. This time I smacked the speaker button before he could hang up the receiver again. "Hello, this is Lina."

"Were you running or something?" Blake's voice came through on the other end as I sat in my chair.

"Uh, no. Why would you think that?" I focused on my voice, trying to make it sound normal.

What does my normal voice even sound like?

"You're all out of breath. Anyway, I'm on a quick break between meetings, and I was gonna grab a cup of coffee. Want to meet me at the café?"

Reece crouched down on the floor in front of me and pushed the bottom of my dress to my upper thigh. He started at my knee and kissed his way up.

Had Blake asked me a question? I said, "Nah, I'm fine," just in case. I put my hand on the top of his head, trying to move him away so I could focus, but he didn't budge.

"You're turning down coffee? Are you sure you're okay?"

Reece's fingertip grazed the edge of my panties, and I let out a squeal.

"Lina, what is going on in there?" Her response would have been comical if I wasn't trying to conceal our boss under my skirt.

"Sorry, umm, I dropped something."

I looked at Reece, trying to warn him that she would figure out that he was in here if he kept it up, but he just gave me a devious smile and licked the crease of my thigh.

Trying to sound like I wasn't hiding a grown man in my office, I asked, "How's your day going?"

She mumbled something that sounded a lot like motherfuckers and said, "Remember when this job used to be fun?"

I squeaked out a "Yup," answering Blake's question, but I couldn't even process this conversation.

Luckily, she didn't notice my weird vocal issue and went on complaining about the meetings she had been attending. I tried to listen and reply as needed, but Reece was proving to be immensely distracting.

He moved over the thin fabric he had been hyperfocusing on, and I slammed my hand onto his shoulder, unsure that I could keep this game up. His eyes met mine, and he winked, whispering, "So beautiful."

Blake suddenly blurted out, "I just hope all of these assholes fucking choke. I want them out so I can go back to running things the way we used to. Except for Reece. I think he's a prick, but you like him, so I guess he can stay."

When he burst into laughter, I realized I couldn't hide him any longer.

"Is he in there with you? Oh God, am I on speakerphone?"

Reece pulled my skirt back down, covering me, and pointed to the door. He mouthed, "I should go."

I shook my head and grabbed the lapel of his blazer. Replying to Blake, I said, "No, it's just me. I've got a frog in my throat or something." I coughed a few times, pretending to fix my voice. "You know what, I have a shoot in a little bit and need to get ready. I'll call you back later?"

She sounded skeptical but still gave me an okay before saying goodbye. I hung up the phone and gave Reece an angry look, "You're going to get us caught!"

He stood up and kissed me again, making me light-headed. "Maybe it would be worth it?"

"I have bills to pay. And your consequences are even worse."

He sat back down on the edge of my desk, "You're right." He glanced down at his watch. "I have to be in the conference room in a little while anyway. Have dinner with me tonight."

I was about to agree, and then I remembered how busy my schedule was for the next several days. "I can't. The boss is working me to the bone, and I won't have any free time for a while."

He gave me a cheeky little grin, "Well I could have a word with him if you want me to."

I put my hand on his knee and pushed it away. "Reece. It's important for me to do a good job for however long I still work here. I've got to have some integrity."

He grabbed my hand, wrapping his fingers around mine. "Okay fine, I won't mess with your schedule. We do need to talk, though."

"Oh yeah, that reminds me. I'm totally irritated with you right now." I glared at him playfully.

"Take a number, babe." The way he smiled after calling me babe almost cleared my mind completely.

Instead of starting with the tough questions, I lifted an eyebrow. "Why don't you have any furniture? Or dishes? Your house is empty."

The way his cheek dimpled when he laughed made him look even sexier than before. "I have furniture."

I tapped the fingernails of my free hand on the arm of my chair. "Let me rephrase that. Why do you only have like six pieces of furniture?"

He picked up a paperclip from my desk and started playing with it. "Well, most of the furniture in my last place was bought with company money, and I didn't feel right bringing it to my new place. I want everything in this house to be mine." He shrugged. "I don't want them to be able to take anything from me."

I stood up, tucking myself between his legs again. As I ran my fingers through his hair, pushing his wild waves down, I gave him a kiss on his puffy cheek. His stubble tickled my lips. "So you'll understand why I can't hire Sylvia Cohen?"

He pulled back, looking at me. "Who said anything about Sylvia Cohen?"

"I met with her yesterday. And since she said you offered to pay for her services, I'm willing to bet you know exactly what we discussed."

He pressed a sweet kiss to my lips. "I only talked to Anita because she asked for a reference, and because I've known Sylvia forever and know just how good she is at what she does. I wanted to make sure you had the best options."

I wrapped my arms around his waist, holding him against me. "How is it any different from you taking handouts from your family, Reece? You want to do this on your own. Can't I do this on my own?"

He pressed his forehead against mine. "Everything going on right now is my fault, and when I found out she was interested in you, it felt like the perfect solution. Please, just let me fix this."

I rubbed my hands across his back. "Reece. You can't possibly believe that. You work for a corporation that does this over and over again. You're just a cog in the big machine."

"No." He sat back and looked directly at me. "It was my data analysis that convinced them to cut your position. I'm the reason you won't have a job at the end of this summer."

"Oh." The truth in his words cut like a knife. I took a step back, but his hand landed on my shoulder, keeping me from going any further. "So I really am about to be out of a job."

"I've been fighting for you in the boardroom. I've

been telling them how your bookings have tripled, and how our increase in clients is solely based on your talent, but they don't see it that way. They are going to lay you off, no matter how hard you work for them." I couldn't respond. I didn't know what to say. He went on, "Then when you mentioned that you wanted to start your own company, I knew I could support you in other ways."

"But you didn't call her and tell her to represent me?"

His free hand flew to his chest. "I swear, I didn't. She's interested in your work, regardless of whose name is on the check."

"I still can't accept it. It's too much money."

"Think of it as a zero-interest loan that you only ever have to pay back if you feel like it later on down the road."

I rubbed my forehead, realizing that I wasn't going to be able to win this.

"Please, Mag. This is more about me making amends than anything else." He flashed me that sweet smile. "It's not you, it's me. But if you really don't want it, I will call Sylvia right now and tell her the deal is off."

I bit my lip, thinking about what my future could look like. I was going to have to throw the plan out the window now. "Can I think about it and let you know?"

"Yes. Any time you want me to pull back, just let me know." He jumped off the desk and pulled me into an embrace. His nose nuzzled my ear, and he left a trail of kisses along my jaw. "I'm sorry I kept all of this from you, but I really thought I could fix all of it before you even knew what was going on."

His lips met mine in a series of sweet, gentle kisses.

My body melted into his before a thought occurred to me.

"I've never had an orgasm." Oh Jesus, why did my brain decide right now was the prime time to spill that secret?

He pulled back a few inches, giving me a devilish grin. "Why are you thinking about orgasms?"

I laid my head on his chest, hoping it would make me disappear. "You were being open and vulnerable, so I thought I would be brave, too. I know it's not the same as what you just shared with me, but I wanted you to know that I've been hiding something, too."

His hand went to my chin and lifted my face so he could meet my eyes. "Wait, so you and flower guy haven't . . . ." He trailed off, leaving me to interpret what he was asking.

"We have. Had sex, I mean. Just not . . . umm . . . successfully, I guess?"

The look he gave me raised the temperature in the room about twenty degrees. "I guess we'll just have to fix this, won't we?"

He gripped my waist and lifted me onto the desk, but I put my hand on his chest. "Not in my office. And not until your mouth is better."

He ran his hands up my thighs, tucking his fingertips under the hem of my skirt. "I don't have to use my mouth to make you come, you know."

I plucked at the top of my dress, letting some air in. "Wow, um, I don't even know what to say to that."

He started to crouch down again, but I called out, "No. Later, okay?"

He glanced at his watch again. "Fine. But only because I have to go anyway." He gave me a quick kiss. "I want to take my sweet time the first time."

Instead of replying, I just bit my lip, thinking about the promise he'd just made.

"Soon." He kissed my forehead and was out the door before I could say another word.

I leaned back against my desk, wondering how I'd gotten myself into this situation and what I was going to do now that I was here.

Chapter Twelve

The next night, after a long day on my feet, I parked my little blue car in the lot of a strip mall I had always avoided. I got out and looked around, making sure I didn't see anyone I knew, and walked toward the door.

"Hey girl!"

I must have jumped about five feet in the air. "Valerie! You can't scare me like that!" I looked around again, whispering, "What if someone sees us here?"

She laughed. "Then they will see that we are healthy human beings?"

I scanned the parking lot for Blake and saw her car pulling in. Thank goodness she was able to leave work to be here, too. I couldn't handle being the only awkward woman in this store.

Blake parked and walked up to where we stood outside the door. "I think I should have worn a hat or maybe some big sunglasses."

Val laughed. "Once you girls get used to being in

here, you are going to make fun of the people who act the way you're acting right now."

Blake said, "I don't know. Why couldn't we have just done this online? That's how I usually do it." Val didn't answer her and just directed us to the door. This wasn't the first time Val had dragged me into an uncomfortable situation, but I had to admit, it always turned out to be fun. I didn't regret a single nightclub or biker bar Val had shoved me into.

We walked into the store, and I was immediately overwhelmed by the bright colors and interesting shapes. A guy who was about our age waved cheerily from behind the counter. "Hey ladies! Welcome in. Please don't hesitate to ask if you need anything."

He was so chipper, I had to double-check that we were standing in an adult toy store, not an Applebee's.

"Hey, Dimitri! I have a couple of newbies with me today. I'll let you know if they have any questions I can't answer."

Oh jeez, she even knew the guy's name. I was learning so much more about my roommate than I had ever wanted to know.

She looked at Blake and me. "I think I know where we should start. Follow me."

There were so many things I had questions about as we walked through the store, but I was way too chicken to ask her about any of them.

We came to a wall that had phallic devices of every shape, size, and material imaginable.

Blake grabbed something bright pink that looked like it had little ears on it and tucked it under her arm. When

I caught her eye, she said, "What? We're here because you need help. I know what works for me. I'm due for a new one of these, anyway." She grabbed another one from the same hook and handed it to me. "Here, I think you'll like this one."

I took it but avoided looking at it.

"Ah! Here it is!" Valerie stood on her toes, reaching for something gold and white that looked like it had the mouth of a suckerfish. "This is pretty much the best thing I've ever purchased. You can use it on your own, but it works best with a friend." I could feel my entire body starting to blush, but before I could say anything, she called out, "Dimitri, could you bring us a basket? My friend Lina is going to have her hands full."

He replied, happier than ever to help, "Sure thing! I'll be right there!"

I peeked down the aisle, checking for other patrons in the store. "Could you please refrain from calling out my name like that? Someone might recognize me."

"Um, at this point, if someone sees you, they also have to be in here, so I think you're safe." She did have a point, but I think she was trying to embarrass me. More than I already was.

Dimitri came up and handed me a basket. "Here you go, love. Let me know if you need me to hold on to anything behind the counter for you."

I nodded. Val started asking him about something with vocabulary I had never heard before, so I started browsing on my own. My phone buzzed in my pocket, and I was desperate for a distraction, so I checked it. It was a text from Reece: *Hey. What are you up to?*

When we'd had our nightly phone call last night, I'd avoided mentioning tonight's plans.

I replied: *You would never believe me if I told you.*

Reece: *Well now I'm intrigued.*

Feeling braver than I ever had in my entire life, I opened my camera and snapped a selfie with the wiener wall behind me and sent it to him.

Predictably, I regretted it immediately.

I watched the bubble pop up, showing that he was typing, but it quickly disappeared. And then it popped up again . . . and disappeared. It popped up one more time, and it felt like an hour passed as I watched those three little dots blinking while I anticipated his response.

Finally, a text came in: *So when am I coming over to check out what you've bought?*

I replied to him: *I don't have any plans after this. Want to come over?*

"What's with the big goofy grin, Lina?" Blake looked over my shoulder, but I locked my phone screen before she could see anything.

My face was hot. "Just texting with a boy."

She clapped her hands together. "How are things with Ezra?"

"No, this is . . . ." Was I supposed to tell her it was Reece? She had specifically said she didn't want to hear any details about us. "Someone else." Riding my wave of bravery from before, I grabbed another contraption, small and shaped like a tube of lipstick, and tossed it into my basket.

"Is that thing still going on between you two?" She didn't sound happy for me.

My phone vibrated again, so I checked the incoming text.

Reece responded: *As much as I would LOVE to come over tonight and help you with your purchases, I can't. Rain check?*

I couldn't say that I wasn't bummed but I understood. I sent him a text telling him to let me know what day worked for him and that I'd be there.

Val had mentioned earlier that these toys might be something I wanted to try by myself for the first time, so it would probably be best if I used my purchases without him.

Val jumped into the conversation. "Are things getting more serious with either of them?"

"Not really. Ezra's been too busy for anything other than a text here and there. Reece and I talk on the phone a lot, but you know why I can't really take things further with him."

Val herded us toward the lingerie aisle, and I felt a little more comfortable. I wouldn't need to read an owner's manual to figure out how to wear clothing.

Blake grinned. "I wonder if Ezra has a brother."

I laughed. "Sorry, he's an only child, but I can ask if either of them have cute friends."

I grabbed a lacy blue outfit that looked like it covered about what my bikini did and tossed it in my basket. Val grabbed a few things and winked at me as she tossed them in, too.

"Blake, we know how you are. Even if Lina found someone to hook you up with, you wouldn't take time away from work to date him anyway."

She groaned. "You guys, I can't even think about

anything other than this damn resort right now. I feel like I need to prove myself to these people, and then in the next breath I want to run for the hills, never to be seen again."

I said what had been on my mind. "At least your job is safe. I'm busting my ass trying to prove myself for a job that won't even exist soon." I sighed and looked at the items in my basket, which were going to cost a fortune. "I should probably start saving every penny for when I have no income at the end of this summer."

"How did the meeting with Sylvia go?" Val asked, realizing that Blake and I had become total downers.

I rifled through my basket, trying to decide how my meeting had gone. "I don't know if I'm ready to do it all on my own. Help would be nice, but it's a lot of money."

Val framed my face with her hands, squeezing my cheeks. "You need to stop focusing so much on money and think about what you really want. You can always make more money later."

I mumbled through my squished lips, "Says the lady who is financially stable."

She stared me down. "If money wasn't a factor, what would you want to do?"

I shrugged as she released my face. "I honestly have no idea."

"Well, at least now you know that you have some choices."

I felt that deeply. For the first time in my life, I had options. In more ways than I was willing to discuss in front of my friends at a sex toy shop.

We walked to the front of the store and placed our items on the checkout counter.

"Don't you ladies worry about the price of anything today," Val said. "I dragged you here, so it's all on me. Consider it an early . . . whatever the next major holiday is, gift." She handed Dimitri her credit card.

I nudged her hip with mine. "Thanks, Val, but it's kind of weird to get a basket full of vibrators for Easter."

Blake let out a giggle. "I think it's the perfect occasion, actually!"

While Val took care of the purchases and Dimitri placed our stuff in black plastic bags, Blake wrapped her arm around me. "I'm not allowed to talk about anything official yet, but you're an amazing artist, and they would be stupid to get rid of you. However, in the event that they do lay you off, I'm sure you'll find something fast. Your Instagram account is growing every day, and we all know people we can recommend you to." She thought for a second. "Ooh, My cousin Macy is pregnant. I bet she would hire you for maternity shots and probably a newborn session when the baby gets here."

The fact that she was helping me find new clients was her way of confirming what I already knew: I was about to be unemployed. "That would be nice. I should focus on building a clientele while figuring out my next step."

Val turned to us, the receipt in her hand. "You know what? Joey and the guys are looking for someone to shoot material for their newest album. They have a venue rented for a few hours in a couple of weeks and were planning on just setting up a phone on a tripod, but I bet they would pay you to do it instead. It wouldn't be a lot of money, because they are broke as hell, but it would be good for the 'gram."

"That actually sounds pretty fun." I immediately thought about texting Reece to ask if he wanted to come with me.

Blake tied the handles of her bag into a bow and looked up at me. "I don't want to talk about work anymore. Have either of you seen any good movies lately?"

I locked myself in my bedroom and dumped the contents of my shopping bag on my bed. Blake had gone home, and Val said she had plans with Joey, but I knew they were just trying to give me a chance to be home alone so I could get . . . comfortable.

But knowing that they knew what I was doing made it really *un*comfortable. I picked up my glass of wine I had poured before coming up the stairs, hoping it would give me some liquid courage.

I took the devices out of their packaging and read the directions. Two of them needed to be plugged into chargers and the other one required batteries. I followed the directions to charge the first two and put the last one in my side table drawer for later.

I felt a bit of relief knowing that the two most intimidating ones needed to charge for several hours. I was off the hook for now.

I popped the tags off of the lingerie that both Val and

I had picked out for me and held them up in front of my mirror.

I made eye contact with myself and thought, *You are a strong, sexy woman, Lina.*

I undressed and picked up the blue lace babydoll dress. I put it on and checked myself out. The word "dress" was used lightly in this situation.

I'd never worn something like this before, but it made me feel powerful. Eager to try the other outfits, I took it off and put on a silky red number with a big bow between my breasts. Before I could give myself the once-over, my phone buzzed on my desk.

I picked it up and read the text from Ezra: *Hey Babe, what are you up to tonight?*

I pursed my lips seductively and snapped a picture of myself in the mirror, sending it to him.

I don't know who I had turned into today, but I liked this girl.

As soon as I set the phone back on my desk, it started vibrating like crazy. I picked it up and giggled a little to see that Ezra was calling me on FaceTime.

I took another sip of my wine and answered the call. This must be how Batman feels when he puts on the batsuit.

I waved to the camera. "Hey, what's going on?"

"I was going to ask you the same thing." He was sitting at his desk in his bedroom at home, so I felt safe enough to show him what I was doing without worrying about having an audience.

"I went shopping with Val and Blake today. We got

some accessories." I pulled the camera down and showed him the rest of my body.

"You look amazing. What else did you get?"

I flipped the camera and showed him the spread on my comforter.

"You should put something else on and show me." He moved over to sit on his bed, which made this feel even more scandalous than before.

The next item in my pile was a hot pink fishnet bodysuit. I finished my glass of wine and set the phone down so the camera pointed at the ceiling. I found it ironic that I was fine wearing next to nothing on this call but being actually naked was too much for me.

I wiggled into the bodysuit and was a little confused about where some of the openings were, but I shrugged and held my phone up, showing myself in the mirror.

"Wow, Lina. You are so beautiful."

I felt my body blush, turning the same color as my. "I wish I would have known how fun dressing up was before now."

"I wish I was there with you right now." He shifted the phone into his other hand, and I wondered what he was up to off camera.

I lowered my voice, trying to sound seductive. "Then why don't you come over? I've got the whole place to myself."

He grinned and sat up straighter like he was going to head out the door and rush to my house. "Let me see what I can do."

There was a knock at his bedroom door, and he put his phone against his chest, blocking my exposed body on his screen. I rolled my eyes. His roommates had the worst timing.

"Ezra, you're all out of milk. Could you give me a ride to the store?" That wasn't one of his roommates, and it was far from breakfast time.

Hearing a feminine voice while we were in the middle of whatever this was instantly killed my mood. I grabbed my robe from the back of my door and put it on.

"Yeah. Let me get my keys and I'll be right out." He pulled the phone back up to his face. "Can we come back to this in, like, twenty minutes? Abby needs a ride somewhere."

I sat on the edge of my bed, "Umm, who's Abby?"

He raised his eyebrow in question. "I thought I told you my friend was coming to stay with me?"

"You did." *You just didn't mention that she was a girl.* "It must have slipped my mind."

"Great. I'll call you back when I get home?"

I nodded in reply, but he ended the call before I could say anything.

I suddenly felt dirty, but not the fun kind. I took off my fancy lingerie and put on some sweats. I didn't want to try any of this stuff on anymore, so I scooped it up and stuffed everything in my side table drawer.

My room felt too small, like the walls were caving in, so I went downstairs and turned the TV on. I opened up my texts to tell Val that the coast was clear and she could come home, but I saw my earlier conversation with Reece.

Now I felt like a hypocrite.

If I could see two guys at the same time, why should I have any say in what Ezra did in his spare time?

I was also aware that I was drawing a huge conclusion over a situation I literally knew nothing about. She could be a friend he had no interest in. Maybe she wasn't into him.

Who was I kidding, my gut told me that there was something else going on. I just didn't know if I wanted to fight for someone's attention.

I watched a stupid sitcom that I had never seen before to keep my mind from self-destruction, but it didn't help.

When Ezra called me thirty minutes later, I didn't answer it. He called me three more times, but I ignored every one of them. There was no way I would be able to get back in the mood, even though I knew I was being immature.

He didn't leave a voice mail, but he sent a text: *Call me when you can, can't wait to see your sexy ass soon.*

My first instinct was to ask him to give me every single detail about this girl, but I knew that would be crazy.

Instead, I spent ten minutes coming up with a reply that didn't make me sound neurotic. All I came up with was: *I just got a massive migraine and need to lie down. I'll call you when I can.*

I had just made it through another episode of the show I wasn't paying attention to when my phone rang again. I grabbed it angrily and answered, "What?"

"Oh, shit, I didn't realize how late it was. I'm sorry." Reece's voice sounded deeper than usual.

"No, I'm sorry, I was just . . . ." I cringed, thankful that he couldn't see me right now. "Watching some TV."

"I just got home from a meeting and was hoping you were up. I couldn't stop thinking about you after that picture you sent me."

"They have you working this late? No wonder you hate it there."

He let out a quiet chuckle. "It wasn't a work meeting. It was a 'Hello, my name is Reece, and I'm an addict' meeting."

The angst in his voice gave me so much more than his words. "That's why you couldn't come over tonight."

The line was quiet, except for his breathing for a few moments. "I go every Thursday night and sometimes Monday mornings if I've had a rough weekend. I've been doing better the last six months, but some days are harder than others."

I rolled onto my side on the couch, imagining that I was lying next to him, as always. "You seem upset. Anything you want to talk about?"

"No, not really. Thanks, though." I heard him moving around before he asked, "How was your night?"

It was easy to pretend his eyes were looking into mine when I answered, "Pretty boring, actually. I've just been laying on the couch since I got home."

"You didn't try anything you bought? Nothing, umm, spectacular happened?"

"Reece, are you trying to find out if I made myself come this evening?"

I pictured him smiling on the other end of the line as he said, "Maybe. I figure one of us should have had fun tonight."

"Well, I'm sorry to report that I discovered it takes

several hours for those damn things to charge." I avoided
thinking about the other boy I had tried to fool around
with this evening.

The longer we talked, the more I knew I was a
chicken without a leg to stand on. I was doing the same
thing to Ezra that I was worried he was doing to me.

Maybe spending my energy on more than one guy at
a time just wasn't for me. My biggest problem was that
the man I wanted to be with the most was a giant risk to
the rest of my life.

I walked across the grassy field in front of the resort with
the Phillips family, talking with Bernice about what kind
of photos she wanted. I had snapped some test shots to
make sure my camera was calibrated for the lighting, and
she'd said she liked them, so I knew I was on the right
track. Taking pictures at sunset was my favorite thing to
do at the beach, and we had just enough time before it
became too dark to get what I wanted.

I heard someone behind me call my name and turned
around. Ezra ran up to us.

"Lina!" He grabbed my hands and pulled me close to
him. "I have been looking for you all day. We need to
talk."

I looked over my shoulder at Bernice and spoke
through my teeth with a smile plastered on my face.
"Now is not a good time, Ezra."

"There will never be a good time for this. Please, just
listen to me."

Bernice stepped forward. "How's your tooth doing? Lina told us you had an emergency and she had to pick you up."

He looked confused but went with it. "Uhh, much better, thank you. Can I steal her for just a quick minute?"

I protested, "I have to work with the sun here. Time is limited."

Bernice waved her hand. "Go ahead." She gestured to her two sons, rolling around in the grass. "I need to straighten them up anyway."

He started to pull me toward the building, but I stopped him. "No. This is so unprofessional." I put my hands on my hips, "If you need to say something to me, you're going to have to do it when I'm not with a client."

"But Lina, you don't understand. I made a mistake."

"You're right. You are mistaken that I'll drop everything and take care of your problem right this minute." I pointed back toward the building. "You need to go. I'm at work, and you have to respect that."

He nodded and waved toward the family standing behind me. "I'm sorry, Lina. I'll call you later."

I turned around and smiled. "Sorry about that interruption. It won't happen again. Ready to head across the street to the beach?"

We wandered in the sand for about an hour, and I got some great shots. They were a sweet family, and despite the boys throwing clumps of seaweed at each other near the end of the session, our time together was delightful.

I walked them back to the resort, dropping them off on the far side of the lobby, close to the entrance to the restaurant like I usually did, so they would hopefully take the hint and stay for dinner.

I shook hands with Beatrice and her husband, thanking them for booking me.

Beatrice shook my hand vigorously. "Are you kidding me? You're a hot commodity right now. All my friends are going to be so jealous that I was able to snag you first."

"Oh, well, thank you so much. I hope you enjoy the rest of your stay at the resort."

Just then, Reece came up the hallway, his hair slightly disheveled, his tie loose. His face was puffy, and he looked exhausted. I felt a flash of panic that Bernice might connect him as the man I took to the dentist instead of Ezra. He reached up and put his hand on my shoulder gently. "You're right, our Maggie really is a hot commodity. We're so lucky to have her." He reached out with his free hand, offering them both handshakes. "I'm Reece Howell, the resort's CFO. It's nice to see that you're in good hands."

Beatrice replied, "Oh, the best, I'm sure." I might have imagined it, but I swore her eyes lingered on his swollen cheek.

Her husband stepped in, saving us from further scrutiny. "I think we need to feed the boys before they cause any damage."

A crashing noise echoed across the tiled entryway, and we all turned to find their boys standing in front of a smashed vase, flowers littering the floor around them. They pointed at each other, screaming accusations, neither one admitting fault. My eyes tracked across the room, and I caught Ezra's eyes boring into mine as he leaned against the reception counter.

I turned back to Reece, who still had his hand on my shoulder. He said, "I have something I need to take care of. I'll call you later?"

His nightly phone calls had become the best part of my day, so of course I answered, "Sure."

Both of us leaned in a fraction of an inch, about to kiss goodbye before remembering where we were. Instead, he squeezed my shoulder awkwardly before turning toward his office.

Instead of confronting Ezra with Reece nearby, I walked through the front door of the resort, and just as I had suspected, Ezra followed closely behind. We weaved over the cobblestones until we stopped in the middle of the most secluded area of the resort, the West Garden. It was the site we used for our most intimate, private wedding ceremonies.

Ezra put his hand on my waist, pulling me close to him. Any other time my heart would be racing because I liked him, but after the FaceTime incident yesterday, I wanted to be anywhere but here.

The hedges were at least seven feet tall around us. He turned so his body blocked the thick cypress archway, affording us some much-needed privacy. "Look, Lina, I know that you're pissed, but you need to hear me out." His blue eyes were pleading, and I couldn't deny them.

"You have three minutes." Any longer and I might start screaming . . . or crying. I wasn't sure which would be worse.

He let go of my waist and brushed his hair out of his eyes, making him look like Ryan Gosling.

"Well?" I tapped my fingers against the strap of my camera, silently counting the ever-passing seconds.

"You can't get mad at me for having another girl over. I made it really clear that I'm not a monogamous guy."

I put my hands on my hips. "Well, maybe I'm not a monogamous girl."

His eyes went wide. "Did you invite some other guy to your place when I had to leave?"

I started to say no, but I tilted my chin up, "Wait, you left to go get milk with Abby,"—I hated that I knew her name—"but you're upset that I might have had someone over, too?"

He stammered, "The way you put a lot of pressure on me to be with you made me think that you were only seeing me."

I threw my hands up in the air. "Well, you thought wrong. I am not the kind of girl who is going to wait around for some guy anymore. The old me is gone." I stopped for a second, staring him down. "And I have you to thank for that."

He reached for me again, but I pulled away. "Lina, don't be like this."

"I'm tired, and my feet are killing me. I am done with this conversation, and I'm going home." I stepped around him, passing through the garden arch. He took a few steps toward me, and I put my hand in front of him. "Don't follow me."

I made it back to my office so I could grab my purse, thankful that not a single person spoke to me on my way.

I slumped down at my desk, replaying the entire conversation with Ezra in my head.

What was I doing?

He was right, this girl was not me. I didn't want to play the field, I wanted a relationship on a solid foundation.

My heart raced at the realization. I didn't want to waste my time playing pretend with Ezra. I wanted the man who showed up consistently, even when he didn't know I needed him. I needed the man who adored me, wanted me, and at the end of the day was my friend.

I wanted Reece. Regardless of what pressure it put on my position at the resort. He was worth it.

Chapter Thirteen

My shutter clicked as I focused on the woman standing under a floral arch in the West Garden. I tried not to think about the last time I'd been here, but I couldn't avoid the ghosts of Ezra and me arguing everywhere I looked. The sky was overcast, making the small space feel smaller than it had been almost a week ago. As much as I would have liked to be anywhere else on site, the lighting for headshots in this garden was the best choice for this time of day.

My client was at least six feet tall and had the skin of a goddess. She made it easy to work even though I was somewhat distracted.

"Move a little to the left. Tilt your head just a tad bit more. Great!" As I snapped my next shot, the sound of a second shutter pulled me out of the zone.

I looked down at my camera screen, flipping through my last few shots, trying to ignore the other shutter snapping again. I said to the literal supermodel standing in front of me, "Thanks, Denice. I think we have the perfect ones already, unless you have anything else you want to try?"

Instead of her eyes meeting mine, she looked at the photographer who had been following me for the past two hours. "If Lina is done, then I trust that you're done, too."

I looked over my shoulder and smiled at the photographer from SB Weekly, desperately hoping that we were finished. He looked down at his camera, mirroring my last several movements. "I think we've got great shots. I'll meet you in the lobby when you've wrapped things up with Denice."

Just like that, Jaf—the journalist the magazine had sent to do my photos and interview—disappeared down the cobblestone walkway. I looked back to Denice. "Sorry about that, I didn't mean to make our session so awkward."

She laughed, her eyes sparkling in a way that made me regret not having my lens trained on her. "Oh Lina, if I thought having an extra camera on me was awkward, I would be in the wrong industry."

"I'm just not used to being on the other side of the lens. It's not for me." I looked back down at my camera screen and selected my favorite one from the session. "It's still too early to tell, but I think this might be the best shot I've ever taken."

Denice let out a squeal and leaned over my shoulder. "Can I take a peek?"

I turned the screen toward her, and she gasped. "Wow, it's perfect."

"I thought so, too." I turned the camera off and let it

hang around my neck. "Thanks again for booking with me. It's surprising that someone who is surrounded by photographers for a living would want to do a shoot on her day off."

She flipped her long chestnut hair over her shoulder. "Well, Brita told me about you, and then I started following you on Insta, and everything you've posted has been gorgeous. I wanted to get in on it before you become impossible to book."

I felt a blush rising through my whole body. "That's so sweet of you. Thank you."

Her hand brushed my arm like she was talking to an old friend, and I felt giddy. "Honestly, though. You've worked with, like, a ton of my friends already, and they just talk about how comfortable you make them feel. It's the truth."

I thanked her, unsure how to handle the praise, and she went on, "Have you ever thought about traveling? I work a lot of fashion campaigns, and they're always looking for additional photographers. I could pass your name around."

I led her toward the front of the resort as I thought about her offer. "You know what, I've been thinking about doing something new, and I'm going to need all the help I can get."

"Please, with photos like you took today, you're not going to need much help at all." She grinned and grabbed my arm again like we were giggling girls at a sleepover. "Oh, you're going to have so much fun!"

Our conversation shifted to her career, and she told me that she hadn't thought she would like a nomadic lifestyle at first but fell in love with it quickly. I walked her through the lobby, like I did with all my clients, even though she wasn't staying at the hotel.

As we walked toward Kathy's office, I realized that the majority of my clients in the past week hadn't stayed here. It was weird to think that they had come all the way here just to work with me.

I guided her to Kathy's desk, having gotten her excited about our bike rentals, and she surprised me with a hug. Of course, I hugged her back, but when I tried to let go, she held on tight. She said something about catching dinner together the next time she was in town, which I assumed was just something she said to people. I then walked to the lobby to meet up with Jaf.

I found him standing next to the large table in the center of the room talking to Ezra, so I said, "Oh, I see that you've met our florist." I'd recently been avoiding not only Ezra but my feelings about the disaster FaceTime, including the conversation we had about it the next day. I had hoped this interaction would be short and sweet so I could get back to stuffing my emotions into the well deep inside of me.

Ezra spoke, bringing my thoughts back to the present. "I was just telling him about all the work I do here at The Pacifica." He looked at Jaf. "Maybe you could do a piece on me if Lina's goes well?"

Jaf smiled at Ezra but didn't respond. Instead, he held a hand out, motioning around the room. "Do you have somewhere we could sit that's a little more private? I have a few more questions for you."

"Sure." My first thought was to bring him to my

office, but I only had one chair. "Let's go to the café. There's a quiet corner in the back I love disappearing in."

He followed me as we walked through the resort and sat at my usual table. Jaf pulled out a notebook and a pen. The things he asked were typical. How long had I been a photographer, what were my inspirations. But one question threw me off.

"What are your plans for the future?"

I thought long and hard for an honest answer, tapping the table with my fingers while I worked out my truth. "Well, if you would have asked me a month ago, I would have said I'm going to work for The Pacifica forever. But now I'm not so sure what my future looks like."

His pen paused above the page. "And why is that?"

I realized that my answer might not paint The Pacifica in the best light, so I backtracked a little. "Don't get me wrong, it's great working here. The new resort management is great. I just think that I'm ready to spread my wings a little. So many of my clients come from all over the world. I would like to get out of my hometown and see theirs, you know?"

He clicked his pen shut. "Well, if you ask me, I think we're going to be seeing your name in much larger publications than our weekly magazine. I'll be glad to say that I knew you before."

I smiled and thanked him. He wasn't the first person to say something like that, but he was the first person I believed.

After saying goodbye and walking him out, I went to my office to do the second half of my job.

While I waited for my files to upload, I dug my phone out of my desk. I had a couple of texts from my mom asking how my day was going, a meme about weird photography clients from Ester, a few messages from my group chat with the girls about what they had for breakfast, and a text from Reece that came in just a few minutes ago.

Of course, I focused on his text first.

Reece: *Knowing that you're somewhere in the same building as me right now and I can't kiss you is killing me.*

It had also been almost a week since I had gotten any private time with Reece, and I couldn't believe how much I missed him. We still stuck to our nightly calls, talking about little things, big things, and everything in between, but not seeing him during the day just made me crave him more.

Instead of letting him know exactly how much I wanted him, I decided to play around. So I wrote: *Oh, you're here? I must have been too busy to notice . . . .*

Reece replied almost immediately: *Wow, here I am being romantic, and you're burning me!*

Me: *What are you up to? I'm just about to do some editing, but I could blow it off till later if you want to accidentally bump into each other somewhere. I won't tell the boss if you don't.*

Reece: *Actually, I heard he's an asshole and everyone hates him, so we probably shouldn't. Wanna go out tonight?*

Me: *Sure, where you taking me?*

Reece: *My best friend is having a soft opening for his new restaurant, and I promised I would be there. Want to be my date?*

I grinned down at my phone as I typed my reply, but before I could hit send, Ezra stepped into my office. I mumbled a hello to him, not glancing up from my screen, and sent my text: *What time should I be ready?*

I read Reece's incoming text: *I'll pick you up at six. Waiting until then to touch you is going to be agony . . . .*

Ezra propped himself on the edge of my desk, looking me up and down. "What's with the smile on your face?"

I clutched my phone to my chest, hiding the screen. I wanted to bask in this giddy, new-relationship feeling, but I knew I needed to tell Ezra my decision.

I relaxed my cheeks into a neutral pose. "We need to talk."

He picked at a bit of dirt under his fingernail. "I was thinking the same thing."

I motioned my hand between us. "This thing that we have going on isn't working."

His eyes shot to mine as he stood. "Wow. I thought this conversation was going in the opposite direction."

"Really?" I shook my head. "Look, you made it very clear that you want to see other people, and I've realized over the past week that I'm not comfortable with that."

He let out a heavy breath and pinched the bridge of his nose. "I know. That's why I came in here. I wanted to tell you that I want to try it. Just you and me."

"Oh . . . ." A month ago, working here and being his girlfriend was all I had wanted. How did my life get so shuffled? "Well, I'm flattered, but I don't want to be an experiment. I want to be with someone who feels like he needs to be with me. Like he couldn't bear going a day without being together."

His eyes blinked rapidly before he said, "This is because you found someone else, isn't it?"

It was my turn to stand up. "Excuse me?"

He laughed, but there was no joy behind the sound. "You think you've found someone better." He put a hand on his hip. "How long do you think it's going to last before you call me again?"

I pointed at the door behind him. "I think it's time for you to leave."

In a flash, his hands cupped either side of my face, and he kissed me, hard.

Instinctively, I shoved his chest away. He pulled back, leaving his hands where they were. "Lina. Don't make this mistake. I'm ready to fight for us."

My lips tingled with frustration. I stepped back, yanking my face out of his embrace. "You need to go. We're done."

His eyes narrowed as they scanned my face. "That's where you're wrong. We belong together."

Had he said these words a month ago, I would have melted right into him. I would have given him the whole world. But now, his words were hollow—I knew he only said them because he was losing me, not because he meant them.

I deserved someone who wanted me from the beginning.

I stepped around him, opening the door so he would get the point. "Goodbye, Ezra."

After he left, I slumped into the chair at my desk. It took me a few minutes to slow the beating of my heart so I could work. I grabbed the computer mouse and started lightly editing the pictures of Denice that had the best composition. My brain was obviously somewhere else, which made it difficult to find the beauty in my work. After an hour or so, I had ten shots that I was proud of.

I hadn't checked my Instagram in a few days, but I knew I wanted to put some of today's images on there. I pulled up my account and gasped when I saw that not only had I shot up to over ten thousand followers, but my engagement had practically blasted out of the atmosphere.

There were too many notifications to even go through, but I scrolled through my latest posts and grinned at the numbers. The only complaints I saw in the handful of comments I read were that they couldn't book me for several months.

This emotional whiplash was the proof I needed to toss the five-year plan out the window, just like the girls had told me to. I didn't need anything I'd thought I'd needed a month ago.

I selected two shots of Denice, tagged her, and threw together a caption thanking her for being a wonderful new friend. Within a few moments, the post had already received a bunch of likes and comments. I clicked my screen off, afraid of getting too excited from the social media dopamine rush.

Maybe it was time to look at the logistics of leaving the nest instead of pretending they were going to keep me here. With a little help, I could totally do this.

Val's voice bellowed from downstairs, "He just pulled up!"

I struggled to finish pulling my leggings on. They had looked cute under my denim dress when it was on the hanger, but now I wasn't so sure.

I heard the door open as I checked my outfit one more time in the mirror. This was going to have to do.

I bounced down the stairs and into the living room, finding Reece standing there, as perfect as always in a baby blue shirt and navy slacks. It looked like we'd matched on purpose. I stood up on my toes, giving him a brief kiss on the cheek before spinning around in a circle. "How do I look?"

"Stunning."

My eyes met his, and I knew he meant it. The way he looked at me made me feel it.

He wished Val a good night and walked me to the car, but he stopped me as I reached for the passenger door. "Nope. You're driving." He tossed me the keys.

"I don't think you want to trust me with this thing."

He rolled his eyes at me. "You'd be amazed at what I would trust you with."

I tried to argue more, but he put his hands on my shoulders, and guided me to the driver's seat. I resisted a little, even though the thought of getting behind the wheel was really exciting. "But I've already driven it before. I don't think I need to again."

"I wouldn't call taking me home from the dentist at thirty-five miles an hour *driving* her. Get in."

I did what he said, got the seat situated for my height, and watched him slide into the passenger seat. "You're so bossy," I told him.

He grinned at me. "You have no idea." My skin was hot under his gaze. "You gonna start the car, or are we going to stay here all night?"

When I gripped the wheel and took a deep breath, he added, "If you're not comfortable, I'll swap spots with you right now. But I have a feeling you're holding yourself back."

I looked at him. "I'm not holding myself back."

He nodded. "Yes, you are. I've seen what you do when something new or adventurous is in front of you. You freeze and try to find the road most comfortable."

"There's a difference between being reliable and not taking chances."

His eyebrow shot up as he tilted his head, letting me know he didn't believe a word I'd just said. "What's stopping you?"

He did have a point. I closed my eyes and really thought about his question. After a minute, I cupped my locket in my hand and answered. "My dad was so adventurous. He was wild and up for anything." I opened my eyes and moved my hand to the logo on the steering wheel. "He would have loved this car."

After a few more seconds, I looked at Reece, who continued to sit and listen. "He was the person who encouraged me to get out of my comfort zone, and I lost that when he passed. In the chaos that became our new lives, I was able to get by without trying new things."

He took my hand in his. "If you want to continue being comfortable, I will support you. But I think you would be a lot happier if you let things go and pushed the limits. You have so much potential that you're not even using."

The conviction in his voice rang true. A lot of things were changing, but I needed to change, too. "You're right. I'm ready to start really living. I want to feel alive."

With that, I started the car and set off down the road, my chest feeling like a weight had been lifted from it. Reece gave me directions, and I got on the highway heading south.

We drove about five minutes before he put his hand on my leg. "Okay, time to see what she can really do."

"What who can really do?"

"The car. And you, I guess. You're more than comfortable driving now. I bet you can get her to 150 without even trying."

I looked at him skeptically. "Are you for real? I've never gone faster than like 90."

He nodded. "There's no one else on the road. Get into the left lane and give her all you've got, Mag."

"What if we get in trouble?"

"It would make for a good story to tell our kids one day."

My jaw dropped.

"Don't worry about it, I've got the best lawyer in the state of California."

Knowing that he wasn't going to let this go, and, okay, knowing that I really wanted to do this, I jammed my foot down on the gas and giggled as the instant acceleration sent my stomach into a flip.

I glanced down at the speedometer as I shifted

through gears, watching it climb . . . 100 . . . 120 . . . 130. I screamed in delight as we flew down the road.

After several minutes of pure adrenaline and joy, I slowed down and moved out of the left lane.

My cheeks were sore from grinning, and I looked over at Reece, who was staring straight at me. "I didn't think you could get any more beautiful than you were, but when you smile like that, I almost can't handle it."

Heat rose in my cheeks. "You're just saying that."

He shook his head. "I knew you were going to be something special that night we first met."

"You couldn't even see me the night we met."

"I know you think I'm crazy, but I knew. I had to make you mine. I was wondering how I was going to find you, and then you showed up on your own."

I reached over and patted his leg awkwardly before putting my hand back on the steering wheel. He laughed and asked, "What was that for?"

"Well, I wanted to hold your hand, but when I let go of the wheel, I panicked. I thought that I might crash your car. So I did . . . that instead."

"You're ridiculously cute." He pointed. "This is our exit."

I followed the rest of his directions, and we pulled into the parking lot in front of a large brick building, perfectly designed for an Italian restaurant. I parked at the valet stand and handed the keys to a kid who looked barely old enough to drive. I took in the ornate decor on the front of the building, and wished I had worn the red dress that Val had recommended.

"I am way too underdressed for this place," I said.

"Nonsense. You look better than anyone else in there right now."

"You better stop complimenting me, or I'm going to start believing it."

Reece took my hand in his. "That's exactly what I want you to do."

I noticed a black motorcycle parked right outside the front door. "That thing looks fast."

"I could've guessed that Sal would keep his bike parked out front. It's his pride and joy." Reece pulled the enormous wooden door open for me and guided me ahead of him. The maître d' greeted us as we walked up to the desk at the front. "Will you tell Sal that Reece is here?"

The man nodded and disappeared into the kitchen.

A few minutes later, a boisterous man in a crisp black chef's coat shouted from the back of the room. "Welcome to Sal's Kitchen!"

He jogged toward us and wrapped Reece in a bear hug. He was a couple inches shorter than Reece but had even wider shoulders. He had tattoos that crept up his neck, and the sides of his head were shaved, forming a short mohawk.

When he released Reece, he grabbed me in a hug, too. "You must be Reece's girlfriend, Maggie." He pulled back a few inches, looking me over. "It's nice to meet the woman who tamed the wild beast!"

The interaction was a little overwhelming, so I just smiled at him and said hello.

He walked us to a table near the back, my eyes sweeping over the gold and glass chandeliers hanging from the low ceiling as we followed him. The restaurant was dark, but comfortable. Oversized booths lined the walls, with smaller tables closer to the bar. The walls that weren't brick were painted a deep red, making the large space feel small, more private. Sal motioned for us to sit first and then took the place next to Reece. He tapped his finger on the table. "Everything on the menu is on the house."

Reece frowned at him. "No, it's bad enough we skipped in front of all those people that were waiting." He scanned the crowded room. "This place is slammed for not even being fully opened yet."

Sal wrapped his arm around Reece's shoulder. "After everything you've done for me lately, the least I can do is feed you." His eyes met mine. "Reece tells me that you're a photographer." Sal seemed genuinely interested, not just asking questions because I was his best friend's date.

"I am. I work at The Pacifica, but I think I'm going to start branching out on my own soon."

"Would you want to come in and do some shots for us? Our social media manager is on my ass because she doesn't like the way I take pictures, but because she's basically doing the service for me for free, I can't complain."

"Yeah, that would be great. I'll check my calendar and give you a call."

The conversation turned to food, and Sal showed us what was on the menu, giving us recommendations. He said the Ragù alla Bolognese was his grandmother's recipe and was his favorite thing on the menu, but he also loved the osso buco. I relished in his excitement, especially as savory smells wafted toward us from the kitchen. You could tell his entire heart was in this restaurant.

He turned to Reece. "So, are you two going to make it to my birthday party?" Reece cringed, and Sal went on. "I promise it won't be bad. You don't even have to stay the whole time."

Reece shook his head warily. "You know I don't live that life anymore."

Sal looked at me. "You should talk this guy into coming out. Just one night. For me." His pout was the cherry on top. Before I could give in, he added, "Ooh, there's going to be a bunch of influencers there. It would be good for business." He smacked the table and said to Reece, "You could hook her up with Francesca."

Reece's eyes turned to ice, but all he said was, "Now is not the time, Sal."

The two of them stared at each other as if in a visual pissing contest for a solid minute before Reece turned toward me. "Do you really want to spend the evening with narcissists who only want to talk about how great they are?"

Sal chimed in before I could answer. "But if you want her business to grow, you should introduce her to those narcissists. You know I'm right."

Reece let out a deep breath. "Okay, we'll go. For an hour, and only so Mag can network. I refuse to be nice to anyone."

Sal grabbed Reece's shoulder and shook it like Reece had just told him he'd won the lottery. "Perfect. It's going to be great." Reece just groaned and gave him a fake smile.

Sal looked at me again. "Take care of this guy, he's one of the good ones."

I promised that I would, and Sal excused himself to go back to the kitchen. Reece picked up his menu and started scanning the pages, so I did the same, even though I already knew what I was going to order.

"So, why don't you want to go to the party?" I had a guess but wanted to hear it from him.

He looked over the top of his menu. "It's going to be a bunch of pricks standing too close to each other in a nightclub."

I laughed at his description. "It could be fun."

His smile was strained. "The only thing that will be fun will be having you with me. The rest won't be worth the hassle."

"We don't have to go. We could stay in or go somewhere else instead. When is it?"

He sighed. "It's tomorrow night, doors open at ten. Sal's right, though, it would be good for your business if we went." His eyes looked back down to the menu. "The guest list is mostly people who have too much money and a lot of followers on social media." He laughed. "They are terrible people that I don't want you to be friends with but would be good for you to meet."

"So we'll go, do some networking, and then head home and put on our jammies like a couple of old people."

He smiled at me from across the table. "That sounds like the perfect date."

The waitress came by and took our drink orders. Reece said he didn't mind if I ordered something alcoholic, but I told him I didn't want to.

"How was work this week?" I asked. Despite the hours we'd spent getting to know each other over the phone late at night, he always managed to avoid talking about work. I wanted him to know he could share that part of his life with me, too.

He sighed, running his hand through his hair. "It's been a lot. The board wants us to cut more positions than we originally planned, and I am struggling to find jobs for everyone within the company."

"I'm sure a lot of them will understand."

"I hope so. I'm sick of being the guy everyone blames. Plus, they announced this afternoon that they want to transition one of us to the director of operations at The Pacifica so they can bring the rest of the corporate staff back to the main office to get the ball rolling on the next property acquisition."

My stomach dropped. "Do you think they'll make you take it?"

He reached under the table and squeezed my leg reassuringly. "No. I would quit before that happened. I'm ready to move on." He took another deep breath. "But I might be taking on more responsibilities until they find someone to do the job permanently. They're looking internally, and I was wondering if you could ask Blake if she would like the job."

"I don't know what she would say, but I'll ask her."

"Izzy isn't exactly helping the situation, so I'd like to find someone soon. She wants me to visit properties on the East Coast so I can scout candidates from our more lucrative properties, but I think our best choice is already here." His fingers tapped the table in a repetitive rhythm. "She's been insufferable lately. It's not like her."

"Do you think there's something going on with her?"

"Well, something big is about to happen, but it can't leave this table." He glanced at me over his menu, his eyes serious, until I nodded. "My parents announced to the board this week that they're retiring at the end of the year, and Izzy's trying to convince them that she should take over."

"Do you think she's the best one for the job?"

"Without a doubt. She loves what she does, and she genuinely has the company's best interests at heart."

"And you don't want it?"

He laughed. "Oh God, no."

I must have given him a wary look because he added, "It's not like I don't care about the company or our employees, because I do. I just think I would launch into a downward spiral pretty quickly if I was in charge of the whole place."

"You think that's why Izzy is acting differently? Is she trying to do too much on her own?"

He thought for a moment. "That could be it. I know things have been weird at home, too. I think something happened between her and her husband, but she won't talk about it. Maybe that and the structural changes in the company are weighing on her."

"That's got to suck." I couldn't imagine trying to run multiple million-dollar companies while also juggling a marriage.

"It does. Especially since her only coping mechanism is micromanaging everyone around her. I think I'm going to give her my therapist's phone number."

I nodded. "I bet that would help."

He didn't say anything else, but I could tell he was mulling something over in his head over the next few quiet minutes. We were supposed to be out on a fun date, so I changed the subject, hoping to lighten things up.

"So tell me about Sal. How did you guys meet?"

He seemed glad to talk about something else, and the tempo of his words sped up. He told me that they met in college and had been friends for almost a decade. "We realized pretty early on that we came from similar families. Five years ago, he had the balls to walk away from them, cutting them out of his life. He opened his first restaurant against their wishes but has been doing great on his own." He looked around the room, awe in his eyes. "This place is his third. Can you believe it?"

"Which means that if he can do it . . . ." I let the end of my sentence fade.

He smiled, his eyes lighting up the room. "Right? Just a little longer and I can, too."

The waitress stopped by the table and took our orders. The table felt much smaller without menus between us.

Without thinking, I said what was at the forefront of my mind. "So, when we first got here, Sal called me your girlfriend . . . ."

The blush spreading across his cheeks was the most adorable thing I had ever seen. He reached across the table and took my hand. "I know you aren't there yet, but the only person I want is you. So when you're ready, say the words and I'm in."

"I'm ready." I squeezed his hand.

He sat back in his seat and bit his lower lip like he was trying to hide a grin. He thrummed the fingers of his free hand against the table again. "I thought you were seeing that florist guy."

"Not anymore." I shrugged slightly. "I just want to be with you, too."

"You mean it?"

I nodded excitedly, and he jumped out of his chair, scooping me into his arms and kissing me deeply.

I pulled back a few moments later. "People are staring at us."

He smiled against my lips. "Good."

An hour, a pile of empty plates, and a dozen hugs from Sal later, we were back on the road, this time with Reece behind the wheel.

He glanced at me and asked, "Your house or mine?"

I grinned at the prospect of sleeping against him for another night. "Mine should be empty for at least a few hours, as long as you don't mind the possibility of waking up in a house full of women?"

"A group of women has never scared me before."

We parked on the street in front of the house, and he popped the trunk open, which was at the front of the car. We got out, and I met him on the sidewalk. He carried a small bag.

"Do you always have a bag packed for sleepovers in there?" I teased.

He laughed as we walked up to the house. "No, but I

hoped that you might invite me in, and I didn't want to leave early just to get dressed in the morning."

I unlocked the door, letting us in. "I admire your ability to think ahead."

He closed the door behind us and wrapped his arms around me. "I know you appreciate a good plan."

We barely made it through the front door before he pulled me into a kiss. His hands burned through my clothes, his tongue dancing with mine. I backed toward the staircase, pulling him with me.

My fingers caressed his chest as I unbuttoned his shirt and pulled it off his shoulders, dropping it at the foot of the stairs. The amber in his eyes turned molten, like my action had flipped a switch.

He gripped the bottom of my dress and yanked it up over my head. As soon as it hit the floor, I grabbed his belt buckle in my hands and pulled him up another few steps. By the time we made it to the loft, I was down to a bra and panties, and he only had his boxers left.

My back hit the closed bedroom door, and his arms framed either side of my head. Our lips slammed together, and I wrapped a leg around his waist. Eager to get him in my room—in me—I slipped my fingers into the elastic of his boxers, but he shook his head.

"We're taking care of you right now. Only you."

I bit my lip and nodded, moving my hands to his lower back.

His eyes were twin flames as he leaned down to kiss

me, gently this time. With a flick of his wrist, my bra came undone, and I dropped it to the floor. His eyes roved over my exposed breasts as he whispered, "You are so beautiful."

Reece's gaze met mine again before he pulled my bottom lip between his teeth, nibbling. Heat erupted between my thighs, and like he knew exactly what was happening to my body, he dropped down to his knees.

I could barely breathe, but a small crack came through my thoughts. Was it really going to work this time? Was I going to be a letdown? Should I just fake it after a few minutes?

He rubbed his nose against the front of my panties and pressed a kiss to my swollen bundle of nerves. I put my hands on his shoulders, replaying all my worries in my head like a bad mantra.

"Shhh. It's just us. Remember?" He ran his tongue up the thin floral fabric, the only barrier between his skin and mine, and I relaxed, letting out a sound that I had never heard myself make.

"There you go." He leaned back a few inches, flashing that devious grin I loved. He laced his fingers into the sides of my panties and pulled them down slowly, kissing my thighs as he removed them completely.

I stood there, naked, on display, and more ready for someone than I ever had been before.

He grabbed one of my legs, slipping it over his shoulder, and I leaned most of my weight against the door behind me. He gave me a sweet kiss between my legs, stealing my breath. Reece reached a hand up, his fingers going right to work, massaging me, entering me, giving me sensations I wasn't sure were possible until this moment.

After a few minutes, he whispered between licks, "You're awfully quiet up there. Everything good?"

I squeaked out something incoherent as he continued his delicious rhythm. Unable to keep quiet any longer, a moan escaped my throat, which made what he was doing feel more intense. I gripped the doorframe, keeping myself upright.

He hummed against my skin, "That's what I like to hear." And then he added another finger inside of me. My hips moved to match his pace, and all the muscles in my body tensed.

I had never had anyone make me feel the way I felt right now.

This? This was paradise.

I finally understood what people meant when they talked about the glory of sex.

His speed and intensity increased little by little, never once making me feel uncomfortable. His hand shifted slightly as he pressed his tongue to my apex, causing a shock of heat to spread all the way to the arches of my feet. "Oh God, is it supposed to feel like this?"

He mumbled an agreement against my skin as he changed the position of my leg, spreading me wider. Without thinking, I called out his name. It was just like in the movies. Explosions. Fireworks. The earth opening up and swallowing me whole.

The wave subsided as he slowed his motion and stood. He scooped me up in his arms, grinning. "Well?"

I could barely breathe or speak. "How have I lived this long without that?"

Chuckling, he responded, "All it takes is a little bit of patience."

He swung open the door to my bedroom and carried me in. As he laid me down on my bed, I asked, "How did you get it to happen so easily?"

He shrugged. "We just make a good team, Mag."

He pressed a kiss to my belly and sat up on his knees, so I propped myself up on one elbow, reaching for him with my other arm. "Where are you going?"

He ran his hands up my body and down my arms, stopping to hold my hands. Those hands were officially my new favorite things on the planet.

"I thought I would try something else for the next one. If you're up to it." He put his finger up in a "wait here" motion and got up, leaving the room. Luckily, the light from the moon came through the open curtains, so I had the best view of his perfect ass.

He ran back in a few seconds later, his open duffel bag slung over his shoulder, a foil packet in his hand.

I grinned. "Ooh, he's prepared for anything."

He dropped the bag to the ground. "Only if you want to." The honesty in his voice was my undoing. I would let this man have anything he could ever dream of, which should terrify me, but it didn't. I felt completely safe with him. Content.

I realized I hadn't said anything when he knelt next to me on the bed and gently flicked at the packet in his hand. "Do you want to?"

I bit my bottom lip and nodded at him. "Yeah, I do."

His empty hand grazed my cheek as he pressed a sweet kiss to my lips. "Good, because if I don't get inside of you soon, it might kill me."

When I admitted I felt the same way, his grin was brighter than the moonlight flooding through the window. He stood up and tore the packet open, tossing the wrapper onto the floor, then slid his boxers off and kicked them to the side.

I unabashedly stared at what was revealed in front of me. "Is that even going to fit inside of me?"

He laughed, thinking I was joking, but I couldn't stop watching him as he rolled the condom on. "If I've done my job correctly, then it will."

He climbed back over me and kissed me. His motions were sweet and gentle, a contrast to the frenzy he had just put me through in the hallway. I wrapped my arms and legs around him as he entered me slowly.

We moved together, working in unison. Our kisses were quiet prayers. I matched him as he sped up, and my muscles tightened around him. I couldn't keep quiet for very long, moaning loudly as he moved inside of me steadily.

I shattered under him over and over again, and he finally found his release after I had found mine multiple times.

He kissed my temple and whispered, "Don't move, I'll be right back."

He stumbled into my bathroom, and I heard a rustling as he disposed of the mess we had made. When he came back into the room, he curled up next to me, pulling me against him. "How are you feeling, Maggie?"

I turned so I could see his face. "I feel like you replaced all the blood in my body with glitter."

He chuckled against my temple. "I'll take that as a compliment."

I ran a finger across his jawline. "How are you feeling?"

He let out a long breath. "Honestly? I've never felt better." He rested his hand on my cheek and nudged his nose against mine. "You are amazing, Mag." After a few moments, he leaned back, his eyes scanning my face. "You don't regret it?"

"The only thing I regret is that my sheets aren't as soft as yours." I pressed my lips into his. "But no, I don't regret you at all."

He smiled against my lips, kissing me again. "I'm so happy that you're all mine, Maggie."

I cupped his cheek in my hand. "It's nice to be yours, Reecie."

Chapter Fourteen

The sunlight shone through the cracks between my curtains, casting patterns of light into the room. I stretched my arms above my head, and Reece shifted in his sleep, pulling me back against him. I turned slowly so I could stare at him. His face was perfectly sculpted, and in this light, he didn't look real.

His eyes were still closed, his breathing soft. "Are you seriously watching me sleep right now?"

I giggled. "Maybe."

He grunted and rolled onto his back, pulling me on top of him. I laid my head on his chest as he said, "I don't want to get out of bed ever again."

"What time do you have to go in today? My first client isn't until eleven." I moved my hips against him, letting him know I didn't want to get out of bed, either.

His hands started on my sides and slid down the backs of my thighs, fingertips tickling the creases between my ass and my legs. "I have a meeting at ten thirty, but there is something very important we need to do first."

"What is it?" I didn't remember making any plans.

His voice was enthusiastic as he said, "We need to spend at least an hour testing out the things you bought at the store." He craned his neck, looking at the light coming through the window. "Looks clear outside, so I'm going to cash in that rain check."

I moved up, kissing his neck. "Hmm, I'll have to check my planner. Not sure if today works," I said playfully.

"I think I can convince you to fit it in." Two of his fingers inched closer and closer until they found the spot they had been looking for, the one that made me shiver.

"You know what, I think I can make right now work."

Our hands and mouths took over, no longer needing words between us. I climbed off of him just long enough to open my nightstand and dump the pile of pink, blue, and gold electronic devices onto the comforter.

I thought this moment would be embarrassing, or cringeworthy, but I was so comfortable in his presence that I was more excited and turned on than anything else.

Reece helped me discover how to use each toy, guiding me, finding what made my toes curl, and I found what left him gasping for air. We moved slowly, carefully, taking note of things that worked and things that didn't.

When he discovered that running his finger lightly on the skin behind my knee caused me to laugh uncontrollably, he laughed with me. When he thrust his hips against mine and I moaned, he did, too.

We found ourselves spent, covered in sweat, spread across my bed. He reached over and took my hand in his. After lying there for a few moments catching our breaths, I turned, facing him. "Guess we better get dressed?"

He kissed my hand and got up, collected the toys off the bed, and went into the bathroom. He turned on the shower and brought our discarded toys to the sink, methodically cleaning the items that were now quite possibly my favorite possessions. His voice was quiet as he asked, "Do you have a coffee maker?"

I stood up, meeting him in the small bathroom. "Yeah. Do you want me to go make some?"

He grabbed my bare hip with one hand, turning me to face him, using his other hand to grasp mine. I followed his lead and put my free hand on his shoulder as we started to dance. He leaned his forehead against mine and whispered, "No, I'll go down in a minute and make some for us so you can shower." His lips met mine in a slow kiss. "You are so beautiful."

"You make me feel beautiful." He spun me around in a circle and pulled me back to him. We continued to waltz around the bathroom, with nothing covering our skin but sweat. I stumbled a few times, but he never missed a beat. "Where did you learn to dance like this?"

"My mother was a competitive ballroom dancer and made me practice with her for hours on end when I was growing up."

"That sounds adorable. I love dancing." I tripped over my own feet, but he steered me to the next step. "I'm just not very good at it."

He laughed. "I hated it when I was a kid, but now I'm grateful for what she taught me. To be honest, I think it's the only thing we ever did together." He dipped me and then spun me around again. "Looks like your shower is warm."

I glanced at the foggy glass door. "You can join me if you want to."

He kissed the skin under my ear. "If I do that, there's no way either of us will make it to work today. I better go downstairs and find your coffee maker."

He let go of me and opened the shower door, guiding me in before grabbing his pajama pants from his overnight bag and pulling them on.

I ran my head under the water and then heard him knock on the shower door. I wiped off the condensation to see him better and asked, "Did you change your mind?"

He gave me a crooked smile and asked, "How do you want it?"

I grinned. "Any way you want to give it to me."

He propped his arms against the doorway, getting a clear view of me. "I meant your coffee, perv. Wow, make a girl come once and all she can think about is sex."

I splashed a handful of water at the door, laughing. "A little bit of cream and sugar, please." He nodded and kissed the glass door before walking away.

I heard him laugh again from the doorway. "What is it?" I asked.

"Someone must have appreciated the mess we made when we got home last night. The clothes we had on are all neatly piled in the hallway." I watched him disappear into the hall before coming back in with our clothes. He put them on the dresser and blew me a kiss before closing the door behind him.

I finished my shower quickly, got dressed, and threw my hair into a messy bun. As I sat on the bed to put my socks and shoes on, Reece's phone lit up and started vibrating on my dresser. I glanced at it and saw the call was coming from someone named FC.

I didn't know what to do. Should I answer it? Should I just let it ring? I was his girlfriend now, so it's not like I couldn't introduce myself . . . but what if it was a work call? We hadn't really discussed any details of that part of our relationship.

The time it took me to decide was enough for the call to go to voice mail, making the decision for me. Oh well.

I grabbed my phone off the nightstand, ready to head out the door, and saw that Val had sent a text to our girls' group: *OMG! There is a shirtless man in our kitchen. I'm so proud of you Liiiiina!!!*

Oh shit. I needed to get down there to save him from her.

I turned the shower back on for him and ran down the stairs. He was leaning over the kitchen island, mug in his hand, laughing at something Valerie had just said. When I came rushing into the room, he turned to me and smiled. "Hey, gorgeous."

That smile was the most beautiful thing I'd ever seen. Butterflies fluttered in my stomach as he handed me a mug. "I was just on my way to deliver this to you."

The smell of the coffee was delightful. Dark and smooth, just the way I liked it. "Thank you." I smiled over the rim of the mug as I took a sip. "This is perfect. I turned the shower back on for you. Your phone rang, too, but I didn't catch it in time."

"Thanks. I'm sure it can wait until I get to the office."

He grabbed his mug, leaned in for a kiss, and went back up the stairs.

I turned to Val, who I had been successfully ignoring until now. She had the goofiest smile on her face that made me turn bright pink. She raised her eyebrows up and down and asked, "Well?"

I put my free hand on my hip. "Well, what?"

My phone vibrated in my pocket, so I pulled it out and checked it. Of course, it was from Blake: *I can't believe I'm not there for this! Give me ten minutes and I will be at your house! Did he make you . . . ?*

Her text was followed by a GIF of a woman's face, her lips making the largest "O" I'd ever seen.

I immediately replied: *Stay at home. We are leaving soon, and I don't need anyone other than Val embarrassing me right now.*

Val looked up from her phone, having read the same message. She glanced back down and sent: *Gonna answer the question, Lina? Did he take you to O-Town?*

She gave me a wink that bordered on pornographic, and I laughed out loud. So of course, I sent another text: *Both of you are immature and need to get out of my business. But yes, my boyfriend took me on quite the adventure last night. And again this morning.*

Then I sent a GIF of fireworks exploding.

As soon as it came through, Val screamed with excitement and clapped her hands. I shushed her, looking toward the stairway. "Keep it down. I don't want him to hear you."

She grabbed me in a hug and kissed the side of my head. "I'm just so happy for you!"

I pushed her away from me jokingly. "Eww, get off of

me. You're not going to act like this every time I have sex with him, are you?"

I took my coffee into the living room and sat on the couch. Blake sent a reply: *Yay Lina! I hate to admit it, but I knew he had it in him. So, this one's your boyfriend for real this time?*

I grinned and sent: *Yup. It's official.*

Valerie added: *I'll make sure to give him a high five for you when he gets back downstairs. Or maybe a smack on the butt like they do after ball games?*

I spun around, mortified. "You better not."

Val laughed. "Fine. You're such a buzzkill."

Blake asked: *So how is it going to work at the office?*

I grimaced and wrote: *I'm not entirely sure. We didn't exactly talk a lot last night . . .*

Before they replied, I remembered the conversation with Reece last night and sent: *Before I forget, Reece said they want to hire a director of operations for the resort so the suits can take a step back. He asked me to find out if you wanted it before he recommended you to the board.*

Blake replied: *Dammit, I regret bringing up work. If I promise to think about it, will you tell us more about the sexxxx!*

I said: *This makes me feel like I'm in high school again. It's weird. I'll tell you both about it when he's far, far away from our house.* And then I sent a winky-face emoji.

Val came in and sat next to me. I asked her what she had going on this week, and she caught me up with the gossip from the record store. I had only met her employees a few times, so I didn't quite know who she was talking about, but the stories were juicy, so it didn't matter.

Reece came down the stairs in a navy suit that accentuated all of his best features. He sat down on the couch next to me, kissed me on the cheek, and finished his coffee.

He joined us in our small talk, asking Val about the store and Joey's tour that was coming up soon. The way he slipped into the conversation felt natural and comfortable, like he had always been there.

He checked his watch and then put his hand on my thigh. "Well, babe, you ready? I bet we could have a quick bite to eat at the resort before my first meeting."

I stood and reached for our empty mugs. "Are you sure we should? It could be a disaster."

"I was serious last night. I'm in this, jobs be damned." He took the mugs from me and carried them to the sink, starting to wash one of them.

"I can do that, you know."

I reached for the other one, and he swatted my hand playfully. "I know how to wash a couple of cups."

I shrugged. "You could have just left them there for later."

He set the first mug on the drying rack. "I don't want Valerie to tell all your friends that when I stay over, I throw my clothes everywhere, use up all the hot water, and leave dirty dishes in the sink."

Val chimed in from the living room, "I would never!"

I bumped my hip into his while he washed the second cup. "So. Breakfast. In our workplace." I lowered my voice. "With you still on probation."

He gave me the side-eye. "I was hoping you would forget about that little issue."

"Wouldn't it be safer to just keep this private for a little while longer?" I leaned against the counter, eager to hear his answer.

His hands paused. "I'm willing to do whatever you're comfortable with, Mag, but I'm honestly not worried. Throwing me in jail would just make more work for their publicity team in the long run." He went back to washing the coffee mug. "Worst case, they fire one of us. I hate my job, and you already have your next big thing around the corner. Nothing they do can hurt us."

I cringed. "I feel like a baby bird about to be shoved out of the nest."

He put the second mug on the drying rack and patted his hands on the towel hanging from the cabinet before wrapping his arms around me. "Look, Mag, it's your choice. You can stay at the resort, and I'll quit. I'll call my lawyer and tell him I'm going to work for Sal, so it won't mess with my probation. Or you can quit and start your own photography empire, or anything else you want to do. Hell, we can both quit and tell them all to fuck themselves on our way out the door." The intensity of his words hit me in the chest, taking my breath away. He kissed me gently, letting air flow to my lungs again. "But I want to be with you, and that means no hiding. We are either all in or we have to admit that we're just playing pretend."

When I didn't respond, he kissed me again and asked, "Are we all in?"

I nodded slowly. "Should we call ahead and request a table up front?" The fluttering in my stomach was from hunger; definitely not from anxiety over eating together in view of all of our coworkers. I agreed that if we were going to be together, we should just do it, but never in a million years did I think we would be going public with our relationship today.

I pulled my shoulders back, forcing myself to feel more confident as we left the house together.

We walked through the main door of the resort just as he twined his fingers around mine.

I felt eyes on us and heard whispers as we walked through the lobby to the café. When Joanna, the hostess, looked at our linked hands and asked, "The usual table, Lina?" I fought the urge to tell her I wanted to sit way in the back.

Reece answered her instead, "Actually, we would like that booth over there." He pointed to a circular table that was small, intimate, and in view of every other table in the restaurant.

I'm sure we talked about important things while we ate, but I was hyperfocused on not freaking out, so I didn't remember a single word.

Reece stood and held his hand out for mine, and I followed him out of the restaurant. He led me to my office, and the cloud of unease I had been trapped in started to dissipate.

Reece wrapped his arms around me, nuzzling his nose into my neck. "Are you okay, Maggie? You've been all wound up since we got here." I leaned into him, loving his warmth and strength enveloping me.

"I'm sorry. I'm not exactly a rule-breaker. I'm just a little nervous."

He kissed me gently while massaging the nape of my neck. "No reason to be nervous. I'm not going anywhere."

I pushed up on my toes and kissed him again. "I just have to get used to us, that's all."

We kissed a few more times before he asked, "See you later for lunch?"

"Yeah, I would like that." With one more peck on my lips, he left for his meeting, and I ducked into my office to prep for my first shoot.

Luckily, I had a perfect client for my morning session. She had flown in from Florida, just to get a set of headshots done. She was witty, beautiful, and knew just how to stand to get the best lighting on her cheekbones. Gigs like this would be more profitable when I was finally on my own since I wouldn't have to share income with the resort anymore. I was looking forward to that.

I was in my office working on her images a couple of hours later when there was a knock at my door. I called out, "Come on in."

The woman that had pulled Reece out of my interview meeting weeks ago—I think her name was Janine—opened the door, clipboard in hand. "Hello, Ms. Herrera. Mr. Howell has requested your presence in the boardroom."

I made sure my work was saved and stood. "He could have just called me on the office phone."

She nodded. "Please follow me."

I did as she said and went with her to the conference

room. Nerves washed over me until I saw Reece coming up from the other direction.

As soon as he saw me, instead of being happy, the corner of his lips wrinkled into a frown. "Fuck. I didn't expect this."

Unaware of what he was talking about, I took one step into the room and then understood that I had just walked into the lion's den. When the nervous assistant had told me Mr. Howell had requested me, it wasn't Reece she was talking about.

A mountain of a man sat at the end of the table and pointed to a chair at the opposite end when I walked in. "Have a seat, Ms. Herrera."

Reece's hands gripped my shoulders, stopping me from moving any further. "What are you doing here, Dad?"

The man stood, making it obvious where Reece had inherited his wide shoulders and height. His hair was white and cropped short, and his suit was dark and powerful.

His peering gaze, which was a hint darker than Reece's, lowered to where Reece's hands touched me. His upper lip lifted in a sneer. "So it is true. You're dabbling with an employee again. You swore up and down that you were up for this job, but look at you, not even a month in and you're breaking company policy."

Reece replied, "Your damn policies are bullshit, and you know it."

The older man's voice dropped an octave. "Are they? An employee called my office this morning and reported your erratic behavior. Can you even imagine how embarrassing that was for me?" He glanced up at the ceiling, exasperated. "When are you going to take this seriously enough to grow up?" He checked his watch. "We have to go. The board is waiting back at my office to discuss damage control."

"No." Reece took a step toward the man, blocking him from leaving the room. The two of them looked like birds ready to fight, with their chests puffed out.

"This is not a negotiation, Reece. Tell your little friend that you're done here and you're sorry you wasted her time. We're leaving."

"I quit." Reece threw his hands in the air, and I suddenly couldn't breathe.

I knew he didn't want to work for his family anymore, but I didn't think he could step away from his responsibilities so easily. I knew in an instant that he would resent me if he went to jail for a probation violation that I caused.

The older man folded his arms across his chest. "You know exactly why that's not an option."

"I hate this job, and I don't want anything of yours. I'm done."

I reached for him, saying, "Reece, wait," but he didn't seem to hear me. His eyes were trained on his father's penetrating gaze.

His father stepped so close their noses almost touched. He spoke so quietly through his teeth that I barely heard him say, "Do I need to contact your probation officer about this?"

"Call him. I'll tell him I'm taking a job somewhere else, somewhere that's better for my sobriety."

A silver eyebrow tilted above Mr. Howell's eye. "Who are they going to believe, Reece? A philandering drug addict who wants to go play with his friends again, or the owner of a successful multi-billion-dollar empire?"

Reece's chest deflated, and he turned to me. His eyes flashed with helplessness. "Mag. I—"

I gave his hand a squeeze, knowing just how big of a jackass Reece's dad had always been, pressuring him to be perfect his whole life. "It's okay, Reece. Go take care of business. You'll know where to find me."

His dad replied before Reece could. "Don't get your hopes up. He won't be contacting you, because he's already gotten what he wanted. I advise you to delete his contact information from your phone."

"That's bullshit, and you know it. You can't just come in here telling my girlfriend lies."

His father let out a deep laugh that rumbled through the floor. "Girlfriend? You know you're not stable enough for a serious relationship." He patted my arm, and it took all my effort to not smack it away. "Whatever he told you to get into your pants was a trick. I'm sorry to say, you're just another notch in my son's belt, a tool he's using to give me and this company the finger."

I knew how much Reece hated this job. That much was true. But maybe he was using our relationship as a way to stick it to his dad and the company rules. Images of our sweet morning flashed in my mind. He hadn't been hesitant about flaunting our relationship at the restaurant.

I put on a brave face and held my tongue, knowing any reply I had would fall on deaf ears. Then he continued with a wave of his hand, "We're done here. You can go."

I stood perfectly still as my heart pounded wildly in my chest. No matter how much I wanted to trust Reece, I couldn't shake the feeling that some aspect of what his dad was saying might be true. He and his father clearly were in some kind of power struggle. I looked to Reece for reassurance, but only found a hint of it in his pleading eyes.

"Mag, you know what you mean to me. I can fix this. Please."

I knew then that there was only one thing I could do to have control in this situation. "Stop. Both of you." They turned, and if I hadn't been so upset and angry, I would have found their mirror expressions comical. "I can't do this anymore. I refuse to work under this scrutiny anymore. I quit."

His father snickered. "Quit if you want. It won't change anything. You aren't the first employee my son has seduced and left. You're just the most recent."

I spun on my heel and fled down the hallway.

Reece called out after me, and I stopped, facing him. "Please, just let me leave."

"Mag, I can explain."

I shook my head. He wasn't denying what his dad had said, he wanted to explain it. Justify it. I couldn't deal with that right now. My head was a storm of all of his father's accusations. I wanted to believe Reece, but now I wasn't sure if I should. I just needed to get away. I needed time to think. "I have to go pack up my things. If you care about me, you'll give me space."

"Let me help you." He reached his hand toward me.

"Not right now." Feeling my resolve slip through the cracks, I turned away from him, making the trek to my office completely alone. I wondered if all of this had been a playboy's elaborate game the whole time.

I shoved the door to my office open and paced around in a circle. I was doing this. I was going to grab my things and never come back.

I didn't know where to start. My eyes jumped from the desk to my cabinet and back to the desk. Luckily, the equipment in here belonged to me, not the resort, but I didn't know how I was going to carry all of it out of here.

I sat down in my chair, pulled out my phone, and sent a text to Blake: *Do you have any boxes? I just quit my job.*

Needing something to fidget with, I grabbed a pen and clicked it over and over and over.

A message came in from Blake: *Trapped in a meeting. Texting under the table. I'll try to get out of here soon to help.*

I replied quickly: *Don't worry about it. The last thing you need is to be put in the middle of my drama right now.*

My eyes lingered on my other messages, and I opened the thread between Reece and me. Weeks' worth of messages, all of them signs that he was opening up, that it wasn't just about sex. Above all, he was becoming my best friend, and I felt like I was his, too.

My gut told me that Reece was a good man. That he had made some mistakes in the past but had been working so hard to improve himself. He had never been anything but completely honest with me, and I should trust him.

According to his father, though, this was a pattern, and I should be wary. I couldn't shake the feeling that I was just a pawn.

Ezra popped his head in my doorway, and I instantly regretted leaving the door open. I set my phone down on the desk, shooting him a glare that should have turned him to ice. "Is there something I can help you with, Ezra?"

His face lit up in a brilliant smile, but his teeth seemed too big, too white. "Oh babe, I'm so sorry all of this is happening to you." He spun me in my chair to face him and crouched down on his knees. "But I forgive you. For all of it."

I blinked a few times, unsure of what he was going on about. "What?"

He took the pen from my hand and cupped both of my palms in his. "Lina, I saw through all of it. That bastard got into your head and was taking advantage of you. Thank goodness I called the corporate office and made sure they knew what he was up to."

I pulled my fingers out of his clammy hands. "No. Reece is my boyfriend." At least, I thought he was. What if Ezra and Mr. Howell were right, and I was just a plaything?

No, that couldn't be true. If anything, he was the most considerate man I'd ever been with. I rubbed my forehead. "Ezra, what have you done?"

He stood up abruptly. "What have I done?" He counted on his fingers. "I told you I would date you exclusively like you asked. I told my friends they can't stay at my house anymore. I supported you when you complained about your easy-ass job and your boring friends. I made time for you at the drop of a hat, even though you're obviously fucking some predator and acting too stupid to see that he's taking advantage of you. And now I'm pulling all kinds of strings, putting my job in jeopardy, to get.him away from you."

I leaped out of my chair, shocked by what Ezra had just admitted. "Excuse me?"

He reached up and swept his thumb across my cheek. "I'm trying to take care of this problem so we can be together." My blood ran hot. I had never been so disrespected by a man in my life. I couldn't believe I had missed this side of him all along.

"Ezra, I don't know how many times I have to tell you this. I don't want to be with you." I folded my arms across my chest, punctuating my words.

His eyebrows bunched together angrily. "You've got to be kidding me right now. You can't possibly want to be with him."

"What if I do?"

"You can't. He's just in your head, Lina. You were practically begging to be my girlfriend just a couple of weeks ago. I'm the one you want to be with."

I took a step closer to the door. I wasn't sure where I was going, but I had to get away from here.

He must have taken my movement as an agreement because he tucked his hand into my hair and pulled me into a kiss.

I screamed and slammed my hands into his chest.

"Get away from me!" I shoved him in the chest again, trying to get him to move out of my personal space. "I want to be with Reece because I love him. He is kind and thoughtful and wants to take care of me. He has his flaws, but he would never call me stupid or say that my friends are boring."

He took a step back, blocking the doorway. "I didn't call you stupid. I said you were *acting* stupid. Because you are."

"You need to go." I pointed to the doorway as the click-clack of stiletto heels echoed down the tile hallway.

He stood tall, his chest filling the space between us. "You are going to regret this. When you call me a week from now sad and alone, I'm not going to be there to pick up the pieces. This is your last chance."

"Get out."

He let out a sigh, reaching for me again. "Lina. You're not thinking clearly right now."

Lizette pushed her way into the office. I would have said her timing was perfect, but I wasn't sure which one of us she was about to start yelling at. "One of you tell me what is going on or I will call security and have you both escorted off the property," she demanded.

Ezra pointed to me. "Lina won't admit that your brother is a monster and is taking advantage of her."

My voice was shrill as I yelled, "He is not taking advantage of me! We are two consenting adults in a relationship, and Ezra needs to butt out of it."

She tapped her shoe on the floor. "You should leave."

Ezra and I replied, "Which one of us?" at the same time.

"Both of you."

Ezra asked, "Are we being fired?"

"Not today, but the offer is tempting."

Irritation over being jerked around for weeks oozed out of all of my pores. I couldn't take it anymore. I grabbed my purse and hung it over my shoulder. "I already quit when your father was an asshole to me earlier, and now I'm glad that I did."

Lizette turned to face me. "Lina, let me clear this up with my father. Reece has his issues, but I think our dad is crossing the line here."

My vision went red. "You've treated me like garbage since day one, and I'm over it. Find someone else to kick around."

I pushed past them and stomped down the hallway. As I slammed the main doors open, my only plan was to get my feet in the sand. I made it across the street, not even looking to see if the little person was illuminated in the crosswalk on my way to the beach.

I hopped on one foot, undoing the straps of my shoes and pulling them off, one at a time, unwilling to stop walking for anything. As soon as I felt the warm sand between my toes, I was able to take a deep breath.

This wasn't the end of the world. This was the beginning of a new chapter. I just had to repeat the phrase in my head a hundred times to believe it.

I made it about half a mile down the beach when I realized that no matter how far I walked, I would still have to go back to get my stuff . . . and I really didn't want to have to do the inevitable walk of shame covered in sand and sweat. Stomping miles and miles down the beach was no longer the best idea I had ever had.

I needed to let Blake know how badly I had just thrown my life in the dumpster, so I dug through my purse. When I didn't find my phone there, I slipped my hand into my back pocket. As soon as my fingers hit denim, I remembered my damn phone was sitting on the edge of my stupid desk. So much for avoiding an awkward return to claim my belongings.

I tossed my purse and shoes in the sand and plopped down on my butt, hoping the vast horizon would give me some clarity. As I dug my toes into the sand, I found my emotions starting to calm. Watching the water sweep up onto the beach, moving back and forth in its never-ending ebb and flow, I knew that no matter what happened to me when I got up and dusted myself off, I was going to be just fine.

Sure, I didn't know how I was going to pay my bills next month, but if my recent reviews were to be believed, I could absolutely handle booking clients on my own.

I closed my eyes, listening to the waves crash on the beach, contemplating what a new plan would look like.

I'd gained a ton of followers on social media that might hire me for their events. I owned every piece of my equipment, cameras, lights, and even a few backdrops for bad weather days. All I really needed was the paperwork and logistics. I bet if I asked my marketing guru of a sister, she would walk me through setting up a business. Hell, she might even do some PR if I begged her enough.

As soon as hope started to build in my heart, I felt the

presence of someone sitting down next to me. His voice was barely audible above the ocean. "Can we talk, Mag?"

I opened my eyes, wiping at the moisture that had built up under my eyelashes, and looked at him. His tie was missing, the first few buttons of his black shirt were undone, and his hair was a mess.

Whatever happened in the time since we had last held hands had taken a toll on him, too.

I felt the skin between my eyes scrunch together when I repeated his father's words, "Dabbling with an employee again, Reece?"

He responded with a grumble before laying his forehead against his propped-up knees. "It's not what you think."

I turned my body, tucking my legs under me, allowing some space to grow between us. My eyes scanned over him, as he hunched over himself. For a man who usually kept himself collected, he seemed to be falling apart. "You're going to have to tell me what he meant by that, or I'm going to assume the worst."

He sat up and looked at me. "My last relationship was a disaster, so I can't really blame my dad for his apprehension. She was not an employee, exactly." His lips pursed as he formed his next words. Those lips that had delivered such ecstasy hours ago now held power to crush me.

He finally continued, "She was a subcontractor for the corporation, working in a different department than mine. I never even saw her at the office." He turned, facing the water. "It was what we did in our time off that my family is concerned about. They don't want me to have those . . . issues again."

I fought the urge to demand he tell me everything about her so I could find her and smack her. Not just to soothe the jealous green monster inside of me, but because she had hurt him, and I hated that to my core.

Something else his father had said rang in my ears. "He called you a philanderer."

Reece cringed. "I told you before, I haven't always made the best choices, and I've done a lot of things I'm not proud of. But I've never cheated on a girlfriend, and I don't intend to. He was just trying to rile you up."

"Well, it worked." I sat quietly, watching the expressions on his face change. He slipped deeper and deeper in thought before he finally leaned to the side and pulled something out of his back pocket.

He flipped the folded paper over and over in his hands. It looked ragged, like it had been opened and folded again many times. "I've been really good at learning how to take care of myself, but he doesn't trust me yet."

"Who cares if he trusts you if you plan on leaving his company?"

"Because sometimes I worry that he's right." His eyes bored into mine, "Not about us—I know he's wrong about us. About my sobriety, though. I feel good right now, but I don't know how long it will last."

"Don't beat yourself up about it. You're doing great." I put my hand on his thigh, reassuring him.

He handed me the paper, which was warm from his hands. "I want you to take this."

I unfolded it once, but he covered one of my hands with his, stopping me from going any further. His voice was painfully quiet as he said, "I've been trying to rip it up since I saw it on the counter, but I just can't do it. I keep staring at it, debating if I should fill it before putting it right back in my pocket."

He took his hand back and tucked it in his lap, so I opened the paper. "This is the prescription they gave you at the dentist's office."

The lines in his forehead were as deep as ravines. "I hate how much power it has over me. I should have torn it up when you took me home, but I couldn't."

"Thank you for sharing this with me." I pinched the top of the paper. "Should I?"

He nodded wordlessly, and I tore the paper in half. I looked up at him, but his gaze was trained on my hands, so I tore again and again until I had a handful of confetti.

"I'm a mess, Mag. But everything I've said is true. I may have fucked up before, but I'm in this. If you'll have me." I stood up, clutching the paper pieces in one hand, and reached for him with my other. He put his hand in mine and stood, following me to the water.

"I know, Reece, but you're my mess. We can grow together." I pushed up on my toes and planted a kiss on his cheek. "Right now, I'll trust you for the both of us, until you can start trusting yourself again, too." Then I turned his hand and poured half of the shredded pieces into it.

He took my hint and smiled before tossing the scraps into the ocean, and I threw the ones I still held, too. They flew in all directions around us. Some floated in the air, some landed in the water, and even a few ended up in our hair.

He wrapped his arms around me, spinning in a circle. I let out a laugh before plucking a little square from his shoulder.

He stood me back down on my feet as he went serious again. "Sometimes I feel like I'm hanging on by a thread, like everything is spiraling out of control. And now I've sucked you right into all of it." He ran the pads of his thumbs gently across my cheek. "Did you really want to quit your job today? I can go talk to him, tell him it was a misunderstanding if you want to stay."

"No. I want this." He leaned back, his eyes squinting like he didn't quite believe me. "I'm scared as hell, but I think I can do it."

He kissed me on the forehead. "I'll call Sylvia's office as soon as I get back. I can probably pull a few strings with her and get her to put you on her calendar tomorrow."

I squeezed my arms tightly around him. "I'm going to try to do it without her. Thank you, though. This has to be sustainable for it to last, and I think if I lean on her, I won't get used to doing it on my own." I paused, taking another look over the ocean. "Maybe I'll go to the library tomorrow. I bet they have *Starting a Business for Idiots* or something."

He pressed another kiss to my temple. "I do have a business degree, Mag. I can help."

I tugged on his arm and started walking back to the sidewalk, stopping only to scoop up my shoes. I was ready to collect my things from my office and start my new life.

"Oh, I'm going to take you up on that offer so much you'll regret it."

He laughed and pulled a tiny piece of paper out of my hair. "I feel bad leaving these little scraps out here."

I took the tiny paper from him, stuffing it into my pocket. "I'll donate money from my first month to a sea turtle rescue, but I don't foresee us needing to rip up papers at the beach again."

He laughed, tucking me under his arm as we walked. "Do you want me to come help you pack up your things, or do you want me to walk you to your car and collect your stuff for you?"

I latched my thumb into his belt loop, letting him lead us toward the resort. "I can do it, but you can come hang out with me while I get organized."

Chapter Fifteen

"You about ready to go?" I heard Reece's voice from the bathroom as I stretched across his bed, trying to decide whether I really wanted to go out tonight.

He walked back into the room, buttoning the cuffs of his sleeve. "Maggie, did I knock you out?"

I sat up slowly, tugging his ridiculously soft sheets up with me. "Fine, I guess I'll get out of bed."

After our talk on the beach this afternoon, we'd gone back to the resort and he'd helped me pack up my things. He also sat with me when I gave the news to Kathy, asking her to cancel my upcoming appointments. It was his idea, however, to give the clients my phone number to reschedule, which made me wary, but both of them told me they knew I could handle it.

Networking at Sal's birthday party had suddenly become more important than ever, so of course I was nervous as hell.

I climbed out of bed and put on the clothes I'd been wearing when we left The Pacifica, remembering how we hadn't even made it from the car to the front door fully clothed. Luckily, Reece had gone back outside after our first round and found my shirt hanging in a bush by the front door.

Oh, the things Dennis would be telling the other neighbors about us.

Reece came back to the bedroom, fully dressed, not a hair out of place, and I felt like I deserved sainthood for not ripping his clothes off of him again. He was focused on his phone, a concerned expression on his face.

"Is everything okay?" I asked as I followed him down the stairs.

"Yeah, just work stuff." He seemed a little preoccupied, but after what we had gone through today, I understood. "You ready to head to your place?"

It was now or never. "Yep. Let's go."

He followed me home in his car so we could ride to the nightclub together, and as we walked through the front door, Val burst out of her bedroom, a wild gleam in her eye.

"You're finally home! I have a few outfits laid out and some ideas for your hair!"

I looked over my shoulder at Reece, who was already headed for the couch. He just smiled and said, "Sorry, babe. I'd offer to help, but it looks like you've got it handled."

Val grabbed me by the arm and dragged me into her room. I figured that tonight would be fun, but the dresses she had lined out on her bed made it look like I was prepping for a Miss USA pageant.

She laughed at the overwhelmed look on my face.

"This is an important night for you, and I want to make sure you look your best."

"I figured we would be going through my clothes, not your random assortment of clubwear." I looked her up and down. "My hips aren't going to fit into any of these."

Valerie picked up something that was made out of half a yard of hot pink fabric and tugged on it. "Everything I have selected will stretch where you need it to. You're going to look amazing."

I scanned the shoes all over the floor and knew I couldn't say anything about them since we wore the same size.

Blake called out as she came through the front door, "I hope you didn't start without me!" She said hi to Reece before walking into the room, arms full of curling irons and products. "Wow, that one looks scandalous!"

I tugged on the pink string that I assumed would hold the fabric to my body. "Oh, there is no way I'm wearing this one."

I looked back at Blake, who wore a little black dress of her own. "Wait, weren't you supposed to be out on a date tonight?"

Her entire body shivered as she grimaced. "I faked an emergency to get the hell out of there before I could even finish my appetizer."

"That bad?" Val asked from over my shoulder.

"I should be used to it by now, but another dude on the dating app turned out to be the absolute worst. I thought this one might be worth my time, but all he wanted to talk about was putting a baby in my belly."

"Gross," I told her. Blake had been playing the online

dating game since her ex cheated on her last year, and she'd had zero luck.

"I know. I'm so over kissing all these frogs. Maybe I just need to be on my own again for a while." She laid down the hair supplies and plucked at a silver dress on Val's bed. "Enough about me, let's get you ready."

We went through several options before I finally agreed upon a black minidress covered in sequins and a pair of black stilettos.

With the impending outfit waiting for me on the bed, the girls sat me down on a stool in Val's bathroom. Blake curled my hair into tight ringlets, and Valerie did my makeup.

"I think this is the fanciest I've ever looked in my entire life." My eyelashes fluttered like butterfly wings, my red lipstick a stark contrast to my smoky eyes.

I went to run my fingers through my hair, and Blake smacked my hand away just before spraying enough hair spray to burn a new hole in the ozone layer. "Try not to touch it."

Valerie made me close my eyes before she sprayed my face with something she said would set my makeup, whatever that meant.

Reece knocked on the door frame before saying, "It's not too late to just go back to my place. We can put on pajamas and I can do that thing I did this morning that you really liked."

Heat pooled in my cheeks as I remembered exactly what he was talking about, but I stopped myself. "Give me two minutes, and I'll be ready to go. I've got too much hair and makeup going on to stay home now."

He replied, "Fine, but don't get too excited. We won't be there long."

I wiggled myself into the dress we had picked out and checked myself out in the mirror. "Is this really what I look like?" I barely recognized myself.

"You're ridiculously hot." Blake snapped a couple of pictures with her phone.

I grinned, excited to be going to a nightclub for the first time in so long. I clasped the straps of the mile-high stilettos and stepped into the living room. Reece stood from the couch and met me halfway, his jaw hitting the floor as his eyes raked over me.

"Wow, Mag. You look . . . ."

I grinned, knowing that I had rendered him speechless. He grabbed me by the waist, pulling me against him. "Is it too much?" I asked.

He kissed my cheek before nuzzling his nose against my ear. "You sure you don't want to just go back to my place? This dress looks amazing, but I really want to—" His hand reached under the hem of my skirt, his fingers gliding up my bare skin.

I sucked in a breath, trying to remember that my friends were standing behind us watching. Right on cue, Blake cleared her throat and Reece stepped back. His eyes were still on me, burning my skin.

I looked over my shoulder and saw that the girls were clearly pretending to talk about something they saw on the wall behind them instead of watching us. I turned back to Reece. "An hour. We'll go for an hour and then back to your house."

I reached down and grabbed a bag Val had packed

for me with my toiletries and comfortable clothes for after the party—not that I thought he would let me wear them for very long—and we were on our way.

Reece and I made it to the club, and I was proud of myself for not falling over like a baby deer in Val's shoes as we went up the stairs to the VIP area. Reece had his hand on my lower back, guiding me to the party, pointing out where we were headed. We entered an area where about a hundred people milled around. If this was a small gathering, I wondered what their big blowouts looked like.

His lips grazed my ear as he said, "First we stop at the bar, then we find our friends."

I gave him a questioning look. "Isn't the point of table service that they bring drinks to us?"

"I learned with this group that if I come in with a drink in my hand, they won't give me one that I don't want."

"Smart." We leaned against the private bar area, and Reece ordered a soda.

The bartender turned to me. "I'll have a Shirley Temple, please."

"Mag, you're so wild." He grinned and pulled me in for a kiss. With these shoes, I could kiss him without stretching on the tips of my toes. One of his hands roved to my bottom, and he lifted me a little, kissing me deeper.

The bartender placed our drinks in front of us, but we ignored them. The music was loud, covering us like a blanket. We were in a room full of people, but his arms around me made it feel like it was just the two of us.

He broke away and pulled cash out of his pocket,

placing it on the bar. His hand had a slight shake to it, the only sign that he was nervous. "One hour."

I nodded. "Just long enough to say hi, and then we can get out of here."

We walked to the roped-off area, and I noticed that every person there looked like a model. It was a pool of lips, legs, and blonde highlights. Insecurity started to creep in, but then Reece's hand squeezed my waist, and I knew I was with the best-looking guy here, and he had chosen me.

As soon as Sal spotted us, he jumped up from the booth and grabbed me in his signature bear hug, this time lifting me off the ground. "Maggie, I'm so glad you're here!" He smacked a wet kiss on my cheek and sat me back down. He grabbed Reece in the same kind of hug but left out the kiss.

"Looks like quite the party, friend," Reece called out to him.

I patted Sal's shoulder, grinning at him. "Happy Birthday. Thanks for having us."

A blonde woman I would have recognized anywhere came up to our group, causing Reece to stand a little closer to me. "You're that photographer, right?" she asked, using a tone that accused me of being dirt on the bottom of her shoe.

I gave her a smile that didn't meet my eyes. "Hi, Aimee. Yes, I'm the photographer."

She turned to Sal. "You know what, if I remember correctly, she's got a hookup with a really talented florist. Weren't you looking for a better company to distribute the arrangements in your restaurants?" Her cold eyes met mine. "I bet you could get Sal a huge discount, huh?"

Reece put his hand on my lower back. "Why don't you crawl back to the bridge you live under, Aimee?"

Hearing him insult someone was jarring, but I was happy that he was sticking up for me. She huffed angrily and stomped back to her circle of friends, a group of women that appeared to contain more plastic than a toy store.

Luckily, Sal had no idea what had just happened, made evident by the way he reached for my wrist. "Come dance with me!"

I looked over at Reece, hoping he would get me out of it, but he just grinned and said, "I hope you two have fun." I handed my glass to him before Sal dragged me to the small dance floor at the front of the VIP area.

The music was blaring so loudly that I couldn't hear my own thoughts, but I did my best to keep up with Sal. He was all over the place, and his moves didn't match the beat, but I loved every minute of it.

He leaned in and yelled into my ear, "He seems happier than he's been in a really long time."

I turned, finding Reece in the crowd. There was a circle of people around him, and he was laughing. I saw a hand reach up and graze his chest, but he didn't react to it. I opened my mouth to ask who the girl was, but Sal grabbed me and spun me in a circle.

We danced for a couple of songs, but after a while, I was hot and out of breath, so I let him find another partner and weaved through the crowd to find my boyfriend.

Reece smiled when he caught my eye and handed me my drink. "Having fun?" He leaned down and kissed me.

"I am. Sal is . . . something else."

He looked over at Sal on the dance floor, surrounded by a flock of girls. "I wouldn't have come here for anyone else." He put his hand on my hip. "Let me show you off a little, and then we can leave."

He kissed just below my ear before biting my neck gently. I knew exactly what he had in mind and couldn't wait to get out of there.

He walked me around, introducing me to every Chad, Brad, Mike, and Brian in the place. They talked about real estate and investment portfolios, so I just nodded kindly and smiled when Reece did.

Then we made our way through the social media influencers and socialites, and he talked them all into calling me to photograph their next event or cosmetic line launch.

He definitely had his work hat on, and his charm was turned all the way up. Trying to remember everyone's names was overwhelming, but there was no way I would lose in this town with a PR rep like Reece.

Twenty minutes later, he was in a deep discussion about accounting with two other guys who were equally excited about the topic. For a guy who'd claimed he was dreading spending time with everyone here, he seemed surprisingly happy. Even his shoulders were relaxed as he talked about bottom lines and accruals. I patted his arm and said, "I'm going to go find a restroom."

He kissed me on the cheek, and I found my way through the dark hallway at the back of the club. I pushed the door to the women's bathroom open and saw three girls standing at the counter touching up their makeup and—okay, so that was what cocaine looked like in person.

I smiled at them, rushed into a stall across the way, and opened the little purse that I had borrowed from Val. It was only large enough for my phone, a couple of cards, and my house key. I wiggled my phone free and checked if Val or Blake had messaged me.

Radio silence. Weird. I sent a text to the group: *I'm having more fun than I thought I was going to. Just saw someone snort a line in a bathroom. Miley Cyrus would be proud.*

I tucked my phone back in my purse, ready to stand up and fix my dress when I heard one of the girls say, "Why did God make Reece Howell so fucking delicious? I want to eat him alive."

Another one spoke up, "Umm, I thought we didn't bring up exes."

"I just want to peel his clothes off and screw him in this club like we used to."

What the actual hell?

I peeked through the crack in the bathroom stall, thankful that I could glimpse a part of all three of them from where I sat.

The one in pink shrugged as she reapplied her lipstick. "Well, he never actually broke up with me when he . . . disappeared. So he's kind of still my boyfriend, right?" She fluffed her perfect platinum blond hair, puckering her lips.

"You mean when he got arrested and had to go to

rehab?" This was from a tall brunette in a gray dress mostly made of string and glitter.

"Regardless of what happened, he's here tonight, and I fully intend on getting him back. That man belongs to me."

I took a deep breath to calm myself before I did something stupid, like launching myself out of the bathroom stall at her. Before I could move, the one in a blue bikini top and shorts asked, "Isn't he here with some girl tonight? Sal said they were pretty serious."

The blonde one threw her head back, laughing. "Did you see her? There is no competition. He's going to leave with me tonight, you can bet on it." She sighed deeply, giving me a flashback of hiding from my tormentors just like this in high school. "It's been impossible to find a man who can fuck like him." She leaned into the mirror, wiping at her smudged eyeliner. "I haven't had a good dick since he left."

The one in gray nodded. "He really does know what he's doing, though."

Bikini Top gasped. "Alexa!"

Alexa, the one in gray, smacked Bikini Top on the arm. "I thought you knew that he and I hooked up a few times in college. Francesca is right about the way he fucks." She turned to the one in pink—Francesca . . . *why was that name so familiar?* "If he doesn't leave with you, I'm going to ask if he'll take me home instead."

My blood turned to ice. I didn't know what to be angrier about, that my relationship wasn't valid enough to respect it, or that I was trapped in a room full of vipers who had slept with my boyfriend.

Francesca gave her an angry look. "Did I mention that he's been texting me quite a lot lately?"

Hold up. What?

The other two said aloud what I was thinking, so Francesca went on, "He called me out of the blue a couple of weeks ago, pretending to ask me about work stuff, and now we've been talking pretty much every day. I know he's going through a weird phase, trying to throw away his family's money and play house with that mousy girl, but with a little time, I can bring him back to the man I fell in love with."

Then I thought back to the phone call that came through at my house the other day. He had been texting someone a lot more than usual, but he'd been working so much. Jesus, could this girl be FC?

Was he really just playing some game with me while he waited to get back with her? Fuck, was his father right about this whole thing?

The walls of the bathroom stall squeezed in closer, like a trash compactor. I was starting to sweat, feeling claustrophobic.

I was going to throw up. I needed air.

I needed to get out of there.

Standing up, I flushed the toilet and made sure my dress covered all the parts it was supposed to. When I swung the door open, ready to defend myself, the girls were gone.

Catching my eyes in the mirror, I realized how silly I appeared, dressed up like a Barbie doll. My eyes welled up, and I blotted them with a tissue before my makeup could run.

I refused to be this girl. I wouldn't let some guy take advantage of me, even if I was falling in love with him.

If he wanted her, he could have her. I wouldn't let him hurt me.

I washed my hands and really wanted to wash my face, but the layers of makeup would have to wait to come off until I got home.

I turned and left the bathroom, moving through the crowd until I found him. Of course, he was standing in a group with Francesca and Alexa flanking him. Bikini Top stood next to them with a smile on her face like she knew I had been in the bathroom that whole time.

He smiled at me, but it wasn't as bright as it had been before. "Mag, I'm glad you're back. This is Francesca, Alexa, and Rachel. They—"

"I'm leaving."

He blinked a few times and shook his head. "Sure, okay, we can go." He stepped toward me, confusion painted across his face. I held my hand up, stopping him.

"No. You're not coming with me." I pointed to Francesca, who had a proud smirk on her face. "Maybe you and your ex can text about it after I'm gone."

He looked at her and then at me again. "Mag, it's not like that."

"But you have been texting and calling her? Telling me it's work?"

"Mag, listen—"

"No, Reece. You listen. I'm not doing this. You can have her. Or the other one, since she said she wants to sleep with you again, too. Apparently, you might even fuck one of them while you're still here, so take your pick."

"Can we talk about this?" He ran his hand through his hair, and I wanted to shove him. I wanted to scream in his face.

I shook my head. "Enough of this bullshit. You're the same guy your father warned me about, and I refuse to play along." I spun on my heel, trying to get out of the club. He followed after me, reaching for my elbow, but I turned, swatting him away. "Leave me alone, or so help me, I will make a scene." I pointed to the girls, catching their smug smiles. "Go back to your friends, and let me go."

I ran down the stairs and out the door. It wasn't until I made it to the street that my eyes blurred and the tears that had been building finally spilled onto my cheeks. I pulled out my phone and tried to open my app to find a car to pick me up, but I couldn't see the screen well enough.

Instead, I used the voice command to call Blake, knowing she didn't have any other plans tonight. She answered on the second ring. "What's up, how's the party?"

I sobbed into the phone. "I need you to come get me. Please hurry."

Blake's SUV came flying down the road, and she screeched to a stop where I was standing on the sidewalk.

She reached across the car, propping the passenger

door open. Just as I reached for the handle, Sal called from behind me. "Maggie, wait! What's going on?"

I spun on my heels, putting my hands on my hips. "You need to go ask your best friend."

He put his hand on the frame, holding the door open for me. "He's the one who begged me to come down here to talk to you."

"Reece knows why I don't ever want to see him again. Maybe he's been keeping secrets from both of us." I slid into the car and grabbed the handle, yanking the door out of his hand.

I turned to Blake. "Take me home. Please."

She hit the gas and we left Sal standing on the side of the road. Lightning flashed across the sky, making me jump a little.

I opened the center console, where I knew Blake kept every drive-through napkin she had ever been given, and pulled one out. I rubbed my face with it, trying to remove some of the tear-streaked makeup painted on my face.

Blake looked through her rear-view mirror and asked, "Who was that guy?"

I turned around in my seat, looking at him through the back window as he got smaller and smaller behind us. "That's Reece's best friend, Sal. The birthday boy." I turned back around in the seat and caught her smile. "What?"

She turned away, trying to hide the look on her face, and said, "He was a little cute, that's all."

"No, Blake. We hate him. We hate all of them." I flipped down the sun visor, checking myself in the mirror.

"Ugh, I'm a fucking disaster." I dabbed at my eyes with the napkin, but nothing was coming off.

Curse Val's really nice expensive makeup.

Blake tapped her fingers on the steering wheel. "Are you going to tell me why you called me like your ass was on fire or why you're acting like a lunatic?"

I laid my head against the headrest, trying to force my body to sit still. "It was all a joke. Like Laney Boggs in *She's All That*."

"Okay, usually I'm good at your random movie trivia, but I'm coming up blank with this reference."

"You know, that 90's movie where they pick the ugly girl to dress up and take to prom, but then she finds out it was just a bet and they were all really horrible people in the end." I reached down and took my shoes off, rubbing the bottoms of my sore feet.

Her eyes scanned the mirrors as she drove us closer to home. "I think I remember that one. She wore glasses and overalls, right?" She paused to check her blind spot before changing lanes. "Didn't that movie have a happy ending, though?"

I threw my hands up. "I don't care how the damn movie ended. Right now I feel like some hot guy picked me out of a crowd to see how hard he could fuck me over."

"Look, I haven't been team Reece for most of this ordeal, but I highly doubt that a grown man would turn his life into a teenage drama on purpose."

I looked out the window, watching the houses in my neighborhood go by as we passed them. "Fine. You're probably right."

We pulled up to the house and Valerie came running out the front door. "I had Joey bring me home as soon as Blake sent me a 911 text."

My eyes started welling up again. "I'm sorry, I didn't mean to ruin either of your nights."

My two best friends followed me into the house and didn't stop me when I dragged a chair from the kitchen table over to the refrigerator.

We kept the good alcohol on top of the fridge, and this called for it.

Still standing on the chair, I twisted the cap off the vodka and took a long glug straight from the bottle. Then I handed it to Valerie and climbed off the chair. She took a drink from the bottle and then handed it to Blake, who did the same. Solidarity.

Blake handed the bottle back to me, and I carried it into the living room. I felt grateful as they sat next to me on the couch, holding me together, but I also didn't want to recount the awful evening I had just lived through.

Val ran her fingers through my hair, still curly and perfect. "Take your time. You don't have to tell us anything unless you're ready."

As she finished her sentence, there was a knock at the door. I knew it was him without even asking. I whispered, "Please send him away."

Blake jumped off the couch and swung the door open, excited to tell Reece to kick rocks. "She hasn't told us what you did, but she doesn't want to talk to you, so I'm guessing you were an enormous asshole. Goodnight."

His eyes met mine, and the pain in them mirrored my

own. "I am an asshole, Mag, but if you give me five minutes, I can make it right."

I turned away from him, pulled my legs up on the couch, and snuggled into Val's side. I felt like that helpless girl with no control over my life all over again.

Val shot an icy glare across the room at him as she said, "You need to go."

Blake agreed, adding, "And don't come back." She shut the door, came back to the couch, and held the bottle of vodka out for me.

I took it from her and swallowed another drink.

Ugh, it fucking burned.

But everything in my life was burning down, too. So what was one more thing? I took another long pull from the bottle and set it back on the coffee table.

My body warmed immediately from the alcohol, but the dress I wore felt too tight. I stood up, pulling at the straps. "I think I'm going to go to bed. I don't want to be awake anymore."

They nodded at me but didn't move from the couch. I had a feeling I would find both of them in the same spot when I came down in the morning.

I thanked them for taking care of me and plodded up the staircase. I dumped out my little purse on the dresser and saw ten missed calls from Reece. As I held my phone in my hand, it rang, and Reece's adorable, cheating face that I never wanted to see again showed up on my screen. I ignored the call, blocked his number, and turned off my phone.

I peeled off the asinine dress that was constricting my airflow and caught the reflection of my locket in my makeup mirror. I didn't want to see this special piece of jewelry and think about anyone other than my dad, but after the way I met Reece, and how he had gone out of his way to fix it when it was broken, it reminded me too much of him.

I yanked at the clasp, took it off, and placed it in the top drawer of my dresser, hoping in time it wouldn't hurt my heart to look at it anymore. Then I dug through my dresser, found an old T-shirt and some shorts, put them on, and climbed into bed.

I lay there for a few minutes staring at the ceiling until I wanted to scream. My legs were restless, begging me to get up and run, but that was the last thing I needed.

I turned to my side, and all I could see was the image of Reece lying there with me. I nuzzled into my pillow and tried to take a few deep, calming breaths.

The stupid bedsheets smelled like him.

I squeezed my eyes shut, and it felt like he was there with me, cracking my heart in half. How could I love someone that I obviously didn't even know?

I needed to move on from this as quickly as possible. Like ripping off a Band-Aid. I jumped out of bed, determined not to let this man dictate my life.

My first step was getting the smell of him out of here.

I ripped the sheets from the bed and threw them on the floor. I picked up the pillows and shook them violently until they fell out of their pillowcases.

Scooping up everything, I stormed down the stairs and into the laundry room. I swung open the door of the washing machine to find that it was full of wet clothes that reeked of mildew. Why could Valerie never remember to move her damn laundry into the dryer? I let out a guttural scream.

Mildew sheets were better than Reece sheets.

If I couldn't wash them, I had to get rid of them.

I stomped through the living room and Val and Blake's heads popped up over the back of the couch like gophers. Knowing they would freak out if I stuffed the sheets into the fireplace, I had to do the next best thing.

"Don't ask," I called out as I secured the sheets back in my arms and flew out the front door.

I got to the side of the house, tossing the lid off the trash can. It was mostly full, but I didn't care. I shoved the entire set of sheets inside and pushed with all of my might, shoving them down as hard as I could. I never wanted to see these smelly, scratchy things again.

Feeling pretty proud of myself, I closed the lid and dusted my hands off on my shorts. I went back into the house, stopping only to pick up the bottle and take another swig before heading back up the stairs.

Thankfully, neither of my friends said a word to me as I lost my mind in front of them.

I threw myself on top of my empty bed, feeling empty inside. My thoughts drifted to the fun times Reece and I had spent together, so I focused on the things I hated about him instead.

I hated that he had come into my life, and I hated that he had ruined my career. But most of all I hated that I missed him so fucking much already.

～

I came downstairs the next morning to an empty house. There was a note on the counter from the girls, telling me that they loved me and that I should text them when I was ready to talk. I glanced out the kitchen window, watching the rain drizzling outside, which made me a little glad that the outside matched my inside.

I started to pour a bowl of cereal but decided I wasn't really that hungry.

I stood in front of the TV, wanting to drone out my thoughts. I scrolled through Netflix but couldn't find anything worth my attention. Finally, I opened Spotify and turned on my sad songs playlist. The words made so much more sense now that there was a deep pit in my chest, especially when I heard them through the surround sound. I lay down on the couch, but then I remembered the last time I was sad on this couch. And the jerk who came over and made me feel better.

I hated this couch.

Soon I'd use my emergency credit card to buy a new one. I didn't care that I needed to save every penny I had so I could buy groceries. The couch had to go. I cranked up the volume and pushed the coffee table off to the side of the room.

Laying down on the floor, I let the music envelop me, wishing I could disappear. As the best breakup songs ever written reverberated through the walls of my living room, I finally let it all out.

I cried for everything I had been holding in.

I cried for the loss of the man I had wanted to spend the rest of my life with. Thank goodness I hadn't told him that.

I cried for losing the comfort of a job that I had once adored. My amazing friends that I wasn't going to get to see every day anymore. Food at the restaurant that was always perfectly cooked.

I cried because I had picked the wrong guy. After our last conversation, I knew Ezra was a conceited dipshit, but he wouldn't have pretended to be faithful when he wasn't.

I cried because if I had picked Ezra, I know I would have been settling and my heart would have gotten broken eventually anyway.

I cried because the mean girls always won. They won in high school, and they were winning now. I'd never be able to move on from the bullies, no matter how old I got.

I cried because, above all, I was alone and scared and didn't know what I was doing with my life.

Then I thought about the sex. Would I ever have something as good as I had with Reece? Those stupid girls in that bathroom were right. He was extremely talented.

How many other girls was he sleeping with to be that good, though? I guess practice really does make perfect.

Dammit, I should probably go get tested.

I heard a knock at the door, and my stomach sank even further. No one would be able to make this better. I yelled out, "I don't care who you are, go away!"

Val propped the door open just a few inches and yelled back, "It's just me. I forgot my lunch in the fridge and thought I could pop in without you seeing me. But when I heard 'Ten' from Jimmy Eat World blasting through the walls, I figured I should probably knock. I'm just going to run in real quick. You won't even notice that I'm here."

I sat up and grabbed a handful of tissues from the coffee table so I could wipe my face before turning the volume down. "It's fine. You can come in."

She sat on the floor next to me. "Do you wanna talk about it yet?"

I told her everything that had happened, from running into Aimee, to listening to the girls in the bathroom insult me, and then finally how I learned that Reece had been texting some other girl for weeks.

She waited until I finished the whole story before she asked, "Don't you want to hear his side of the story? Maybe he has a really good explanation for texting his ex-girlfriend."

"No. I don't ever want to hear from him again."

She laughed, "You're acting like a little kid over this."

"I am not!" When I heard the words leave my lips, I cracked a smile. "Okay, so maybe I am. But I'm allowed to be miserable."

She was gentle, but firm when she said, "Being miserable is your choice, and I'll go get you some ice cream if you want me to, but I think you're really just scared."

"You're not the only person who's told me that lately. Everything is completely different."

"Which is a good thing." She wrapped her arm around me. Her hair, which was wet from the rain, brushed against my face. "If things were stagnant, life would be boring."

"I like when things are boring."

"No, you like when things are controlled and safe. You have been striving for control since I met you. What you can do now is choose how you'll control the madness."

"How do I control the fact that the man I was head over heels for is still pining over his ex."

"You don't. But you can remember what a badass you are and cowboy the fuck up."

I laughed. "Cowboy the what?"

She shrugged. "It's something my grandpa used to say when things got hard. Do you know who the toughest motherfuckers are? Cowboys. Do you think they wallow in sadness when shit goes down? No. They put on their boots, and they fix their problems."

I balled up my hands and propped my chin on my fists. "I hate when you make sense."

"Wait right here." She got up and disappeared up the stairs. A few minutes later she came down, my planner in her hand.

She opened to this week and started pointing at appointments for the resort that I had documented. "Let's start by calling these people." She flipped through several pages. "There's a ton of clients in here. I'll help you reschedule all of them if you want me to."

I sighed. "Maybe. I think I need a few days to think about it. I need a plan."

"Fuck the plan. What's to think about?"

Then it hit me. "How do I even start a business? Reece said he would help me with this stuff, but that's not an option anymore." I lay back on the floor, ready to let the misery eat me alive.

"Umm, hello. Earth to Lina. I own a successful

business, too. I can help you with all the planning, and . . ." her tone changed, going deeper. "I have a bit of a secret I was waiting to tell you about."

I looked up at her from the floor, and she bit her bottom lip. "Secrets don't make friends, Val." I hadn't thought we'd had a single secret between us.

"Well, things at the store have been really great for the past few years. You know this, though." I nodded, wondering what she was hiding from me. "And I've been collecting your rent in an account for the past two years . . . just in case you wanted it to start your own business. As a loan, until you start making money."

This time I sat up, completely shocked. "You've been saving my rent?"

Her shoulder bunched up. "I didn't really need it, but I knew that one day you might. Along with some other cash I've stashed away, I've got about twenty-five grand at your disposal if you need it."

"Valerie! Are you fucking with me?"

I jumped toward her, wrapping my arms around her.

She laughed. "Lina, you work so hard, and you're so talented. It's about time that you start seeing yourself for who you are. Whatever you need from me, money, business advice, help holding one of those reflective circle things you use during shoots sometimes, I've got your back."

"Thank you. So much." The stress about starting my business started to turn into excitement. One good thing was going to come out of all of this.

Val leaned into me. "I do think you should call him and get his side of the story, though. At least so you don't look back years from now and wonder what could have been."

My thoughts snapped back to why I was so upset. "I think things between Reece and me are done. I don't know if I can put what he was doing with that girl behind me."

"What did you say her name was?"

I grimaced, spitting out her name, "Francesca." As Valerie pulled her phone out of her pocket and started scrolling, I remembered an earlier conversation. "You know what, Sal had brought her up when we were out at dinner the other night. I wonder if he was trying to tell me that Reece was being unfaithful."

"Hmm, that's a possibility." She continued looking through something on her phone.

"What are you doing?" I twisted to see her screen, watching her scroll through pictures on Instagram.

"I'm investigating." She had found Sal's account and was going through pictures from the birthday party. It left an acidic taste in my mouth. She stopped on a picture of a group of girls standing together, drinks in their hands. "Is she in this one?"

I pointed to her, wishing I could punch her in her ugly, Botoxed face.

"I think I know her." She tapped the screen, showing the tagged accounts on the picture, and then clicked Francesca's account. "Yes! I met her at a charity event a few years ago."

"Great, so she's rich and way above my league, too. Perfect for Reece."

"I'm going to ignore that." She pulled up Francesca's profile and handed me the phone.

"Holy shit, Val. Her last name is Cohen." I thought back to Reece's phone calls. "FC is Francesca Cohen." I scrolled through her pictures, careful to not accidentally like one of them. I found a picture of her and Sylvia, with the caption, "Happy Mother's Day to the best mom in the world!"

I handed Val's phone back to her and laid back down on the floor.

"Ugh. The woman he tried to hire to run my business was his ex-girlfriend's mother."

Chapter Sixteen

Three days later, Val met me for a bite to eat at a taco shop down the road from the resort. It had been unseasonably rainy outside, to the point that the clients I had skipped out on this weekend canceled their bookings on their own, at least according to Kathy's secret texts.

I had spent two days setting up my business license, wrestling with a do-it-yourself website builder, and reaching out to clients on the list Kathy had emailed me. I had told her I was worried that she could get fired for giving me their information, but she'd said she didn't care at all, after what I had just gone through.

So I told her that as soon as I could afford her, I would take her with me. She thought it was a sweet sentiment, and I promised myself I would make it happen somehow.

Val tapped my planner, which sat next to my plate on the table, bringing my thoughts back to the present. "Is this thing filling up?"

"Yeah, actually, it is. I've got a shoot every day for the

next three weeks, which might become overwhelming, but I'm excited about it."

"Did you book a lot of people from the resort?"

"I'm amazed at how many people let me scalp them from The Pacifica. I had no idea how much we charged them for resort and processing fees, so everyone was delighted to pay less for the same service."

"Did you hear from anyone else?"

"Yeah, actually. Denice, the model I met a little while ago, gave me contacts for friends that wanted to book. Ooh, and Brita Jackson shared a link to my website on her social media." I wiped my face with a napkin. "I'm going to be so busy the next few months because of them."

She smiled at me across the table. "That's amazing news, which I'm not surprised to hear at all." Then she leaned forward on her elbows. "But that's not who I was talking about."

I pressed my fist to the sharp pain in my chest. I knew who she was talking about and had been keeping myself busy so I wouldn't think about him. "I blocked his number the other night. I don't want to hear his excuses."

She shifted in her seat. "But what if he didn't betray you? Maybe it was a miscommunication."

"Miscommunication is not a thing. If he wanted to tell me anything, he could have. Keeping secrets is just as bad as lying, and I'm not going to be walked all over."

Commitment meant not keeping things from each other. He'd said he wanted to be all in with me but couldn't be completely honest. I didn't want to find out what else he had been hiding.

I rolled up my napkin and tossed it onto my empty plate. "I'm thankful that I met him and that I realized I was unsatisfied with my life because of him, but I'm moving on." Sure, I didn't really feel that way on the inside, but hopefully, the more I said it, the more I would believe it.

Val played with the straw in her cup, chewing on her bottom lip. After a few moments of silence, I couldn't take it anymore. "Just say it. Whatever you're holding in, say it."

"Joey said they hung out last night, and Reece was like a ghost. He didn't eat or drink and barely spoke. He's really upset that you ran off, and he thinks that if you let him explain himself, you'll forgive him."

My body felt hot as I rubbed my fingers against my temples. "Oh, so I got to spend weeks thinking I was so important to him even though he lied to me about talking to some other girl the whole time, and now he wants me to go out of my way to forgive him."

Her shoulders slumped forward. "Lina, it's not like that at all. Joey said that he really was talking to Francesca about work."

"Well, when he told me about his ex, he said she worked for the family company, but they never worked together. Sounds like he's blowing smoke up Joey's ass, too." I leaned back in my chair, staring up at the ceiling. "I feel like such an idiot for falling for him."

She propped her chin on her fist. "Why do I get the feeling this is less about Reece's secrets and more about something you're not telling me?"

I blinked my eyes several times, trying not to cry at my

next thought. "Do you remember those girls who used to make fun of me in school? The ones that would call me caterpillar face across the quad?"

"I haven't thought about those bitches in years. Besides, thick eyebrows made a comeback, so they can suck it." She crossed her arms and leaned forward. "Why are you bringing them up?"

"Hearing those women in the bathroom say all that shit sent me right back to being that scared teenage girl. Remember how they spent a whole month pushing me into random guys in the hallway so it looked like I was throwing myself at them? And I ended up looking like the weirdo for it?" My bottom lip began to tremble. "The birthday party was just the adult version of trying to get to class without being torn apart by wolves. I don't want to go through it again."

"Oh, honey." She scooted forward in her seat and put her arms around me. "It makes me so mad that their actions are still affecting you like this."

"I didn't think they were that deep in my head, but in that moment, those girls were right there in the room tormenting me. I didn't know anything would ever make me feel so small again. The girls from the bathroom are obviously friends of his, or at the least coworkers, so a part of me worries that even if we did get back together, I'd have to see them at every social gathering, and I can't take it. It's better that I just cut him off cold turkey."

She squeezed my arms before releasing them and moving back to her chair. "The girls from high school are living small, miserable lives. They were unhappy with themselves all those years ago, and I guarantee they are still unhappy now. The same thing goes for the girls in the bathroom. They just wanted to take their suffering out on you." She took my hand in hers. "Do you really think Reece or Sal will let any of them get invited to any parties after the way they behaved? I'm willing to bet that when word gets out about how awful they were to you, the group will blacklist them, if they haven't already."

I frowned at her. "I hate how you make so much sense sometimes."

Val stood, picking up her trash. "I need to get back to the store, but I think you should at least let him explain himself. Then you can tell him to go to hell and I'll support you to the ends of the earth." She rested her hand on my shoulder. "I just don't want you to throw away something great because of one bad night."

I kicked off my wet boots at the front door after finishing a maternity shoot with the heiress of a Canadian liquor company. It had rained for the entire two-hour session, which—according to the weather reporter on the radio during my drive home—was record rainfall for the county.

Chloe had been a glowing mama, with just a couple of weeks left of her pregnancy. We had spent the afternoon at the Santa Barbara Botanical Garden, and the addition of a frilly pink umbrella just added to the magic of capturing her under redwood trees and strolling across the wooden bridges. The clouds had covered the sun just as we finished the shoot, surrounding the city in a dreary darkness, making me want to do nothing but curl up in my bed.

I made it up to the loft, uploaded the pictures to the computer, and changed into some warm leggings and an oversized sweater.

It only took me an hour or so to get the sneak peeks ready and post about Chloe and her adorable baby bump on social media. I finally began to feel confident being my own boss.

I turned off my computer and shuffled into my bedroom with a tired brain and a tired heart. I was happy doing my own thing on my own terms, but I knew it would take a little while for the crushing sadness to fade. I had hoped to avoid my heartbreak by surrounding myself with happy families and smiling couples, but it just emphasized the contrast between their lives and mine.

Thankful for how busy I had been since leaving the resort, I lay on my bed, listening to the rain hit the window. After a few minutes of trying to get cozy on the bare mattress, I pulled out my phone and started searching the web for comfortable bed sheets.

I found a set that had really great reviews that was also affordable, but I hated the idea of buying them online and having to return them if they weren't right. They wouldn't be as soft as Reece's, but they were better than the old blanket I had slept on this week.

I decided to make a trip to Target later instead and laid my phone down next to me. Snuggling into my uncovered pillow, I closed my eyes and took a few deep breaths, thinking of all the positive headway I was making with my company. If I had made this much progress in less than a week, I wondered where I could take it a month from now, or even this time next year.

The storm outside must have gotten worse; the tapping on the window got louder, like a branch from the old oak tree was crashing against it. After the fifth time the tree smacked the window, I grew more curious about the storm and got up, pulled the curtains to the side, and peered into the darkness.

Lightning flashed, and I thought I saw something in the tree. A pebble hit the glass, and I heard Reece's voice call out, "Maggie! Open the window!"

I clicked on the flashlight I kept on my nightstand and wrestled with the window, sliding it open an inch at a time. Water pelted my face as I yelled, "What are you doing in my tree?"

In the light, I saw his arms and legs wrapped around the thickest branch, like he was clinging for his life. "I thought it would be romantic if I pretended to break in like you broke into my house, but then I got up here and found that it's too far away from the ledge to reach." He paused, gripping the tree tighter. "I also learned that I'm terrified of heights."

I brushed off the wet hair stuck to my forehead as the wind whipped around me. It was kind of adorable that he'd gone to all this effort, but it still hurt that he'd been talking to his ex for weeks without telling me.

"Please, Mag. Please forgive me. If I climb down, will you let me in the house?" Lightning flashed again, the complete terror in his eyes giving me a little sympathy for his predicament.

"Tell me why you lied to me first."

"I didn't mean to keep anything from you. I was only talking to her about marketing, I swear. If you meet me at the door, I'll show you all the texts."

Another burst of lightning lit up the entire yard, and he yelped. He'd piqued my curiosity by offering to show me his text messages with Francesca. "Fine, I'll let you come inside. But this doesn't mean I forgive you."

He yelled out a thank-you and started a slow descent down the tree. I wiggled the window closed, grabbing a towel before running down the stairs to meet him. I wasn't sure if I could really forgive him, but I worried that Val was right. I didn't want to look back on this years from now and wonder what he might have said. I knew what I believed, but I also knew I needed to hear him out. Once I'd heard his lame excuse, I could send him on his way and get back to my new life.

My skin was itchy, my clothes too tight, as I reached for the doorknob. I counted to ten under my breath, trying to focus. I didn't know if I'd ever been this apprehensive before. Knowing there was no avoiding it, I swung the door open.

If I wasn't so mad at him, he would have taken my breath away, standing under the front porch completely drenched. His hair fell across his forehead, and his baby blue button-up clung to his chest. I looked over his shoulder to avoid staring at his abs shining through his shirt and noticed the absence of something obnoxiously green. "Where's your car?"

He turned around, pointing at the black Porsche parked on the road. "I traded it in for something I could afford. It was the only way to prove to my dad that I was serious about leaving as soon as my probation's over and that I don't want anything from him anymore."

That car had been his favorite possession, so hearing that he had gotten rid of it knocked me back a few pegs. I tossed the towel at him. "You can dry off while you tell me everything. But if you piss me off, I'll throw you back out into the storm."

He rubbed his hair with the towel, and I had to turn around and walk away before my treacherous body threw itself at him. I sat at the kitchen table because as much as I hated that stupid couch over there, I didn't want him to get it all wet with his terrible clothes that I totally hated, too.

He dried himself off as best as he could and then laid the towel on the wooden chair before sitting down. "Mag, you saved my life."

I leaned back in my chair. "All I did was let you in during a storm. It's not that big of a deal."

He leaned forward, filling the space between us. "No, the night we met. You saved me." He picked at the edge of his fingernail. "I was in a really dark place, the kind I wasn't sure I would wake up from. I was in the kitchen staring down a bottle of bourbon, knowing it was about to win. I took a drink, and that's when I heard something upstairs."

He clutched his head in his hands, staring down at the table. "I put the bottle down when I heard another thunk and ran up the stairs to find out what it was. Then I saw you, and I knew you had been sent to stop me from destroying myself." His eyes met mine, red-rimmed and deadly serious.

The caramel smell of his breath that night came back to me. It must have been the alcohol. "I didn't stop you that night, Reece. You did."

"After you ran off, I poured the bottle down the sink and called my sponsor. You'll never know how thankful I am for you bursting in like that."

I crossed my arms across my chest. "So you're saying that you only wanted to be with me because of some misplaced sense of gratitude?"

"That's not what I'm saying at all. I just want you to know how important you are to me."

I didn't want to hear him grovel. I wanted answers. "When Sal asked us to come to the party, was the real reason you didn't want to go because you knew she would be there? You didn't want the two of us in the same room together?"

"Absolutely not." He reached for my elbow, but I moved out of his reach. "I promise. I knew she would be there, but she wasn't even on my radar. I only want to be with you, and she knows that." I wanted so badly for this to be the truth. I wanted to believe that he felt for me what I felt for him, but I couldn't just ignore what he'd done.

"So why were you texting and calling her behind my back?"

His eyes lingered on my neck. "Where's your locket?"

I glared at him. "I took it off. Answer my question."

He pulled his phone from his front pocket, unlocked it, and laid it on the table in front of me. "I wasn't, I swear." He scrolled through texts between Francesca and him, moving slowly enough for me to read them. They started out as public relations issues with the resort—questions about advertisements and social media insights. Then a complaint from Reece about Aimee, him requesting to have her removed from the property account for being rude to employees.

"Her mom is Sylvia, and she works for her company. She's our public relations manager. That's all. She's not my friend, and the thought of being with her again makes me want to throw up." As he scrolled further, the topic turned to me and how Sylvia would be stupid if she didn't beg to represent me.

Everything he showed me made sense, but a question lingered. "Sylvia said you didn't recommend me to her. But it looks like that was a lie too."

He stopped scrolling and brought his hands back to his lap. "I promise it wasn't me who called Sylvia. It was Brita."

"I talked to her yesterday. She's helping me with some marketing. I could always ask her to verify your story."

He let out a long breath like he was about to say something I wasn't going to like. "She's also a really good friend of mine from high school. I was more nervous that she would be at Sal's party than Francesca." He paused, his voice going a bit quieter. "Because I asked her to hire you for her engagement pictures."

My blood started to boil. I stood up and took a few pacing steps across the kitchen. "So let me get this straight. Everyone who's hired me and shared my photos on social media and hyped me up are just friends of yours? Every bit of my success was engineered so you could what? So you could fuck me?"

He stood, closing the proximity between us. "It's not like that. I called Brita and asked her to hire you because you're a great photographer. I had seen your work when I was planning the budget for The Pacifica takeover, and it blew me away. Your name wasn't even on the file, it just said 'resort photographer.'"

When I gave him an incredulous look, he put up his hands. "I had no way of knowing that the person I had put on the chopping block was the same girl who had burst into my life after climbing through my window. When Brita mentioned that she was looking for a talented and unique photographer, I recommended you. It was before I even knew you."

"Did you go to high school with the Santa Barbara Weekly guy, too? Was any of this real?"

He rubbed his arms, but I didn't care how cold he might be. "Listen, Maggie. That was all you. I don't know anyone at the magazine." He looked into my eyes for a few seconds before adding, "I know you're done with me, and I know I broke your trust, but I need you to know, even if I never get to see you again, that I'm so fucking proud of you."

I had to look away from him then, tears threatening to spill down my cheeks. Yes, I was angry with him, but he really had been one of my biggest supporters through this entire roller coaster.

He reached for my wrist, taking it gently. "Every bit of your success has been because of your hard work and talent. You were so scared a month ago, with your checklist. But you faced everything on your own, and you're kicking ass."

I turned away from him again, putting my elbows on the counter, leaning my weight on them. "I want to believe you. I do."

Reece came up behind me, his movements tentative as he put his hand on my shoulder. I leaned into his touch, remembering how safe I had always felt in his arms. He confessed, "I messed up, more than once. And I'm probably going to mess up again and again, but I want to spend every day of the rest of my life making it up to you." His voice cracked. "I love you, Maggie."

My chin began to tremble, the ache in my heart overwhelming. "People who love each other don't keep secrets."

"I've spent so many years keeping secrets that it became a habit. I really just wanted to help you, and since Francesca worked for us, I didn't see the issue in talking to her."

I glanced over my shoulder at him, giving him a glare. "You really saw nothing wrong in talking to your ex on a daily basis?"

He rubbed his hand around my back in soft circles. "In my mind, I wasn't talking to an ex. I honestly thought of her as a coworker. Now that I know how she twisted my words and used our relationship to mess with you, I see how I should have told you about her all along."

I blinked a few times, trying to make sense of his words. Yes, she had twisted his words, but he was the one who reached out to her in the first place. He wasn't innocent in this. "You were together for years, and I'm supposed to believe that there's nothing between you two."

"There had been nothing there during most of our relationship, but I was so deep in my addiction that I was just going through the motions. I talked to her after you rushed out the other night, to find out what she had said, and I made it very clear that I would never be interested in her again."

When we had sat on the beach the other day, he had said their relationship was a disaster for a long time. Another worry popped to the forefront of my mind. "How do I know you won't get bored of me and just hang on to this because you feel obligated to be together?"

He brushed my hair out of my face. "Mag, I'll understand if you tell me to leave, but when I'm with you, I feel like I'm alive again. Like my missing piece was found. I don't want to go another day without you. Think about what we have, how we are together. You can't for a minute believe that I'm with you because of an obligation."

All the sweet conversations we'd shared these last few weeks flooded my brain. The inside jokes, the secrets shared in the dark. No one had ever pushed me to grow as much as he had, or believed in me as much as he did. He was the missing piece I had been searching for, too.

Was all of that worth giving up over one little issue?

I hugged my arms tightly around myself, knowing the answer to my question. "I want to forgive you. And I want to bring you upstairs with me." I stood up straighter, facing him. "Because I love you, too." I let out a wobbly breath. "But I'm scared."

His arms wrapped around me slowly, pulling me against his chest. He left a gentle kiss on my temple, as his wet clothes soaked into mine. He was so cold that I shivered. He whispered, "I'm scared, too, but I want to put in the work. I want to do this with you. Only you."

One thing I'd learned from being with Reece was that I couldn't let fear rule my life anymore. I wouldn't have made such strides if I had clung to my stupid rules, and I didn't want to revert back to being that scared girl. Damn those women for playing into my insecurities! It was time to let go of my worries and give in to trust.

I wanted to be with him. I needed to be with him.

I pulled away from him, unbuttoning his shirt. "We have to get you out of these before you catch a cold."

He leaned down and gave me a sweet kiss. "I'm so sorry."

I returned his kiss, slipping my tongue between his lips and pushing his open shirt down his arms. I pulled away to say, "I'll try to be calm and reasonable next time you do something ridiculous."

He laughed, rubbing the tip of his nose against mine. "No, you won't." He grabbed my ass, lifting me up so I could wrap my legs around his waist.

I giggled against his neck. "You're right, I won't. No keeping anything from me again, though?"

"I promise. No more secrets, even ones I think are helpful." He carried me up the stairs toward my bedroom but paused halfway there. "Wait. Tell me where your locket is."

I smiled and pressed a kiss to his cheek. "I put it on my dresser when I got mad at you. Seeing it made me miss you too much."

He swung open the door to my bedroom and tossed

me onto the bed, preparing to jump on top of me. He stopped, looking around the room. "Are your sheets in the wash?"

I bit my bottom lip and pulled my sweater off, tossing it on the floor. "About that . . . ." I stretched my arms above my head, watching his eyes trace the curves of my breasts. "They've probably made their way to the dump by now." His gaze rose to mine, full of questions. I just shrugged. "They smelled like you, so I threw them out."

He climbed over me, trailing kisses up my tender skin. "Guess I'll have to take you shopping for new ones."

I ran my fingers through his damp hair. "Or I'll just steal the ones from your place."

He gently bit the skin above my collarbone, making my breath hitch as he whispered, "You're my favorite thief."

Epilogue

The band played their instruments in front of the enormous white drop cloth backdrop. Nothing was plugged in, so the sound wasn't quite right, but because I was only snapping pictures, it didn't really matter.

It had only been eight months since I had started my journey as a small business owner, and it was one of the best decisions I had ever made. It was still hard to believe how successful I had become in such a short amount of time, but here I was, halfway across the world, living out all of my hopes and dreams.

The alarm on my phone went off, letting me know that we needed to wrap this shoot up so we could clear the equipment in time. I glanced out the window of the third-floor studio we had rented and got butterflies for the hundredth time at the sight of the Eiffel Tower in the distance.

The lead singer, Trent, walked up to me. "What do you think, Lina? Are they good enough for the cover?"

I smiled, shoving down the knee-jerk reaction to say

something self-deprecating that always bubbled up when discussing my work. "I think *Rolling Stone* is going to love these. Give me a few minutes and I'll give you a preview."

As the band's roadies and the assistants I had hired began to tear down the set, I uploaded the images to my computer. I called the band over to show them my work. They crowded around my laptop, pointing out the ones they liked the best and making fun of each other for the shots with embarrassing facial expressions.

Trent waved to someone who had just walked into the room, motioning for them to come over to us. "Hey Reece, you have to check these out."

I looked up, meeting those amber eyes with my own. They still took my breath away. I reached up and touched my locket, saying a silent thank-you to the universe that he had come into my life and changed everything.

He carried a tray of coffees, and his muscles peeked out from under the rolled-up sleeves of his black button-up. He gave me a peck on the cheek and looked at Trent. "I told you when we started this tour that she was the best in the business."

Reece passed the coffees out to the band and slipped right into his role of band manager, discussing logistics for the upcoming events. He'd only been doing this for six months but was extremely successful already, which is how we ended up on this European tour together.

I was able to book as many or as few clients as I wanted as we traveled. Having access to people all over the world and a huge social media following had given me the creative freedom I didn't know I had been missing.

After they picked their favorite shots and I closed my

laptop, the room emptied out. Reece took me by the hand, pulling me through an arched doorway. "Come out to the balcony with me?"

He guided me in a dance, something he did whenever we were alone. Reece twirled me in a circle before placing me in front of him, facing the city before us. He tucked my head under his chin and put his arms on either side of me, grabbing the railing. I pulled my sweater tightly against myself, fighting the winter chill.

We stood like this, watching the sun set over Paris for a few minutes before he pulled his arms around me tightly. "I love you so much, Maggie."

"I love you too, Reecie. I can't believe this is our life. It's absolute perfection."

"Not quite." His words were slow and shaky.

I craned my neck to look at him. "What on earth could make this any better?"

He reached into his pocket and pulled out a box, holding it out in front of me. "Marry me?"

I didn't even give him a chance to open it before I burst into tears and spun around to face him. My hands cupped the sides of his face, pulling him into a kiss.

"Is this a yes or a no?" He chuckled deeply, knowing the answer already.

"Yes, yes. Oh my God, yes!"

He slipped the ring onto my finger, looking into my eyes when he said, "I love you forever."

I kissed him again before replying, "I love you too. Forever and ever."

Author's Note

I didn't set out to write a book with a recovering addict as a main character, but the longer I got to know Reece in my head, the more I knew he needed to exist just the way he is.

There are a lot of addicts in my life, and I've seen them go through the stages of recovery year after year. The pandemic caused many people I love to struggle with their addictions, plunging some of them into relapse. I saw firsthand how the stigma of addiction can be detrimental to someone's health and wellbeing.

Addiction does not discriminate. It doesn't care if you're rich or poor, where you grew up, or who you know. Giving Reece a kind, loving, and genuine personality was my way of normalizing addiction and showing that it happens in all communities and deserves compassion.

If you or someone you know is struggling with addiction, I urge you to seek help. All it takes is one conversation, and you could save a life.

Holy crap, you guys, Lina and Reece made it into the world! This story changed more times than I could count over the past few years, even surviving through my midlife crisis.

I know I said it in the dedication, but first and foremost, I need to thank my village. May we continue raising our children, gossiping about our partners, and juggling trips, careers, and carpools together forever. Lina's story would not be what it is without feedback and encouragement from all of you.

An enormous thank-you goes to Bethany. You took an 80,000-word pile of random scenes and spent weeks guiding me through the creation of something I'm really proud of. I could not have done this without you.

I want to thank all my editors, readers, and grammar nerds who helped me hash out my story. Jessica, Brennan, Karen, Nur, and Clara, I owe you more than you know. Thank you for pointing out all the words I used too often in my early drafts. I promise to stop shrugging so much all the time!

Thank you, Kailli and Cindy, for being my biggest fans! Your feedback and kind words kept me going when all I wanted to do was slam my head into a keyboard.

I also need to scream from the rooftops about how

great my parents are. They have a stocked kitchen pantry that's open for me and mine 24/7, and they never hesitate to offer all the childcare so I can lock myself in a room and scream into the void whenever I need to (or, you know, write a book or two).

I would like to thank my cute husband. It means the world to me when you listen to me brainstorm ideas when you get home from a 12-hour shift even though you really want to go to sleep. I love you forever and ever.

ZJ . . . you already have the heart of a romantic, which scares the hell out of me now that you're starting to become obsessed with boys, but I know it will guide you to a happy, fulfilling life.

And finally, thank you, dear readers. Knowing that my stories are worth your time means more to me than all the stars in the sky. Seeing my books on your shelves, in your Little Free Libraries, and even on scientific expeditions to uninhabitable places is a dream I never thought would come true.

FOLLOW THE AUTHOR

Instagram | Facebook
DeeRollingsBooks.com

Join my Newsletter to access exclusive content, news, and
get access to bonus scenes coming soon!

BOOKS BY DEE ROLLINGS

Discordant Memories

The Pacifica Resort series:

A Liar and a Thief

Love and Reservations

First Loves and Last Resorts

Love and Reservations

He's her Mr. Wrong . . . and her new roommate.

Resort manager Blake Thomas has no patience for weddings — she's seen far too many lovestruck couples pass through her doors. She'd rather pursue her "weird" hobby of geocaching than try to find The One.

But when a last-minute eviction notice turns her life upside down, Blake is forced to move in with a man she'd rather keep tucked away in her past. And Sal has one condition in exchange for free rent: he needs a fake girlfriend to impress his estranged parents.

Determined to avoid reawakening painful memories, Blake avoids her new "boyfriend" by throwing herself into house-hunting, her best friend's wedding, and an offer for a major promotion.

But as long-buried sparks ignite, she begins to realize that their scheme is becoming all too real. And Sal is hiding more secrets than Blake ever imagined . . . .

A sweet and steamy, first person POV contemporary romance, the second novel of **The Pacifica Resort, Love and Reservations** *will have your heart fluttering from beginning to end.*

First Loves and Last Resorts

**When you've given up on love . . .
but he finds you anyway.**

Lizette Howell-Xu is married to her work. She didn't even cry when her husband of fifteen years left her for his very muscular, very male personal trainer. But now it's time for her ex to break the news to his family—and he's asking Lizette to help him do it. All they have to do is find a way to talk to his parents alone . . . At a family reunion, that's easier said than done.

Convincing herself that she needed a vacation was the easy part; juggling lost luggage and a major business opportunity from a tiny cabin in Michigan is trickier, especially while pretending to still be married. Luckily Ben, the rugged handyman with a British accent, doesn't mind offering Lizette his desk, especially since he's in on her secret.

But the more Lizette gets to know him, the more willing she becomes to step away from her computer and spend some quality time with a man who finally stirs something deep inside of her. Something she hasn't felt in years.

As their romance threatens to turn into a family scandal, Lizette must decide what parts of her life are the most important, which may mean breaking a few hearts . . . including her own.

First Loves and Last Resorts, the third book in **The Pacifica Resort** series, is a first person POV romantic comedy that will leave you swooning.

A car accident, amnesia, two supposed lovers, and many dark secrets. In a race against time, who will come out on top?

Catrina Banks wakes up with bruises on her body and no memories from the last six months. An illustrious painter, she feels as though someone has stolen the colors from her canvas.

Under the teeming hospital lights and white coats crowding around her, Catrina faces questions she has no answers to. How did she end up in a city far from home? What was she doing there? Where is her phone, her ID, and most of all: *Who assaulted her?*

Struggling with intermittent flashbacks, Catrina tries to piece her life together. Cradling a gray hoodie and wedding bands she has no memory of, Cat returns home with her boyfriend Danny.

Even after she's safe at home, she can't shake the weird feeling that something is *off*, nor can she ignore the haunting glimpses she gets of a different life with another man.

Discordant Memories is a **gripping romantic thriller** that *will have you on the edge of your seat, desperate to flip the pages to find out what happens next.*

About The Author

Dee Rollings was born and raised in the big city, but her heart lives in the forest. She does her best writing on the porch of her tiny house in the woods when she's not wrangling her kid or her dogs and having one-sided conversations with chipmunks.

She's a multi-genre author, penning both romantic thrillers and romantic comedies, but there is one thing for sure about all of her books—they'll make you think a little differently about society and the world, exploring topics such as addiction, grief, womanhood, and self-worth.